The Galosh
and other stories

MIKHAIL ZOSHCHENKO

The Galosh

and other stories

Translated from the Russian with an introduction by
JEREMY HICKS

THE OVERLOOK PRESS
Woodstock & New York

This edition first published in the United States in 2006 by
The Overlook Press, Peter Mayer Publishers, Inc.
Woodstock & New York

WOODSTOCK:
One Overlook Drive
Woodstock, NY 12498
www.overlookpress.com
[for individual orders, bulk and special sales, contact our Woodstock office]

NEW YORK:
141 Wooster Street
New York, NY 10012

⊚ The paper used in this book meets the requirements for paper
permanence as described in the ANSI Z39.48-1992 standard.

Cataloging-in-Publication Data is available from the Library of Congress

Printed in the United States of America
ISBN 1-58567-631-4
1 3 5 7 9 10 8 6 4 2

Contents

Introduction

To the English-speaking reader, Akhmatova, Bulgakov, Gorky, Mandelstam, Pasternak, Solzhenitsyn and Tsvetaeva are far more familiar names than Mikhail Mikhaylovich Zoshchenko (1894–1958). Yet in his lifetime, Zoshchenko was more popular than any of these writers of the Soviet period. The English-speaking world's general unfamiliarity with his work is entirely due to the difficulties of translation and the distorting influence of the Cold War. The collapse of the Soviet Union enables us to read Soviet writers in a new way, and removes a huge obstacle to understanding and translating him.

Little is known of the detail of Zoshchenko's life, even in Russia. Uncertainty as to the year of his birth caused his centenary to be celebrated a year late, in 1995. Nevertheless, we know that he was born in St Petersburg, the son of a Ukrainian painter who died when Mikhail was still a child. Despite being a poor student, particularly weak at Russian composition, he completed a *gimnaziya* education in St Petersburg in 1913, enrolling at the department of law at St Petersburg University in the same year. When war broke out in 1914, he was quick to join up, becoming an officer in a grenadier regiment. He distinguished himself through his bravery and was decorated. In 1916 he was gassed. This caused him heart trouble, which remained with him throughout his life. He nevertheless joined the Red Army, leaving it in 1919, after which he attempted a wide range of jobs from cobbler to postmaster until his literary debut in 1922 with *The Tales of Nazar Ilich, Mr Bluebellyov*. This was the culmination of attempts at writing dating back to at least 1914. Some of the best examples of Zoshchenko's work of this early period are his elaborate letters to his future wife, Vera Kerbits-Kerbitskaya, which bear clear signs of his recent reading of Nietzsche. Zoshchenko married Vera in 1920, and a year later they had a son, Valery (who died in the early 1990s). However, Zoshchenko seems always to have been an isolated and lonely figure even in his personal life, and certainly appears never to have been very much of a family man, temporarily moving out of the marital flat when his son was an infant.

Zoshchenko made his reputation with short stories published in the Soviet satirical press from 1923 onwards. The period from 1923 to the end of the 1920s was an extremely fruitful one for satirical literature. In

1921 Lenin had introduced the New Economic Policy (NEP) – a recognition that the country was in a ruinous state and that before genuinely redistributive policies could be attempted, there must first be some wealth to redistribute. It signalled that the Bolsheviks were willing to put their collectivist vision of economic organization and even some of their political agenda on hold in order first to rebuild the country. This meant tolerating private agriculture, private traders and skilled bourgeois specialists in many spheres, including the cultural. The initial years of the Revolution and Civil War had led to a breakdown: what art and literature survived belonged primarily to the spheres of journalism, performance and the spoken word. Satire in that period had been highly politicized and aimed at boosting morale by ridiculing the interventionist powers and White forces fighting the Soviet government. NEP introduced quite different conditions. It meant tolerating the literature of so-called 'fellow-travellers',[1] writers whose works, though not openly anti-Soviet, were not inspired by any notion of the Bolshevik Party's needs. NEP created an interval of relative freedom of speech. However, its very relativity must be stressed, since the Soviet government had already developed the habit of intolerance towards freedom of expression. Hence NEP also brought with it the foundation of the institutions of Soviet censorship: in 1922 the government created a body called the Central Directorate for Matters of Literature and Publishing (usually abbreviated to Glavlit). Its consent was a condition for the publication of any printed material. This was a profoundly contradictory situation: a government committed to collectivist economics permitted private enterprise; and some freedom of expression was granted by a government hostile to the very notion of 'liberal' freedoms. These paradoxes typify the ambiguous nature of the 1920s, and it was these inconsistencies that appear to have been so conducive to the flourishing of satire.[2]

A major figure championing the cause of satire was the poet Vladimir Mayakovsky, whose illustrated verse posters are amongst the most accomplished works of satire of the Civil War period.[3] His satirical verse after 1922 was aimed at exposing the self-seeking, careerist, bureaucratic, petty-bourgeois practices summed up in the peculiarly Russian word *meshchanstvo*. This had been the prerevolutionary Russian intelligentsia's favourite term of abuse, and was appropriated by the Bolsheviks in the years preceding and following the Revolution to mean those lacking selfless devotion to the revolutionary cause.[4] Mayakovsky's poems excoriated all such petty-mindedness, so much so that his poem 'Terminally-in-a-Meeting',[5] which was published in *Izvestiya* in 1922, was praised by Lenin for its attack on the bureaucratization of Soviet society.[6] This was an authoritative precedent, which was to be invoked by satirists and those sympathetic to them to counter critics who from 1923 onwards argued that the Soviet Union did not need satirical literature. Satire, argued such critics, was necessary in prerevolutionary times, when social ills could not be denounced and fought openly, but only through literary means: but since the Soviet state had set up the proper legal procedures for uncovering and eradicating social ills, satirical literature was no longer necessary.[7] Though such debates continued throughout the 1920s, Soviet readers made it clear that they wanted satirical literature. In 1922 the magazine *Krokodil* was established as a weekly satirical supplement to the Moscow newspaper *Rabochaya gazeta* (The Workers' Newspaper). It outlived this newspaper, and indeed still exists today. It soon gained wide popularity, and became one of seven satirical magazines in the years 1922–28 in Moscow and Petrograd/Leningrad which had a combined print run of over half a million copies.[8] The scale of their popularity can be seen when one considers that this was the approximate daily circulation of the officially promoted *Pravda*. In the course of the decade, more than 200 satirical titles were published,[9] and there were many more that had satirical sections. One such was the somewhat populist newspaper *Gudok* (The Whistle), for which Mikhail Bulgakov was among the writers employed to write satirical pieces in this period. Other prominent writers who made reputations writing for the satirical press at this time were Ilya Ilf, Yevgeny Petrov, Valentin Katayev, Pantaleymon Romanov and Vyacheslav Shishkov. However, it was Zoshchenko whose name became synonymous with this satirical press.

His stories bear the imprint of their semi-journalistic origin in their highly topical character. For example, 'Economy Measures', published in 1926, was written in response to a Party-led economy drive. Other stories were written for specific occasions, such as International Women's Day ('A Forgotten Slogan' and 'Domestic Bliss'). Their topicality was probably an important factor in making Zoshchenko's short stories, like the magazines in which they were published, tremendously popular. Zoshchenko was read by all levels of society. He became a star, his stories were memorized and retold, performed at variety shows and quoted everywhere. Books of his stories sold out almost immediately. One more substantial collection, *Much-Esteemed Citizens*, went through ten editions in the two years after its initial publication in 1926. It is estimated that Zoshchenko sold as many as one hundred *million* books.[10] There were even cases of impersonators profiting from his star status. Zoshchenko made this impact through his seemingly simple style, his use of colloquial language, his topical subject-matter and his brevity. These qualities enabled him to reach what he termed the 'new' reader: the mass of the common people who were wholly or largely unaware of prerevolutionary literary traditions, many of whom had only just completed basic literacy courses.

Zoshchenko's stories achieve their most characteristic and powerful effect through the use of an unsophisticated but highly colourful language put into the mouths of characters who themselves typically tell the story; this technique is known as *skaz*.[11] Zoshchenko, who was perfectly capable of writing standard literary Russian, adopts a mask, which swears richly and frequently, employs macaronic speech (corrupted loan-words), distorts other people's speech when reporting it and often uses the wrong Russian word with grotesque or absurd effect. In 'Pushkin', for example, a character complains that NEP is a 'utopia', clearly thinking that the word derives from the Russian word *utopit´*, meaning to drown. 'Monkey Language' reports a dialogue between two men at a meeting, in which they try to outdo each other in employing foreign loan-words such as 'quorum' and 'plenary', which they have heard at political meetings but not really understood. Such uses of language are central to Zoshchenko's art, and are hard to translate.

In part, this language is an object of satire. One of Zoshchenko's purposes is to portray the confusion of ordinary Russian people at the rapid influx of a complicated Marxist political vocabulary. But it is not as simple as that. Zoshchenko's use of such language also has a sincere, democratizing dimension actually in line with the aims of the Revolution. In an article published in 1927, he wrote:

> The thing is that I'm a proletarian writer. Or rather, in my stuff I'm parodying the sort of imaginary but genuine proletarian writer who might exist in the present-day environment . . .
>
> I'm just parodying. I'm a temporary substitute for the proletarian writer. That's why the themes of my stories are so full of a naïve philosophy that is at just the right level for my readers.[12]

Zoshchenko's writing also has a simple and vigorous beauty. It gathers speed and force through its rhythmic, staccato sentences. Often they lack a verb. Sometimes they contain a single word, often an adjective. They may be connected by nothing more than an 'and' or a 'but', and strong logical sequence and subordinate clauses are extremely rare. The effect is to encourage us to read fast. But we do so at our peril, because the details in Zoshchenko's stories are telling. If we fail to notice them we may miss the point.

In the economic and social conditions of Russia in the 1920s contemporary writers might justifiably have quoted Juvenal's 'It's hard not to write satire.' Overcrowding and the housing shortage mean a family live in a bathroom ('The Crisis'), the ubiquity of theft and the scarcity of consumer goods such as padlocks mean that a cyclist has to carry his bicycle with him wherever he goes ('Hard Labour'), and poor organization and a shortage of tubs in Russian steam-baths mean you risk having your clothes stolen, and worse still, you can't even wash there ('A Bathhouse'). Here and elsewhere Zoshchenko's stories hyperbolically strain the boundaries of the plausible (in one story a character downs three litres of vodka and in another a flea is seen bouncing around someone's apartment). However, they are nearer to the reality of Soviet life of the period than we might imagine. The housing shortage was an acute problem in the 1920s. In an attempt to ease the shortage, and at the same time make a virtue of a necessity, the government divided up many large apartments so that all the inhabitants shared the kitchen, toilet and bathroom facilities (if there were any), and each family unit had a single room to themselves. This arrangement was dubbed 'the communal apartment'. The conversions were typically rushed and as in the story 'Casual Work', the walls were often made of plywood and so thin as to conceal very little. If it exemplified the collective ideal, the communal apartment embodied some of its worst aspects – above all, its self-righteous intrusion into the individual's personal life and the resulting lack of privacy. It was also a breeding-ground for numerous petty squabbles, such as the fierce brawl that breaks out over a scourer in 'Nervous People'.

Moreover, the quality of Soviet-made consumer goods was terrible in this period. Heavy industry was the government's priority, and there was simply a shortage of the know-how and quality control procedures that would raise the quality of such goods. Another factor was the ubiquity of bribery, theft, embezzlement, creative accounting, and the abuse of high (or low) position. They seemed to thrive in the uncertain atmosphere of the times. Revolutions by their nature demand mass law-breaking. Respect for law and order was soon sacrificed in the conditions of hyperinflation and the collapse of the money economy, drastic food and fuel shortages and even famine. Furthermore, the government itself had dispensed with any notion of the inviolability of private property. Thus the prevailing atmosphere of the stories, in which consumer goods are scarce and prone to disintegrate, but nevertheless so alluring as to drive people to all manner of underhand practices in their pursuit and to any measures in their defence, has a substantial basis in historical fact.[13] Indeed, Zoshchenko claimed to have based thirty to forty per cent of his stories on material he had gath-ered from the newspapers, particularly from readers' letters.[14] An excellent example of this is 'A Bathhouse', which he wrote on the basis of at least three letters to the Leningrad newspaper *Krasnaya gazeta* (The Red Newspaper) from readers irate about the terrible conditions they had had to endure in Soviet bathhouses: one letter objected to the changing-rooms of a bathhouse being next to a hairdressers', so that the people who had just washed got covered with hair, and another complained that wardrobe tokens were easily lost, and thieves were taking advantage of this to get hold of other people's clothes, details that Zoshchenko employs or hints at in his story. This elaboration on topical factual material, which Russians call a *feuilleton*, was a leading genre in Soviet journalism of the period. Zoshchenko transformed the feuilleton by employing more sophisticated literary techniques than had previously been the case, central to which is his creation of a nar-rative mask using a raw, accessible idiom.

But although he employs a mask and exaggerates his characters' language, Zoshchenko does not quite or does not solely laugh at their expense. That he does so has too often been the assumption of both Western and Soviet critics. This has similarly influenced translations of Zoshchenko's short stories. Critics and translators alike have taken the comic aspect of the narrator's language and the impossibility of his quest for a quiet and comfortable life to be an indication that he is the butt of the satirical humour. For Western critics, including the émigré press for whom he was one of the few acceptable Soviet writers, Zoshchenko was slyly satirizing a typical Soviet worker, showing him as he really was rather than as he was portrayed by propaganda. For Soviet critics, Zoshchenko ridiculed his characters in order to expose and denounce the *meshchanstvo* tendency to put self before society.

Though there are partial truths in both of these accounts, to feel the full bitter-sweet smack of these stories we must also sympathize with their characters, and perceive a tragic dimension to their predicament. Zoshchenko received many letters from his readers asking him for moral guidance. None of them seems to think that Zoshchenko is ridiculing them. Moreover, for his part, Zoshchenko seems to have valued this audience, their way of thinking and their way of writing, to the extent of publishing a collection of such letters (*Letters to a Writer*) in 1929.

The complex mixture of reactions elicited by his short stories is clear when they are compared with the *Sentimental Tales*. This is the name Zoshchenko gave to a group of stories first collected and published in 1927. These are ten or more times longer than most of his short stories, and, though still comic, they are far more literary. They demand a far greater familiarity with Russian literary tradition, which they parody mercilessly. Their main characters are from the intelligentsia, and the stories deal with their reactions to the Revolution. Without exception, these characters' culture and refinements prove to be a veneer: when confronted by stark and hungry realities, they abandon all morals. Moreover, they have nothing to offer the new society. This is presented as their fault rather than that of the society. Zoshchenko seems to have little sympathy for these characters.

By contrast, Zoshchenko's short stories are aimed at a mass audience, and demand no familiarity with literary traditions. Nevertheless, these miniature tragicomedies suggest parallels with the pathos of Chaplin and the aporias of Beckett. Furthermore, they do draw significantly on the Russian classics, in particular on the tradition of moral satire or tragicomic writing in Russia that goes back through Nadezhda Teffi, who wrote for the prerevolutionary satirical journal *Satyricon*, through Chekhov and Leskov at least as far as Gogol. Gogol's prescription for the true comic writer's art, 'laughter through tears', seems an apt description of the ambivalent tensions at work in Zoshchenko's short stories. Zoshchenko deliberately sought comparison with Gogol, despite his general reticence with regard to prerevolutionary literary traditions. Many of his stories are variations on Gogol's 'The Overcoat,' in which an introverted clerk saves up for a new overcoat which will protect him from the elements and win him social acceptance; but it is stolen shortly after he acquires it, and after being humiliated by the authorities whose help he requests in recovering the coat, he dies. The loss of an object, often an item of clothing, that has a deep psychological or metaphysical importance to a character is a plot that often recurs in Zoshchenko's stories. 'Love' and 'Thieves' are just two examples in the present selection, but 'The Galosh' is perhaps the most interesting rewriting of Gogol's theme. Here the search for a galosh lost in the rush-hour squeeze leads the narrator into the labyrinth of Soviet bureaucracy. He eventually emerges brandishing the lost galosh as tangible proof that the Soviet system works. The only problem is that he has lost the other one in the process. Unlike Gogol's clerk, Zoshchenko's narrator is not crushed by his experiences, though they are every bit as demoralizing. Zoshchenko extends Gogol by challenging us to find something sympathetic or admirable in people who are far less deserving of our sympathy or admiration than Gogol's Akaky Akakiyevich. Moreover, the very repetition of a similar plot produces a horrific realization that the same humiliating sequence may never end.

Zoshchenko most explicitly invited comparison with Gogol by entitling a 1928 collection of his stories 'Who Are You Laughing At?', an adaption of the mayor's address to the audience at the end of *The Government Inspector*: 'What are you laughing at? You're laughing at yourselves!' This critical attitude to laughter was one Zoshchenko himself expressed by repeatedly stressing the serious side of his work, at one point even going so far as to claim that the humour of his stories was unintentional:

> People call them [the short stories] humorous. In fact, that's not quite right. They are not humorous. By humorous we mean stories that are written so as to make people laugh. But I did not write to make people laugh; this occurred despite me, it is a peculiarity of my work.[15]

Developing the widely held Russian view of humour as trivial entertainment existing in contrast with satire – comic art with a moral mission in the manner of Gogol or Saltykov-Shchedrin, Zoshchenko stresses that his purpose was high-mindedly didactic rather than simply to amuse. His stories may look crude, unfinished or simplistic, but they are none of these things. They possess a polished disorder which continues a vital and powerful Russian comic tradition.

In recent years critics both Russian and Western have asserted Zoshchenko's relevance in the post-Soviet era by suggesting that the enduring value of his stories lies in key psychological motifs, such as guilt feelings.[16] This approach aims to link Zoshchenko's short stories of the 1920s with his later work, especially his semi-autobiographical psychoanalytical narrative *Before Sunrise*. Alexander Zholkovsky, for example, argues that the fear of crime in stories such as 'Guests' reveals a deep-seated psychological uncertainty rather than anything about 1920s Russia. There is an attractive economy to this response to the challenge of bringing Zoshchenko in from the Cold War. It is further to be commended for championing the cause of *Before Sunrise*, a work that the Soviet censorship prevented from being published in full until 1972, and the first part of which was savagely maligned on publication in 1943. Yet to accord this work more importance than the early stories, or to read those stories in the light of the neuroses revealed in *Before Sunrise*, is to embrace the false notion that a persecuted work is necessarily a better work than one that the Soviet censors pass. Such readings assume that the comic is merely trivial, and that we must look beyond it to find Zoshchenko's content. They fail adequately to appreciate that Zoshchenko's 'content' is inextricable from the comic aspect of his stories. After all, we would be reductive readers of Beckett or Kafka if all we looked for were what the works reveal about the author's neuroses. Moreover, the psychoanalytical readings encourage us to extract Zoshchenko from the context of the Soviet 1920s. Yet as we have seen, his satire is saturated with that context. He exaggerates it and transforms it, thus making it universal. He turns the disappointments and let-downs of everyday Soviet life into a vision of an existence structured in such a way as to humiliate and destroy the average citizen and to undermine the noble aims proclaimed by the Bolsheviks.

Zoshchenko's stories dramatize a conflict. They propose a generalized account of the world typically informed by ideology, and test it against individual experience. The generalization is often an optimistic assessment of events, but it can also be a fear generated by rumour or some other vague notion. These abstractions collide with characters' actual experience of the world. A good example of this is Zoshchenko's most famous story, 'A Bathhouse'. After repeating some gossip he has heard on the merits of American bathhouses, the character-narrator then claims that 'Soviet bathhouses are fine too. But worse. You can get washed in them though.' But the character himself fails to get washed: after waiting for over an hour to get a tub, he steals someone else's, but then finds himself constantly being splashed with dirty water by people washing their clothes. He eventually gives up and decides to finish washing at home. His original statement about Soviet bathhouses, 'You can get washed in them', is not borne out by his experience. Does this man trust the experience of others, the claims of ideology, the generalized account that passes for truth, or does he insist on the importance of his own lived experience? It would seem that a major theme of existential thought is lurking in these tiny stories on ephemeral themes.

The conflict between ideological abstraction and personal experience is played out repeatedly in Zoshchenko's stories. The characters almost invariably choose the ideological abstraction rather than dare to trust their own experience. The reader of course can perceive the disparity between the two, which is very often the source of the stories' comic power. It would be wrong to assume that a character's view is ironic, and is simply to be torn away to arrive at the truth; i.e. that Zoshchenko is employing a mask to ridicule those who claim that Soviet bathhouses are all right. The fact of the matter is that there is an ambivalence towards optimistic assessments, and it is this that makes the short stories tragicomic rather than simply comic. A character often expresses an optimism in the face of the evidence, a kind of Soviet *credo quia absurdum*, which attempts to transform the squalor into splendour, if not through the power of political reform, then through the power of imagination and faith. Typical of this tendency is 'The Cross', in which the character-narrator praises the workings of Soviet officialdom even though his concrete experience of bureaucracy has driven him to a state of nervous exhaustion. He is not a rebel. He is a conformist, a herd animal whose experience contradicts his conformist views.

The period in which Zoshchenko found his audience, the 1920s, provided ample material for the expression of the tension between the dulled and discounted individual experience on the one hand and the general weight of received views on the other. Zoshchenko scaled this tension down to microscopic dimensions with no loss of intensity, and achieving universal resonance. Other great writers of the time faced the same conflict tragically as prophets, martyrs and heroes. Zoshchenko's characters face it comically as cowards, as sheep experiencing a moral crisis.

Zoshchenko's own fate, however, was tragic. By the end of the 1920s he had begun to see his life-long depression as linked to the 'irony' of his stories. This view coincided with political pressures that led to a tightening of control over the satirical press. By the end of 1930 all the Leningrad satirical publications had been closed down, and only the far more politically rigid Moscow-published *Krokodil* remained. The few short stories Zoshchenko was able to publish in the 1930s were mostly published there, but didactic notes began to dominate and they were generally inferior to his 1920s work, with notable exceptions, some of which have been included in the present volume. Consequently, during the 1930s Zoshchenko began to move away from magazine-published satirical literature towards longer satirical pieces, such as his comic history of morals, *The Sky-Blue Book*, which includes reworkings of many of his earlier short stories. He also began to write works of a more sober tone and children's stories, including a series about Lenin.

Considering that he turned to the genre partly in order to escape the attentions of the censor, it is an irony that it was a children's story that led to Zoshchenko's most serious confrontation with the Soviet authorities. In 1946 'The Adventures of a Monkey', first published the previous year, was reprinted in the Leningrad literary journal *Zvezda*. In it a monkey escapes from the zoo, then, having spent a day observing Soviet life, willingly returns to its cage. The accident of the story's publication in a serious literary journal made it seem like a mordant satire. Indeed, this was how the Party's leading spokesman on cultural affairs at the time, Andrey Zhdanov, read it: as a satire on Soviet life, suggesting life in a cage was preferable to life in the Soviet Union. Accordingly, in a notorious Party Resolution of 1946, he condemned the story as slanderous and malicious. Zoshchenko, along with Anna Akhmatova, was attacked in the most abusive language. This was part of a general crackdown on the partial relaxation of ideological control that had been permitted during the war, and was intended to quash hopes of its extension into the postwar period. There were rumours that the real reason for the attack on Zoshchenko was that Stalin wanted revenge on him for ridiculing a man with a moustache in one of his children's stories about Lenin. Whatever the true explanation, Zoshchenko was expelled from the Writers' Union and found it extremely difficult to publish until after Stalin's death in 1953. In the destalinizing Thaw of 1954 he again found himself the target of abusive criticism. When asked by visiting English students whether he agreed with the Party Resolution of 1946 about him, he felt compelled to reply that he could not. In particular, he objected to the accusation that he was a coward, which was based on the fact that he was evacuated out of Leningrad in 1941 at the beginning of the blockade. As a former soldier, he was intensely hurt by this accusation. When asked to take back his objections to the Party Resolution he publicly refused, provoking still more opprobrium, which this time broke him and may have hastened his death four years later.[17]

Zoshchenko's reputation has been steadily gaining ground since the 1960s. Russians are now able to read his work freely and a number of monographs on him have appeared. He is increasingly seen as a writer worth rescuing from the Soviet past. In the West, he has not been translated for a good many years. The present edition is intended to overcome that neglect.

The selection concentrates on his comic short stories, most of them written in the 1920s, because I consider these his greatest achievement. Their tragicomic view of the world is perpetually relevant. They are also a social document giving us a picture of everyday life in the Soviet Union in the 1920s and 1930s, and of the reading tastes of tens of millions of unsophisticated Soviet readers. The most celebrated stories are included, and of these, 'A Bathhouse' and 'A Dogged Sense of Smell' are in their original magazine-published versions which will be unfamiliar even to specialist readers.[18] Nearly half of the stories contained in this selection are translated into English for the first time; I feel these are just as characteristic as those that have been translated previously. The present volume offers the most extensive selection of Zoshchenko's short stories so far translated into English.

Concentration on Zoshchenko's best work has meant the exclusion of much else that is of interest. His first published stories of 1922–23 are not without merit, but generally represent a number of experiments, opening up other literary paths which Zoshchenko did not take, and fail to exert the same fascination over the reader as his post-1923 short stories. Similarly, I have not included any of the *Sentimental Tales*, in part for reasons of space – a single one of them would have meant the sacrifice of ten other stories – but also because they exemplify a special aspect of Zoshchenko's work, his attitude to the intelligentsia and to elite notions of art. The children's stories are not really comic, and hence do not belong in this collection. All Zoshchenko's other works, such as *The Story of a Retempering, Letters to a Writer, Youth Restored, The Sky-Blue Book* and *Before Sunrise*, are much longer and would have to be translated separately, although I have included two short stories that were rewritten for and incorporated in *The Sky-Blue Book.*

These exclusions make for a consistent selection which affords the reader a sustained view of Zoshchenko's grotesque and comic world. His short stories are the greatest expression of one of the greatest feats of the peoples of the Soviet Union: their gallows humour, their laughter in the face of absurdity and evil. The tragedy of the Soviet Union has universal repercussions, and its portrayal as tragicomedy has universal relevance.

Notes

1 Trotsky is said to have coined the term. See Leon Trotsky, *Literature and Revolution*, trans. Rose Strunsky (1925), London: Red Words, 1991, pp. 89–90.
2 Lenin's class-based conception of freedom of speech is briefly set forth in his 'Decree on the Press', included in Martin McCauley (ed.), *The Russian Revolution and the Soviet State 1917–1921: Documents*, London: Macmillan, 1975, pp. 190–91.
3 See Nina Baburina (ed. with introduction and notes), *The Soviet Political Poster 1917–1980*, trans. Boris Rubalsky, Harmondsworth: Penguin, 1985.
4 For a history of *meshchanstvo* see Boym under Further Reading.
5 The title has also previously been translated as 'In Re Conferences' and as 'Incessant Meeting Sitters'.
6 Vladimir Lenin, 'The International and Domestic Situation of the Soviet Republic' (6 March 1922), in *Collected Works*, 45 vols, 3rd edn, ed. David Skvirsky and George Hanna, Moscow: Progress, 1963–70, XXXIII, pp. 212–26 (p. 223).
7 These arguments are summarized in Leonid Yershov, *Sovetskaya satiricheskaya proza 20–kh godov*, Moscow and Leningrad: Izd. Akademii Nauk SSSR, 1960, pp. 43–50. There is a brief summary of them in Richard Chapple, *Soviet Satire of the Twenties*, Gainsville: University of Florida Press, 1980, pp. 15–16.
8 Yershov, p. 61. The five most significant of these were *Krokodil*, the most popular, with an average circulation of 150,000, *Smekhach* [The Laughster] (1924–28), which Zoshchenko edited for a time, with over 100,000, *Pushka* [The Cannon] (1926–29)

between 75,000 and 115,000, *Begemot* [The Hippopotamus] (1924–28) 70,000, and *Chudak* [The Eccentric] (1928–30) 100,000. S. Stykalin and I. Kremenskaya, *Sovetskaya satiricheskaya pechat ´ 1917–1963,* Moscow: Politlit, 1963.

9 Yershov, p. 49.

10 Estimate by Kirill Kuzmin of the Zoshchenko Museum. However, many of these were small, pamphlet–size selections usually of five stories printed by the satirical magazines, especially *Begemot.*

11 For a discussion of *skaz* and its usages see Hicks, *Mikhail Zoshchenko and the Poetics of 'Skaz',* under Further Reading.

12 'O sebe, o kritikakh i o svoyey rabote' [About myself, my critics, and my work] (1927) in *Uvazhayemyye grazhdane* [Much-esteemed citizens], pp. 584–86 (p. 586). This is my translation, but see Further Reading for a reference to a translation of the complete article.

13 The allure of consumer goods and groceries in the stories may also have psychological roots in Zoshchenko's own behaviour: his family told me (August 2000) how, having observed the joyous reaction of someone who had just bought a bottle of wine, he would himself buy some of the same kind, hurry home to lock himself in his room and open it, impatient to experience the same joy. When no such miracle occurred he would not even bother to drink the wine he had bought. His room would be littered with decaying groceries bought in the hope that they would confer a perpetually unobtainable happiness.

14 Zoshchenko made this claim in 'Kak ya rabotayu' [How I work] (1930), in *Uvazhayemyye grazhdane,* pp. 586–91 (p. 589).

15 'How I work' in *Uvazhayemyye grazhdane,* pp. 586–91 (p. 590).

16 E.g. Scatton and Zholkovsky; see Further Reading.

17 For an account of the criticism of Zoshchenko in the Party Resolution of 1946, and of the later incident with the English students, see György Dalos, *The Guest from the Future: Anna Akhmatova and Isiah Berlin,* trans. Antony Wood, London: John Murray, 1998; New York: Farrar, Straus and Giroux, 1999.

18 See 'A Note on the Translations', page 23.

Jeremy Hicks,
London, 2000

A Note on the Translations

In my translations of Zoshchenko's short stories I have naturally attempted to avoid what I see as the major defects in previous translations. I am not speaking of inadvertent errors and inaccuracies. The greatest shortcomings of previous translations lie in their misconceived approaches to the language of Zoshchenko's narrator. This is not the conventional language of literary narration, but an idiom in which elements of dialect and slang, as well as the stylistic features of the spoken language, predominate. This is what literary critics call *skaz* narration. Its translation is a particularly thankless task, in that slang and the spoken language change fast and vary widely from place to place and class to class, to a far greater degree than the received language of literary narration. This is particularly true of English. A translation rendered into a slang specific to London in 2000 may sound alien to native speakers of English in, for example, Belfast, Cardiff, Dublin, Edinburgh, New York, Toronto and Sydney. It may even sound hopelessly dated to an inhabitant of the same city in five years' time. It seems to me that one of the main weaknesses of previous translations of Zoshchenko is precisely the fact that they are too specific to a sort of slang used during a very brief period. As a result they have quickly become outmoded and irrelevant.

An illustration of this problem are the Russian words *morda*, *rozha* and *rylo*, which refer to an animal's face, and can also be used to refer insultingly to the human face. A typical approach to their translation has been to attempt to find a direct slang equivalent in English, such as 'mug'. However, this word now sounds hopelessly dated (there is nothing so contemptible as the previous generation's slang), and evokes the wrong sort of associations (effete rather than f-off). However, a word evoking the right sort of associations, such as 'gob', is very soon likely to sound as dated as 'mug', and may already seem alien to many native speakers of English. My solution is to use the neutral word 'face' but qualify it where possible with an insulting adjective such as 'ugly' or 'fat'. Likewise, where the dictionary suggests such old-fashioned equivalents as 'scoundrel', 'villain' or 'rogue' for *podlets* and other terms of abuse, I have preferred to use the word 'bastard', usually with a qualifying adjective. This may lose a certain subtlety, and it definitely adds vulgarity to the original abuse, but does so in order to render more faithfully the unliterary feel of Zoshchenko's texts in such a way as to avoid seeming outdated or inadvertently incongruous. Where a character's language has to be lexically substandard, I have attempted to employ familiar and slightly vulgar language that is not excessively specific to a given time or place. Nevertheless, I have been unable to stop myself from slewing towards British English, whilst doing my best to avoid a tone or vocabulary that would render my translation unacceptable to a North American reader.

Yet the spoken feel of Zoshchenko's stories is not solely a question of finding the right slang. In attempting to recreate it I have gone for oral rhythm. I have also deliberately avoided vocabulary of an elevated register, except where the narrator appears to be quoting someone else or some terminology he has heard or read in the newspapers (previous translations often failed to convey the characters' and narrators' use of jargon specific to the times); I have drawn attention to such matters in the endnotes. I have attempted to keep the clumsiness, the sharply discordant mixture of registers, the tautologies and malapropisms of the original, even when they are effectively puns. For example, in 'Quality Merchandise', Goosev tries to say that his foreign powder is much better than the Russian stuff with which he has hitherto been ruining his face. He uses the word *lichnost´* (personality) where he should have said *litso* (face or person). Previous translators have for the most part accepted that such subtleties will be lost in the English text, one version of this sentence being: 'For how many years did I pollute my face.' In my translation the passage reads 'How long have I been defacing my complexity', when Goosev means 'complexion'. I regard such attempts to render characters' and narrators' linguistic incompetence as an extremely important aspect of the stories, and one which need not necessarily be lost in translation.

The grammatical errors and incorrect usages of Zoshchenko's narrators are an extreme example of a general difficulty with the use of a non-standard language for narration in the stories: it appears to have led many critics, readers and translators to see them simply as comic, to see the narrator simply as an object of ridicule. As I argue in the Introduction to this book, Zoshchenko's humour works by fostering a certain sympathy for the narrator as well as by undermining him and making him look ridiculous. If a translator misses this duality, then, since translation is a form of interpretation that tends to exaggeration, the result is likely to be an accentuation of the comic to the detriment of the tragi-comic. A good example of this in previous translations has been the way in which Russian narration in the present tense has been rendered by the present tense in English. The Russian language permits narration in the present tense even in standard narrative forms, whereas for English it is distinctly abnormal. The same grammatical form occupies a different relative position in the stylistic system of each language, and creates a quite different effect on the reader. Narration in the present tense in English has strong comic overtones, and the use of this form in previous translations of Zoshchenko has tended to provoke belly laughter at the expense of the narrator and to turn the stories into slapstick, as in the case of 'Lemonade' and 'A Bathhouse'.

The assumption that there can be an exact lexical, grammatical or stylistic equivalent (whether contemporary with Zoshchenko or present-day) into which these stories can be translated appears to me misleading. The English language often has fewer suitable terms, which will have to do more work. An example of this is the form of address *brattsy*, which may be rendered as 'brothers'. It has been translated as 'fellows', 'chaps', 'friends', and 'guys' or even 'lads' are also possible, but most of these are words with a highly limited shelf-life. I have preferred 'comrades' in certain contexts, which though it corresponds to the more formal Russian term *tovarishchi*, at least encourages the reader to see the specific and dissimilar aspect of Soviet culture of the 1920s. In my translations I have attempted not solely to make Zoshchenko and his culture accessible to the modern reader, but also to draw attention to its unique and unrepeatable characteristics.

The present tense and time- and place-specific slang are clearly more direct and expressive than the alternatives. In eschewing or moderating my use of such forms I run the risk of losing the stories' immediacy. But since making the narrator too much of a figure of fun would undermine the tragi-comic purpose of Zoshchenko's project, it is a risk I have decided to run. Translation is always an attempt to minimize losses, and to fail better.

A note on texts

An academic edition of Zoshchenko's works has yet to be published. As source texts I have primarily used Tomashevsky's 1986–87 collection along with Dolinsky's 1991 edition which attempts to fill in its gaps. These however are incomplete, and where necessary, I have used earlier texts.

A major difficulty with Zoshchenko is that he rewrote his stories throughout his life in order to get them republished. This meant altering stories to suit the tastes of extremely rigid censorship norms, where considerations of ideology and not artistic merit prevailed. Notoriously, even 'A Bathhouse' was rewritten in the 1950s to suit the virulently anti-Western political direction of the time, excluding all mention of America. In this light the convention of treating the last version published in the author's lifetime as authoritative cannot govern our choice of text.

But by what other criterion should a text be selected? The late Yury Tomashevsky, in the 1986 edition, evokes a notion of the will of the author as a standard. This is not a reliable criterion, since Zoshchenko's will changed over the course of time, as is clear from the fact that he frequently altered his stories even when there was no political imperative to do so. Nevertheless, I have for the most part followed Tomashevsky's judgement, except for a few instances where I have opted for original magazine variants, when I considered them superior. But my own taste is admittedly no less subjective than that of Tomashevsky. The only satisfactory solution to this problem would be an edition that included all published variants in its notes, and thus permitted the reader to choose.

At the end of this volume I have indicated story by story which edition of Zoshchenko's works I have used as source text, also giving details of first publication. In the few instances where I have employed the magazine-published variant of a story as a source text, I also include a reference to a book-published version.

Jeremy Hicks,
London, 2000

The Galosh

and other stories

A Thief

Vaska Tyapkin was a pickpocket by profession. He was mainly active on the trams.

But don't envy him reader, it's a worthless profession. You go through one pocket – crap: a lighter, maybe; you go through another – more crap: a handkerchief, or ten cigarettes say, or maybe even worse, an electricity bill.

It's a joke, not a profession.

And as for more worthwhile things, like watches or wallets, not bloody likely.

It's a mystery where passengers keep them these days.

And people have become so damned mean. You've got to keep your eyes open, or it'll be *your* pocket they'll clean out. And they really will clean you out. It's easily done. You're eyeing the conductor's bag and that's it, they've already cleaned you out. For crying out loud . . .

And as for their valuables, the passengers are so mean they probably wear them on their chests or maybe on their stomachs. Places like that are tender, you see, and you can't tickle them at all. You hardly need scratch them with your finger and there'll be shouting: They've robbed me. A disgusting sight.

It's a bloody worthless profession.

A semi-respectable old pro, an armed robber, advised Vaska Tyapkin to change profession for his own good. To change trades.

'It's now summer-time,' he said. 'Look mate, why don't you take a trip,' he said, 'to the dacha belt. Pick out a dacha and turn the place over. And while you're at it breathe the air. We could any one of us fall ill with TB. It's easily done.'

'He's right,' thought Vaska. 'You work like an elephant, without the slightest gratitude or word of thanks. Yes, why don't I go to the dacha belt. After all, there's the air and a change of job. What's more, I'm completely worn out, I could catch TB.'

So that's what Vaska did. He went to Pargolovo.

There he was walking along the main road, and the streets. The air really was wonderful, it was dacha air, it was perfect, but you couldn't make a living here. And with all this air, he really felt like a bite to eat, he wanted it all the time, as if he had a hole in his belly: as soon as he'd eaten he wanted more.

Vaska started to pick out a dacha. He saw one inhabited dacha, it looked superb. On the fence was a notice: 'Dr Koryushkin – Gynaecologist'.

'If he's a doctor,' thought Vaska, 'so much the better. These doctors always keep some silver in the sideboard.'

So that day, Vaska climbed into the shrubs that grew behind the flowerbeds in the doctor's garden and started to watch what was going on. And what was going on was that the nanny had come out into the garden to go for a walk with the five-year-old bourgeois toddler. The nanny was strolling around in the heat of the sun, and the little boy was running around the garden playing with his toys. He had heaps of these toys: puppets, clockwork fly-wheels, trains . . . And one toy was really interesting, it looked like a spinning-top. You wound it up with a winder and it made a frightening whistling noise and spun round on the ground by itself like a merry-go-round.

And Vaska became so intrigued by this toy, he nearly fell out of the bushes. Just controlled himself in time.

'They haven't wound it up all the way, the stupid idiots,' he thought. 'If they wound it up all the way, then it would really spin.'

But the nanny had flaked out in the heat of the sun. She'd had enough of winding it up, you see.

'Wind it up, wind it all the way up,' Vaska whispered to himself. 'Wind it up, you stupid cow . . . Damn you.'

The nanny and the little boy disappeared. Vaska came out of the bushes. He went into the yard and looked at what was where. You've got to know every tiny detail: where the chimney is, and where the kitchen is too. Then he presented himself at the kitchen. Offered his services. He was turned down.

'Get out of here,' they said. 'You'll try and steal something. It's written all over your face.'

They're right, they guessed, for crying out loud – and Vaska stole an axe on his way back. Well, you said it . . .

The next day, Vaska was in the bushes again. He lay there trying to think where he should begin.

'I've got to climb,' he thought, 'in the window. Into the dining room. If the window's not open today, that's not the end of the world. I can wait. Maybe they'll forget to close it tomorrow. I'm in no hurry.'

Every night Vaska went over to the house and tried the window to see whether it would give. After a week it did, they'd forgotten to close it.

Vaska slipped out of his jacket to make himself lighter, calmed down the grumbling in his stomach, and climbed up.

'There's a table on the left,' he thought, 'and a sideboard on the right. The silver's in the sideboard.'

Vaska climbed into the room: it was dark. Though it was a clear night, it's always hard to see what you're doing in other people's residences. Vaska felt around with his hands – was that the cupboard? He opened a box. There was rubbish in the box – crap: children's toys. Dammit. Yes – puppets and fly-wheels . . .

'For crying out loud!' thought Vaska. 'I've got into the wrong room. Blow me if I'm not in the nursery. For crying out loud.'

Vaska lost heart. He thought about going into the next room, but was scared. He'd lost his bearings. If you end up in the doctor's room, he'll stick a lancet in you just out of habit.

'For crying out loud,' he thought. 'I may as well take some of these toys. Toys cost money too, you know.'

Vaska started to get the toys out of the box. He came across the spinning-top. The same one they had been playing with the other day in the garden.

Vaska smiled.

'It's the same one,' he thought. 'I'll certainly give it a spin later. Definitely. I'll wind it up all the way. But right now I'm in a bit of hurry comrades.'

Vaska started to hurry and dropped something, it clanged as it hit the floor.

Then he saw that the little boy was stirring on the bed. He got up and went over to him on bare feet.

At first Vaska was startled.

'Go to sleep,' he said. 'Go to sleep for crying out loud.'

'Take your hands off!' shouted the boy. 'Take your hands off my toys.'

'You little . . . ' thought Vaska, 'I could get caught.'

Meanwhile the boy was bawling and starting to cry.

'Go to sleep, you little squirt!' said Vaska. 'I'll crush you like a louse.'

'Get your hands off. They're my toys . . .'

'Wrong,' said Vaska, shoving toys into his sack. 'They were yours it's true, but now you can whistle for them . . .'

'What?'

'You can, I said, whistle for them.'

Vaska threw his sack out of the window and then jumped out himself. He jumped out awkwardly and bruised his chest.

'For crying out loud,' he thought. 'I could catch TB from this.'

Vaska sat down in a flowerbed, rubbed his chest and caught his breath.

'I'd better,' he thought, 'run as fast as I can.'

He pulled the sack up onto his shoulder, and was about to start running when he remembered the spinning-top.

'Stop!' thought Vaska. 'Where's the spinning-top? I haven't forgotten the spinning-top have I? For crying out loud.'

He felt the sack, it was there. Vaska took the spinning-top out. He really wanted to give it a spin. He just couldn't wait.

'Why not?' he thought, 'I'll wind it up just to see.'

He wound it up all the way and let it spin. The spinning-top buzzed and rocked from side to side.

Vaska burst out laughing. He fell over on the ground laughing.

'That's what it's like,' he thought, 'when it's at full tilt. For crying out loud.'

The spinning-top hadn't even finished spinning when suddenly someone in the house shouted:

'Thief! . . . Stop thief!'

Vaska jumped up, and was about to run when someone whacked him on the head. But they didn't hit him full on. Amateurs. Though Vaska crashed down onto the ground, he jumped straight back up.

'That must have been a stick that hit me,' he thought, 'Either that or a tarred rope.'

Vaska ran off, covering his head with his hands.

He ran a mile, and then remembered he'd forgotten his jacket.

He was so upset he was nearly in tears. He sat down in a ditch.

'For crying out loud. I'd better change professions. This is a worthless profession, it's worse than the first. I've been deprived of my last jacket. I think I'll try armed robbery instead. For crying out loud.'

And Vaska set off for town.

1923

A Speech About Bribery

The manager of the Zapletyukhin line, engineer Mordoplyuyev, stood up from the table and, raising his glass, said in a slightly unsteady voice:

'So, dear comrades, please allow me to propose a toast to the total eradication of bribery on our beloved Zapletyukhin line . . .'

'Hip, hip . . .' shouted engineer Sliva.

'Hooray!' chorused the railway workers.

The line manager made a sign with his hand, and everything went quiet.

'I am very happy,' said the line manager, 'to hear your unanimous shouts . . . Now permit me to make you happy in turn. Dear friends, on our line, bribes have gone down by fifty per cent . . .'

'Hip, hip . . .' shouted engineer Sliva.

'Excuse me,' said the line manager, 'don't interrupt . . . Yes . . . This evil has been reduced by fifty per cent, this evil which must be completely eradicated in the very near future. But I am going to be stern and implacable . . . Bribery . . . The word alone drives me mad with indignation . . . Dear friends, now that we are gathered in this close comradely company, permit me, your old manager, whose hair is white with age, to say a few words about bribery . . .'

'Go on! Go on!' shouted the railway workers.

'Dear friends,' said the manager, swaying slightly, 'there is no crime worse than this. Murder, exceeding one's authority, they're nothing compared with this evil. And if I had my way, I'd introduce the most terrible forms of execution. Break them on the wheel, burn them at the stake or quarter them, as far as I'm concerned those are the right punishments for this crime . . . But here I should add that if we take a glance at the contemporary situation, we see that there are two types of bribe: monetary bribes, and bribes in kind. The monetary form is of course far nicer . . . Oh I mean, excuse me, what am I saying?.. Yes, so the monetary bribe, I was saying, is more convenient. More portable, if you like . . . That is, from the point of view of the criminal . . . Imagine, some Nepman comes to see you . . . and you're waving your arms: "No I can't," you're saying, "don't even bother asking comrade . . ."

'But the sly bastard, he'll slip his hand into his side pocket . . . He gets out a pig-skin wallet . . . And meanwhile you're staring at his ugly, thiev-

ing face, trying to guess how much that dog-nose is going to take
out . . .

'Oh, I mean, excuse me, what am I saying? So yes, you, um . . . get
really indignant.

' "Excuse me," you say, "my dear comrade, what's this, a bribe, an
insult?"

'And the banknotes are crackling sweetly between the bastard's fingers . . . you know, that lovely unforgettable rustling . . . You count them
with your eyes: two, three, five, come on, hurry up. Then into your
waistcoat pocket . . . Oh I mean, what am I saying?

'So, yes, so you shout: "I'm pressing charges," you shout, "your sort,
esteemed comrade, should be shot."

'But you can feel a kind of beating in your waistcoat pocket, a trembling, you can feel a pulsation . . . Hm, hmm . . . What was I talking
about, can anyone remember?'

'Bribery,' said engineer Sliva.

'Yes,' said the manager, 'bribery. Hm, pulsation . . . Hm, hmm . . .
But a bribe in kind, that's much worse . . . It's unwieldy, and you can get
ripped off. Like when they sent me a fish, but the bloody thing stank to
high heaven, you remember comrade Sliva . . .'

'Hip, hip . . .' shouted engineer Sliva.

'Hooray!' chorused the railway workers.

The line manager swayed, sat down, and emptied a glass of wine in
one gulp, casting an affectionate eye over his staff.

1923

A Crime Report

The duty militiaman dipped his pen in the inkpot and said:

'Citizens . . . shush . . . stop pushing, one person at a time. Who shoved who?'

'It was him. He shoved him,' said a woman, elbowing her way through to the table. 'He shoved him . . . "Ooo," he said, "you granny from hell."'

A man with a sack who the woman had pointed at stood there quietly, sniffling gloomily. Next to him stood the victim and a few witnesses.

The victim spread his hands and muttered, in embarrassment:

'It wasn't my idea . . . I don't care . . . It's these people who want to . . . The witnesses.'

'He shoved him,' said the woman again. 'He shoved him, and then he said "Ooo, you granny from hell" . . . I was sitting opposite him on the tram, I was going to see my nephew in the village of Smolenskoye.'

'Shush . . .' said the duty officer, 'wait your turn, woman.'

'What's there to wait for?' The woman was upset. 'What's there to wait for? The times are over when people could just be shoved in broad daylight. We've been shoved enough.'

'Shush . . . Shut up,' said the duty officer, dipping his pen in the inkpot again. 'Who are you anyway?'

'Me?' asked the woman. 'I'm a witness . . . I was going to my nephew's . . . You can't have people shoving, in broad daylight, it's not right. He might have shoved him to death . . . And my nephew might just work in a Communist Party Cell . . .'

'Wait a minute woman,' said the militiaman, 'it wasn't you who was shoved . . . We'll speak to you later . . . Just be quiet for a moment.'

'So what if it wasn't me . . .'

'Shush . . . was it you who was shoved?' the militiaman asked the victim.

'Yes, it was me . . .' said the victim. 'Only it wasn't my . . . I don't care. So I was shoved. It happens. After all it was in a tram. It was these witnesses who demanded it: you must go to the militia, they said.'

'I'm sorry, I beg your pardon,' said one of the witnesses. 'I saw it too . . . You can't let him get away with that . . . You've got to report the crime . . .'

'That's what I said,' the woman piped up again, 'a crime report, you've got to get a crime report . . . But the citizen militiaman is trying to shut me up . . . I'll go right to the top . . . It's not right, in broad daylight . . .'

The militiaman dipped his pen in the inkpot for a third time and started to write the crime report, from time to time asking: name . . . sex . . . former title . . . The duty officer took a long time writing, painstakingly tracing out the letters. Then he asked:

'Where was it? In what location?'

'On the tram,' said the woman, 'on the tram, comrades. That's what I've been saying, on the tram, sir . . . I was going to the village of Smolenskoye. Where else would I have been? Going to see my nephew . . .'

'Location? Street?'

'We were going up Semyonovskaya street . . .'

'What,' said the militiaman, putting down his pen. 'Up Semyonovskaya? That's not our district. That, citizens, is the second district. You'd better get round there, off you go . . . '

'What do you mean?' exclaimed the witnesses. 'You've already written it down now, why bother . . .'

'You've got to go to the second district.'

'And what if I'd been murdered.'

'Murdered where?'

'Where else . . . On Semyonovskaya . . .'

'The second district.'

'Come on,' cried the woman . 'Off we go citizens. It wouldn't be right just to leave matters there . . . Where's the victim?'

There was no victim. He'd disappeared, taking advantage of the pause in proceedings. The citizen with the sack, who'd been silent until now, got angry.

'What's the matter with you?' he said, turning to the woman, 'why are you making such a song and dance?'

'Who's making a song and dance?' the woman piped up, putting her basket on the table again. 'Who's making a song and dance?'

'You're making a song and dance. It was you who kicked up all the fuss in the first place, you granny from hell . . .'

The woman threw up her hands, startled.

'Citizens, what's this,' she said, 'did you hear that, he's cursing me.'

'You can now,' said the militiaman, dipping his pen in the inkpot for a fourth time. 'Now it's our district. Shall I write out a crime report?'

'Come off it,' the woman exclaimed, 'why bother writing out a crime report? Comrade militiaman, have a heart . . . What is there to report . . . We're just having a quiet, orderly chat . . .'

The woman took her basket and headed for the way out. The witnesses disappeared one by one. The citizen with the sack was the only one left. For a long time and quite unnecessarily he quizzed the militiaman about the whereabouts of the second district, then he gave up and, sniffling gloomily, left.

1923

An Anonymous Friend

There was a man called Pyotr Petrovich who lived with his spouse, Katerina Vasilyevna. He lived on Malaya Okhta. And he lived well. He was rich. Home comforts, and a wardrobe, and chests full of goods . . . he even had two samovars. And more irons than you could count − about fifteen of the things.

But even with all this wealth, the man lived a boring life. He sat on his goods, looked at his spouse and didn't show his face out of doors. He was afraid to go out, in case of theft. Didn't even go to the cinema. Otherwise, he thought, all his stuff would be stolen while he was out.

But then one day Pyotr Petrovich got a letter through the post. It was a secret letter. No signature. It said:

> Oi you [it said], you old fart, you spare boot. You're living with your young spouse and you can't see what's happening around you. That wife of yours, you old fool, is living it up with some peasant. Seeing as I'm your anonymous friend and so on, I'm telling you: if you, you old fart, go to Labourers' Gardens at seven o'clock in the evening on Saturday the twenty-ninth of July, then you'll see with your own eyes what a roving butterfly your spouse is. Wake up, you old fart.
>
> Respectfully yours,
>
> 'An anonymous friend'

Pyotr Petrovich read this letter and was stunned. He started trying to figure out what could have happened and how. And he remembered: Katerina Vasilyevna had received two letters, but she hadn't said who they were from. In general she was acting suspiciously: she had started making frequent visits to her mother and demanding money for small purchases.

'There's a fine state of affairs!' thought Pyotr Petrovich. 'I've been nursing a viper . . . But keep calm, don't let them laugh at you. I'll track them down, punch them in the mouth. End of story.'

On Saturday the twenty-ninth of July, Pyotr Petrovich pretended to be ill. He was lying on the sofa and keeping an eye on his spouse. She wasn't up to anything in particular, just doing the housework. But towards evening, she said:

'Pyotr Petrovich, I've got to go and see mother. She's fallen danger-
ously ill.'

And she powdered her nose, put a hat on her head and left.

Pyotr Petrovich got dressed as quickly as he could, took a stick in his
left hand, put on his galoshes and headed off after his wife.

He arrived at Labourers' Gardens, turned up his collar so that he
wouldn't be recognized, and started walking round the park. Suddenly,
he saw his spouse sitting by the fountain and looking into the distance.
He went up to her.

'Ahah,' he said, 'Hello. Waiting for your lover are you? Well
Madam,' he said, 'Katerina Vasilyevna, a punch in the mouth's too
good for you . . . '

She was in tears.

'Oh,' she said, 'Pyotr Petrovich, Pyotr Petrovich! It's not what you
think . . . I didn't want to tell you, but now I'll have to . . . '

And with these words she took a letter from her sleeve.

The letter told in tragic tones of how only she, Katerina Vasilyevna
alone, could save a man who would otherwise perish and whose life
stood on the edge of a precipice. And this man begged Katerina Vasilyevna to come to Labourers' Gardens on Saturday July the twenty-
ninth.

'Strange,' he said, 'who wrote it?'

'I don't know,' replied Katerina Vasilyevna. 'I felt sorry for him and
so I came along. But I've no idea who this man is.'

'All right then,' said Pyotr Petrovich, 'so you came here. Now you're
here you might as well carry on sitting there and don't move. I,' he said,
'will hide behind the fountain. I'll see what kind of character we're
dealing with. I'll,' he said, 'give him a beating.'

Pyotr Petrovich hid behind the fountain and sat waiting. His spouse
was sitting opposite him, pale and barely breathing. An hour passed,
nothing happened. Another hour, still nothing. Then Pyotr Petrovich
crept out from behind the fountain.

'Oh, stop snivelling, Katerina Vasilyevna,' he said. 'Clearly someone's played a trick on us here. Shall we go home then . . .? We've had
a nice long walk . . . It wasn't your bastard of a brother up to his tricks,
was it?'

Katerina Vasilyevna shook her head.

'No,' she said, 'this is something serious. Maybe you scared the
anonymous man, and he wouldn't come over.'

Pyotr Petrovich spat, took his wife by the arm, and they left.

And so the couple arrived home. It looked as if a bomb had hit it.
Trunks and chests of drawers smashed to bits, irons strewn all over the

place, samovars gone: they'd been burgled. There was a note pinned to the wall:

> You rotten bastards, couldn't drag you out of the house any other way. Always sitting there being miserable . . . And those suits of yours, you old fart, don't fit me. You're a mangy midgety size, you old fart. That's a bit of a mean trick.
> Do give your spouse my sincerest regards and warmest kisses.

The couple read the note, groaned, sat down on the floor and burst into tears like little children.

1923

A Victim of the Revolution

Yefim Grigoryevich took off his boot and showed me his foot. At first glance, there was nothing remarkable about it. Only a closer inspection of his toe revealed some scratches and abrasions that had now healed.

'They heal up,' said Yefim Grigoryevich. 'There's nothing you can do about it. After all it was nearly seven years ago now.'

'What are they?' I asked.

'Those?' said Yefim Grigoryevich. 'Those, esteemed comrade, are what I suffered in the October Revolution. These days, now six years have passed, everyone's trying to muscle in on it, of course: me too, they say, I took part in the Revolution, I too, they say, shed blood and sacrificed myself. But you can see the marks it left on me. Marks like that don't lie . . . I, esteemed comrade, though I have never worked in any factories and by birth I am a former *meshchanin* of the town of Kronstadt, all the same, in my time I was singled out by fate: I was a victim of the Revolution. I, esteemed comrade, was crushed by the engine of revolution.'

Then Yefim Grigoryevich gave me a solemn stare and, binding up his foot, continued:

'Yes sir, I was crushed by an engine, a truck. And it wasn't as a passer-by or as some petty pawn, through not paying attention or poor eyesight, on the contrary, I suffered for a reason in the Revolution itself. Did you know the former Count Oreshin?'

'No.'

'Well, it was like this . . . I used to be in service with this Count. I was his floor-polisher. I had to polish their floors twice a day, whether I liked it or not. And once with wax, of course. Those Counts really loved it to be done with wax. As for me, I couldn't have cared less, it was just a waste of money. Though of course you do get a shine. But these Counts were very rich and as far as that goes, they spared no expense.

'So, you see, this is what happened: I polished their floors, say, on a Monday, and on Saturday the Revolution took place. On Monday I did their polishing, on Saturday there was the Revolution, and on Tuesday, four days before the Revolution, their doorman came running over to my place and called me over:

' "Come with me," he said, "they're shouting for you. The Count's been robbed blind, and you're the chief suspect. Look sharp about it or they'll twist your head off."

'I threw on my jacket, gobbled something to keep me going and hurried off to their place.

'I came running over to the house. Naturally I rushed into their rooms.

'I saw the former Countess herself writhing in hysterics and stamping on the carpet with her heels.

'She saw me and said through her tears:

' "Ah," she said, "Yefim, *comme-çi comme-ça*, was it you nicked my diamond-encrusted twenty-four-carat gold lady's watch?"

' "What are you talking about," I said, "What do you mean, former Countess? What do I want a lady's watch for, when I'm a man? You've got to be joking, if you'll pardon the expression."

'But she was sobbing:

' "No," she said, "it was none other than you who nicked it, *comme-çi comme-ça*."

'And suddenly the former Count himself came in and contradicted to all present:

' "I," he said, "am an excessively rich man, and I could just forget about your former watch right now and be done with it, but," he said, "I'm not just going to let this go. I don't wish," he said, "to soil my hands on your gob, but I'm going to start proceedings against you, *comme-çi comme-ça*. Get out of here."

'I just looked out the window, of course, and left.

'I got home, lay down and just lay there. I was feeling really depressed. Because I hadn't taken that watch of theirs.

'I lay there for a day, for two days: I stopped eating food, all I could do was think where that encrusted watch could be.

'And then suddenly, on the fifth day it hit me.

' "Now I remember," I thought, "I found that watch of theirs myself and stuffed it in a powder-container. I found it on the carpet. I thought it was a medallion, so I stuffed it in there."

'I threw on my jacket straight away and, without even having a bite to eat, I ran outside. The former Count lived on Ofitserskaya Street.

'So there I was running down the road, and I could feel something wasn't right. What's this, I thought, people are walking in a strange sideways manner and looking like they're afraid of rifle fire and artillery? Why's that, I thought.

'I asked some passers-by. They replied:

' "The October Revolution took place yesterday."

'I pressed on and came to Ofitserskaya Street.

'I ran up to the house. There was a crowd. And there was a motor vehicle standing there too. And it immediately struck me: I don't want to fall under that motor vehicle, I thought. But the vehicle was stationary . . . All right then. I went nearer, and asked:

' "What's happening here?"

' "What we're doing," they said, "is putting some aristocrats in a van and arresting them. We're liquidating that class."

'And then suddenly I saw them being led out. The former Count was being led out to the motor vehicle. I pushed my way through the crowd and shouted:

' "It's in the container," I shouted, "your watch, the damned thing! It's in the powder-container."

'But the Count, the swine, didn't pay me a blind bit of notice and got in.

'I rushed towards the motor vehicle, but the damned thing spluttered to life at that moment and the wheels threw me aside.

' "There you go," I thought, "there's a victim for you." '

At this point Yefim Grigoryevich took off his boot and, with an air of disappointment, started inspecting the healed-over marks on his foot. Then he put his boot back on and said:

'There you are esteemed comrade, as you can see I too have suffered in my time and am, so to speak, a victim of the Revolution. I'm not making a song and dance about it, but I'm not about to let anyone take liberties with me. Which reminds me, the Chairman of the Housing Co-op is measuring my room in square metres. Right down to the place where the chest of drawers stands. He really is taking liberties. You've got about half a metre of floor-space under the chest of drawers, he said. What does he mean, half a metre – that's where the chest of drawers stands! And it's not even mine, it's the landlord's.'

1923

Classy Lady

Comrades, I can't stand women in hats. If a woman's got a hat and silk stockings on, or she's carrying some little pug-dog, or she's got a gold tooth, then if you ask me, that kind of classy lady isn't a woman at all, but a waste of space.

In my time I've fallen for one of these classy ladies of course. I went out with her and took her to the theatre. And it was in the theatre that it all came out. It was in the theatre she exposed the full extent of her ideology.

I met her in our block, in the yard. At a meeting. I saw some personage standing there. Stockings on and a gold tooth.

'Where are you from, citizen?' I asked, 'What number?'

'I'm,' she said, 'from number seven.'

'All right,' I said, 'you can carry on living there.'

And straight away I liked her really badly. I started going round there regularly. To number seven. I would go round there in my official capacity. I'd say, so how are things here citizen, have you had any problems with the plumbing or the toilet ? Or, is everything working?'

'Yes,' she'd say. 'Everything's working.'

And she'd just pull her flannel scarf around her and not a word more. She'd just make eyes at me. And her tooth flashed in her mouth. After I'd been going round there for a month, she got used to me. Starting answering in more detail: saying 'The plumbing's working all right, thank you, Grigory Ivanovich.'

Time passed and we saw more of each other, and began to go for walks together. We'd get outside and she would tell me to take her on my arm. I'd take her on my arm and trawl along, like a pike after its prey. And I didn't know what to say, I felt embarrassed in front of all the people.

Then one day she said to me:

'Why are you,' she said, ' always dragging me around the streets? It's making me dizzy. Since you're a man of influence and you want to take me out,' she said, 'you should take me, say, to the theatre.'

'If you want,' I said.

As it happened, the next day the Party cell sent some opera tickets. I got one, and Vaska the boilermaker gave me his.

I didn't check the tickets, but they weren't together. Mine was downstairs and Vaska's was up in the gallery.

So off we went. We sat down in our places. She sat in my seat, and I sat in Vaska's. I was sitting up at the very top, and couldn't see a damned thing. But if I leant out over the safety-rail I could see her. Not very well though. I felt bored, really bored, so I went downstairs. I saw it was the interval. And she was walking about during the interval.

'Hello,' I said.

'Hello.'

'I wonder,' I said, 'whether the plumbing works here?'

'I don't know,' she said.

She made for the buffet. I followed her. She walked along the buffet looking at the counter. There was a plate on the counter. It had cakes on it.

And strutting like a peacock, like one of those bourgeois bastards we didn't manage to finish off, I was hovering around her.

'If you wish,' I offered, 'to eat one of those cakes, go ahead, I'll pay.'

'*Merci*,' she said.

And suddenly she walked over to the plate in her decadent way, grabbed a cream cake, and chomped away on it.

But I didn't have enough cash to feed a cat. At the most I could afford three cakes. She was eating, and I was feeling around in my pockets, worrying, trying to see with my hand how much money I had left. What I had you could have easily fitted up a dove's nose.

She ate one cream cake, and stuffed away another. I was starting to wheeze, but I kept quiet. I suddenly felt some bourgeois embarrassment. She'd say: he wants to take me out and he hasn't got any money.

I was circling around her like a cockerel, while she was chuckling and fishing for compliments.

I said:

'Isn't it about time we took our seats? I think the bell's rung.'

But she said:

'No.'

And took a third cake.

I said:

'Don't you think that's a lot on an empty stomach? You might feel sick.'

But she went:

'It's all right, I'm used to it.'

And took a fourth.

Then the blood went to my head.

'Put it,' I said, 'back!'

She was frightened. Opened her mouth. The gold tooth was shining there.

But I completely lost it. Whatever happens, I thought, I won't be going out with her anymore.

'Put' I said, 'the bloody thing back!'

She put it back. Then I said to the man behind the counter:

'How much is that for the three cakes we've eaten?'

But the man was indifferent, pretending he didn't understand.

'For the four cakes you've eaten, that'll be such and such.'

'What do you mean,' I said, 'four, when the fourth is there on the plate?!'

'No,' he answered, 'it might be situated on the plate, but there's a bite taken out of it and it's got finger-marks on it.'

'What do you mean,' I said, 'a bite taken out of it! Excuse me, but that's just your ridiculous fantasies.'

But the man was still indifferent, waving his arms all over the place.

Well, then a crowd gathered of course. Bloody experts.

Some reckoned a bite had been taken, others didn't.

So I turned out my pockets: all sorts of rubbish fell out onto the floor. People were laughing. But I wasn't laughing. I was counting my money.

I finished counting the money. Just enough for four cakes. I needn't have got into a f. . .lipping argument.

I paid. I turned to the lady:

'You may finish it,' I said, 'citizen. It's paid for.'

But the lady didn't move. She was too embarrassed to finish it.

Then some fellow poked his nose in.

'Give it here,' he said, 'I'll finish it.'

And he finished it up, the bastard. On my money.

We took our seats. Finished watching the opera. Then went home. By our block she said:

'That was rather lousy of you. If you haven't got any money you can't go out with ladies.'

I replied:

'Money can't buy happiness, citizen. If you'll pardon the expression.'

And that's how we split up.

I don't like classy ladies.

1923

Love

The party ended late.

Sweating with exhaustion, Vasya Chesnokov, wearing a master-of-ceremonies button-hole on his soldier's tunic, stood before Mashenka and said in a pleading tone:

'Wait a while my darling . . . Wait for the first tram. Come on, really, why do you have to go . . . Wait for the first tram . . . We could sit here, and wait and everything, but you're going . . . Wait for the first tram, come on. Look, you're sweating, and I'm sweating . . . You know, you could catch cold in the frost . . .'

'I don't care,' said Mashenka, putting on her galoshes. 'What sort of a gentleman are you, if you won't accompany a lady home on account of the frost?'

'But I'm sweating,' said Vasya, almost in tears.

'Come on, put your coat on!'

Vasya Chesnokov obediently put on his fur-coat, firmly took Mashenka's arm and went outside with her.

It was cold. The moon was shining. Snow crunched under their feet.

'What a restless little lady you are,' said Vasya Chesnokov, ecstatically examining Mashenka in profile. 'If it was any other woman but you, I wouldn't have gone out to accompany her, not for anything. I swear it's true. I only came out of love.'

Mashenka laughed.

'You may laugh and grin,' said Vasya, 'but, Marya Vasilyevna, I really do passionately love you and adore you. If you said, Vasya Chesnokov, go and lie on the tramlines, on the rails, and lie there until the first tram comes, I'd do it. I swear I would . . .'

'Stop it, you,' said Mashenka. 'Look at the miraculous beauty around us, with the moon shining. Look how beautiful the city is at night! What miraculous beauty!'

'Yes, wonderful beauty,' said Vasya, looking with a certain surprise at the chipped plasterwork of a building. 'Really, very beauty . . . And beauty too, you see, Marya Vasilyevna, only works if you really have feelings . . . You see many learned men and Party members deny the feeling of love, but I, Marya Vasilyevna, don't deny it. I might feel like this towards you unto the moment of my own death and to the point of self-sacrifice. I swear . . . If you said: Vasya Chesnokov, beat your head against that wall, I'd do it.'

'Here we go again,' said Mashenka, not without a certain pleasure.

'I swear, I'd do it. Do you want me to?'

The couple came out onto the Kryuchkov Canal.

'I swear I would,' said Vasya again, 'or if you want, I'll throw myself into the canal. Shall I, Marya Vasilyevna? You don't believe me, but I'll show you . . .'

Vasya Chesnokov took hold of the railings and pretended to climb over.

'Ahhh!' shouted Mashenka, 'Vasya! Don't do it!'

A gloomy figure suddenly popped up from a corner and stopped by the lamp-post.

'What are you yelling for?' said the figure quietly, carefully examining the couple.

Mashenka screamed in terror, and leant against the railings.

The man came closer and pulled Vasya towards him by the sleeve.

'Right you, you slag,' said the man in a low voice. 'Get that coat off. Be quick about it. One word out of you and I'll whack you on the head, and that'll be the end of you. Got it, you bastard? Get it off!'

'Ba-ba-ba,' said Vasya, by which he meant to say 'I beg your pardon, what do you mean?'

'What was that?' The man pulled the fur-coat by the lapel.

With trembling hands, Vasya unbuttoned the coat and took it off.

'Take your boots off too,' said the man. 'I need your boots too.'

'Ba-ba-ba,' said Vasya, 'I beg you . . . the frost . . .'

'What's that?'

'You don't touch the lady, but I've got to take my boots off,' said Vasya peevishly, 'she's got a fur-coat and galoshes, but I'm the one who has to take my boots off.'

The man looked at Mashenka calmly and said:

'If I take hers off and carry it in a bundle, I'll get caught. I know what I'm doing. You got them off?'

Mashenka looked at the man in terror and stood immobile. Vasya Chesnokov sat down on the snow and started to unlace his boots.

'She's got a fur-coat,' said Vasya again, 'and galoshes, but I'm the one getting undressed for both of us . . .'

The man squeezed into Vasya's fur-coat, stuffed the boots into his pockets and said:

'Sit there and don't move, and don't so much as chatter your teeth. If you shout or move, you're dead. Got it, you bastard? And you lady . . .'

The man quickly wrapped the coat around himself and suddenly disappeared.

Vasya went soft and sour and sat down lifelessly on the snow, staring in disbelief at his white-socked feet.

'A fine end to the evening,' he said, looking at Mashenka maliciously. 'I walk her home, and I lose my property. So that's how it is.'

When the thief's footsteps were completely out of ear-shot, Vasya Chesnokov suddenly began to twitch his feet on the snow and cried out in a thin, penetrating voice:

'Help! Thief!'

Then he got up and ran across the snow, jumping up and down and hopping from toe to toe in pain. Mashenka remained by the railings.

1924

Host Accountancy

During the holidays the accountant Goryushkin arranged a dinner at his place. There weren't many guests.

The host met his guests in the hall with a sort of ecstatic shriek, helped them take their coats off and dragged them off to the sitting room.

'Here he is,' he said, presenting a guest to his wife, 'here's my best friend and colleague.'

Then, pointing to his son, he said:

'And this, look over here, is my dopey little boy . . . Lyoshka. He's a clever little rogue, I can tell you.'

Lyoshka stuck his tongue out, and the guest, slightly embarrassed, sat down at the table.

When everyone was gathered, the host, with a triumphant sort of look, invited people to take their seats at the table.

'Take your seats . . .' he said warmly. 'Take your seats. Help yourselves . . . Nice to have you . . . Tuck in . . .'

The guests started up a friendly clunking of spoons.

'Yes, sir,' said the host after a short silence. 'Everything's become pretty expensive, you know. Everything you touch, it all eats away at your wages. The rouble's rising, prices are rising.'

'You can't afford anything,' said his wife, mournfully swallowing her soup.

'You're damn right,' said the host, 'you really can't afford anything. Just take a pathetic little thing like soup. It's nothing. Rubbish. Pretty much like water. All right then, try and guess how much this water costs!'

'Mm . . . yea,' said the guests uncertainly.

'I mean it,' said the host. 'Take something else, salt. A nothing product. Complete rubbish, pathetic stuff, but go on, have a guess how much that costs.'

'Yes, but,' said the dopey little Lyoshka, grimacing, 'the way some guests start using the salt, soon there'll be none left.'

A young man in pince-nez glasses, who had just sprinkled some salt in his soup, pushed the salt-cellar away from his place in fear.

'Go on sir, sprinkle away,' said the hostess, moving the salt-cellar towards him.

The guests were tensely silent. The host ate his soup heartily, looking at his guests benevolently.

'And now for the main course,' he declared animatedly. 'Come on gentlemen, take your main course, the meat. But now permit me to ask what the cost of that meat was? Heh? What does it weigh?'

'Four pounds and five ounces,' his wife informed him gloomily.

'We'll say five to even up the figures,' said the host. 'At, shall we say, fifty kopecks a pound in new money? So, for each person it works out as . . . How many are we?'

'Eight,' Lyoshka counted.

'Eight,' said the host. 'At half-a-pound each . . . At the very least, twenty-five kopecks per person.'

'Yes, but,' said Lyoshka in an offended tone, 'some guests slap mustard on their meat.'

'That's true,' the host cried, laughing good-naturedly. 'I nearly forgot the mustard . . . All right then, add mustard to the bill, and what with one thing and another, it'll come to a rouble each . . .'

'Yes, a rouble each,' said Lyoshka, 'but probably that time when Pal Yeliseyevich smashed the glass with his elbow, he probably made it come to a bit more . . .'

'Oh yes!' the host cried. 'Just picture it, the guests arrived, and then one of them, accidentally of course, knocked the glass out of the mirror. That meal cost us. We sat down and added it up.'

The host became absorbed with his memories.

'Mind you,' he said, 'this meal also cost a kopeck or two. We could add it up.'

He took a pencil and started calculating, counting up everything that had been eaten in detail. The guests sat there quietly, immobile, apart from the young man who had carelessly sprinkled salt in his soup, who was constantly taking off his sweat-covered pince-nez glasses and wiping them with his napkin.

'Yes sir,' said the host. 'Five and a bit roubles . . .'

'What about the electricity?' asked his wife, outraged. 'And the heating? And paying Marya?'

The host clasped his hands and laughed, slapping himself.

'That's right,' he said, 'the electricity, the heating, paying Marya . . . And accommodation? There's a point gentlemen, the accommodation! So that's eight people, eight square yards . . . Forty-five kopecks a yard . . . And then it's three kopecks a day . . . Umm . . . I'll need to do this one on paper . . .'

The young man in pince-nez glasses began to fidget around on his chair, then suddenly he got up and went into the hall.

'Where are you going?' shouted the host. 'Where are you going, my dear Ivan Semyonovich?'

The guest said nothing, put on someone else's galoshes and left without saying goodbye. Next, the others started leaving too.

The host remained sitting at the table with a pencil in his hand for a while, and then declared:

'One-fifth of a kopeck in new money, each.'

He declared this to his wife and Lyoshka – no guests remained.

1924

A Dogged Sense of Smell

Comrades, you know they can do amazing things with science these days, incredible! A dog for example. Take a simple dog: four legs, a tail, ears and so on. They can even get a simple dog to grab a criminal by the trousers and unmask him there and then.

I used to take a sceptical attitude towards the abilities of dogs. But not now, now I fear and respect dogs. There really is something amazing about a dog's sense of smell. Or maybe that wasn't it after all. Anyway, this is what happened.

The merchant Yeremey Babkin had his coonskin-coat swiped.

The merchant Yeremey Babkin started howling. It broke his heart to lose that coat.

'That coat,' he said, 'was so good it hurts me to lose it, citizens. It's a crying shame. I'll spare no expense to find the criminal. Then I'll spit in his face.'

And so Yeremey Babkin called for the militia sniffer-dog. This man in a peaked cap and puttees appeared, and with him this dog. A brown dog with a sharp snout and it didn't look too friendly.

This man pushed his dog towards the footprints near the door, said *tsst* and stood back. The dog sniffed the air, eyed the crowd (some people had gathered of course) and suddenly went up to Old Fyokla, a woman from number five, and started sniffing her skirt. The woman tried to hide in the crowd. The dog took hold of her hem. The old woman moved away – and the dog went after her. It clamped onto the old woman by the skirt and wouldn't let go.

The old woman fell to her knees before the officer.

'Yes,' she said, 'you've caught me. There's no denying it,' she said. 'The five buckets of yeast – it's true. And a vodka-still – it's all true. Everything's in the bathroom,' she said. 'Take me to the militia.'

Well, of course the crowd all went 'ooh!' and 'ah!'

'What about the coat?' they asked.

'I don't know anything about the coat,' she said, 'and I don't care, but the rest is just as I said. Take me away and punish me.'

So they led the old woman away.

The officer took hold of his dog again and rubbed its nose in the footprints, said *tsst* and stood back.

The dog looked up, sniffed the empty air and suddenly went up to

Citizen Chairman of the House Committee.

The Chairman of the House Committee went white as a sheet and fell flat on his back.

'Kind people, class-conscious citizens!' he said. 'Tie me up. I,' he said, 'collected money for the water, but I spent that money on myself.'

Well, need I say, the tenants jumped upon the Chairman of the House Committee and started to tie him up. Meanwhile the dog went up to a citizen from number seven. It started tugging at his trousers.

The citizen turned pale and fell to the ground before the people.

'I'm guilty,' he said, 'I'm guilty. It's true,' he said, 'I wiped a year off my work-record. A young stallion like me ought to be serving in the army, defending the Motherland, but I'm living in number seven and benefiting from electricity and other communal services. Grab me!'

People didn't know what to do.

'Just what,' they thought, 'is this amazing dog?'

So the merchant Yeremey Babkin blinked his eyes, looked around him, took out some money and gave it to the militiaman.

'Take your mangy dog,' he said, 'back to its pig-sty of a kennel. Let's forget about the coonskin-coat,' he said. 'It's gone. Ah well, never mind . . .'

But the dog was already onto him. It was standing in front of the merchant with its tail twitching.

The merchant Yeremey Babkin didn't know what to do, he moved away and the dog followed. It came up to him and sniffed his galoshes.

The merchant started babbling and turned pale.

'Well,' he said, 'if that's the way it is then God sees the truth. I,' he said, 'am a son of a bitch and a swindler. And that coat,' he said, 'comrades, it wasn't mine. I borrowed it off my brother and didn't give it back. I could weep for shame!'

People fled whereever they could. The dog didn't even have time to sniff the air, it just grabbed two or three people at random and held onto them.

They confessed. One had lost state funds at cards, the other had taken a swipe at his wife with an iron, what the third admitted is too embarrassing even to mention.

People ran off in all directions. The yard emptied. There was only the dog and the militiaman left.

And then suddenly the dog went up to the militiaman with its tail wagging.

The militiaman turned pale, and fell before the dog.

'Bite me,' he said, 'citizen dog. I,' he said, 'receive three ten-rouble notes for your dog food and take two for myself . . .'

What happened next I'm not sure. I locked myself in my room. The dog didn't grab me by the leg. It probably didn't quite manage to. And what would I have done if it had? I would have fallen on my knees before the crowd:

'Comrades,' I would have said, 'I am the worst criminal of all: though I didn't touch the fur-coat, I take advances from magazines, publish the same story twice, and all the rest of it. Beat me, wretch that I am.'

1924

A Forgotten Slogan

(Letter to the Editor)

Esteemed comrade editors and dear typesetters,

Having learned from the newspaper that you're bringing out a special ladies' issue, I'm writing to ask you to add my humble voice to it.

Dear writers, move over a bit! Let me have a little space to report on the women's question and on equality.

What's going on, dear comrades, with regard to women's equality? Has this lovely slogan really been forgotten? Is there really nothing left of it?

It was only 1918 when this slogan was first announced to complete raptures all round: equality. That means that any poxy little insignificant lady is equal to a man and if she goes anywhere with him, she pays on the same basis and out of her own pocket.

But within five years this slogan has been forgotten, and a different picture now meets the eye of the beholder. Whether you go to the theatre with some lady or take her to the cinema, you have to pay the entrance money at the theatre and at the cinema. And if the lady has her minor little sister with her, then you have to pay for her too. And, what's more, if her old mum tags along too, then you fork out free for the mum as well. Even though the mum's eyes are weak and even with her glasses on she hasn't got the faintest idea what's going on, and so you're throwing money away in vain and down the drain.

Or let's say you get on the tram with a lady, you'll have to pay the conductor her tram fare too. And if you only take out enough change for one, then there'll be no end of tears and scenes later.

Why's that, esteemed comrade typesetters? What kind of equality is this then? Why should people suffer, when a wonderful slogan was proclaimed a while back? The law can't just be reversed!

Move over just a little bit more, dear, venerable writers. Dear typesetters, please don't be angry that I'm making you typeset, I'm only trying to make an effort on behalf of your brothers, us men.

So then, in 1918 the wonderful slogan was proclaimed, and in 1919, deciding not to put matters off to the bottom of the in-tray, I started to look for a woman to share my life with who would be in accordance with the slogan. But I couldn't find one.

Some ladies just laughed at the slogan, saying that they didn't want any such slogan. Others, quite the opposite, said the slogan was very nice, but then, when it came down to it, it was go on, get your money out: pay for the tickets, give up your seat, and buy the fruit-drops . . . So much for the slogan!

I went on searching for two years, and eventually I was successful.

Move over just a little bit more, esteemed writers. Permit me to finish my fable. Set it in bolder type, dear typesetters.

So I found a lady. I found her in a workers' club, where she was fervently defending this slogan.

She wasn't pretty of course, this lady, but I wasn't looking at her exterior, I was looking at her interior.

Her exterior was certainly modest: her hair was shaven off and one of her lips drooped down, which gave her face a sad expression. But her face was a ruddy, healthy colour.

When I approached her, she was spluttering and saying that she'd never allow a man to pay for her.

'That's what you say now citizen,' I said. 'But I bet, if the ship was sinking, it'd be ladies first, and the men can go and drown and choke in the sea.'

'No,' she said, 'we'll all drown together.'

'All right,' I said, 'in that case I'm pleased to meet you.'

We got to know each other. We started to go out together. And she really did pay for herself and spoke about other ladies with contempt.

When we'd been going out together for two months, I made an official proposal. Let me,' I said, 'be your companion in life. You,' I said, 'pay your way and I'll pay mine. You buy your ticket and I'll buy mine. I like this way of doing things,' I said, 'and it's entirely in accordance with the slogan.'

She said:

'All right,' she said. 'But we'll split the costs of the wedding.'

'Fine by me,' I said.

So I got married.

Move over just a little bit more, dear writers. I've nearly finished.

So then, I got married in May, and in June my wife was sacked from her job for being married.

So she came home laughing.

'You're my husband,' she said, 'you'd better support me.'

I went to her work to sort things out, but they wouldn't listen and as for the slogan, they just grinned.

Esteemed editors and dear typesetters, what's going on? How did I do this to myself? What have I done to deserve to live with an ogress?

What happened to the wonderful slogan? Can it really have been completely forgotten?

1924

A Bad Habit

In February, comrades, I fell ill.

I went to the city hospital. So there I was, you see, in the city hospital, getting better and having a really good rest. It was all peace and quiet, a land of plenty. All clean and orderly, you even felt untidy for being there. If you wanted to spit, they had a spitoon. If you felt like sitting down, they had chairs, and if you felt like blowing your nose, blow it into your hand as much as you like, but on the sheets – whatever you do, just don't do it on the sheets. That's not allowed, they said.

Well, you get used to it.

And why shouldn't you? They go to such a lot of trouble over everything, they take so much care over you, you couldn't ask for more. Some man's lying there, all covered in scabs, let's say, and they come along with his lunch, make his bed, stick a thermometer under his arm, shove an enema up him with their own hands, and even show an interest in his health.

And who is it shows an interest? Important, forward-thinking people: doctors, physicians, nurses, and of course the medical orderly, Ivan Ivanovich.

I felt so grateful to all these staff that I decided to give material thanks.

They can't all get something, I wasn't going to go that far, I thought. I'll give it to one of them, I thought. But who to? I started observing them closely.

And I saw that it had to be Ivan Ivanovich, the medical orderly, who ought to get it. A prominent and imposing figure of a man who was making even more of an effort than the others and really giving it everything.

Right then, I thought, I'll tip him. So I started to think how I could slip him something without damaging his self-respect and without getting in trouble.

I soon had an opportunity.

The medical orderly came up to my bed. Greeted me.

'Hello,' he said. 'How are you today? Have we had a stool this morning then?'

Ahah, I thought, now's the time.

'Of course we had a stool,' I said, 'but one of the patients took it. But if you're looking for a seat, then sit down at the foot of my bed. We'll have a little chat.'

So down the medical orderly sat, and just sat there on the bed.

'Well,' I said to him, 'how are things, what's going on in the world, are the wages good here?'

'The wages,' he said, 'aren't good, but your more civilized patients, even though they're at death's door, still manage a contribution.'

'I'd love to,' I said. 'I may not be at death's door, but I don't object to making a contribution. In fact I've been thinking of nothing else for some time.'

I took out the money and gave it to him. He accepted it kindly and did a little curtsey with his arm.

And the next day it all started.

I was lying there all nice and quiet, and no one had bothered me until then, when suddenly it was as if my material thanks had driven medical orderly Ivan Ivanovich round the bend. In one day he must have come over to my bed ten or fifteen times. He was constantly straightening the pillows, dragging me off to have a bath, trying to give me an enema. He wore me out with the thermometer alone, the son-of-a-bitch. He used to take my temperature once or twice a day, and that had been it. But now he did it fifteen times. The baths used to be lukewarm and I liked them like that, but now they were piping hot no matter how much I screamed.

This was just too much for me. I gave him some more, the bastard, just leave me alone, I beg you, but this sent him completely mad and he tried even harder.

A week passed. I could see that I couldn't take any more.

I sweated so much I lost fifteen pounds, became thin and stopped eating.

But the orderly was still trying his best.

Once he even nearly threw me into a tub of boiling water, the bastard. My God. The bath he ran for me, the bastard, it burst a corn on my foot and the skin came off.

I said to him:

'What the hell do you think you're doing throwing people in boiling water? You're not getting any more material thanks from me.'

And he said:

'Won't I? All right, be like that then. You can go and croak,' he said, 'and don't count on the aid of science.'

And he went away.

Now everything is as it used to be: they take my temperature once a day, give me an enema when necessary. The bath is lukewarm once again, and no one bothers me any more.

It's not for nothing there's a struggle going on against tipping you see. Oh no comrades, not for nothing!

1924

Electrification

What's the most fashionable word these days, eh comrades?

The most very fashionable word you could possibly find these days is, of course, electrification.

It's a matter of immense importance, the illumination of Soviet Russia, I'm not arguing with that. But even this, for the moment, has its not so good sides.

I'm not saying, comrades, that it's expensive. It's not expensive. It's worth every kopeck. I'm not talking about that, I'm not making all this fuss over that and not wasting ink over that.

But there was this case, listen.

We were living in this building. The building was big and all the lighting was kerosine. Some people had basic oil lamps, others had bigger ones, others didn't have anything at all – they used church candles for their lighting. It was a right mess.

And then they started to install lighting.

Our official representative was the first to have it installed. So he went and installed it. He's a quiet man, doesn't make a song and dance about things. All the same, he walks in a strange way and is constantly blowing his nose in a thoughtful manner.

But he hasn't made a song and dance about it.

Then our beloved landlady, Yelizaveta Ignatyevna Prokhorova came along one day and suggested we got lighting installed in the apartment.

'Everyone's getting it installed,' she said. 'Even the official representative himself has had it installed.'

So what could we do! We got it installed too.

They installed it, lit us up. My God! Everything was rotten and revolting.

Before, you'd go off to work in the morning, come home in the evening, drink some tea and go to bed. And with kerosine lighting you didn't notice anything much.

But now, we switched the light on and looked around: there was someone's torn slipper lying on the floor, the wallpaper was torn away and dangling, there was a bedbug galloping off – to get away from the light, some unidentified rag lying there, a lump of spit, a dog-end, a flea bouncing about.

My God! It was enough to make you scream out loud. Just looking at the spectacle made you sick.

There was a sofa that stood in our room. I thought it was pretty good. I even used to sit on it in the evenings. But now, you switch on the light: my God! What a mess! Some sofa! Bits sticking out, hanging off, all its insides falling out. I can't sit on a sofa like that. And that's that.

'Well,' I thought, 'I don't exactly live in luxury. Makes you feel like just getting away from it all. You can't bear to look at it. You can't concentrate.'

I saw my landlady, Yelizaveta Ignatyevna walking around looking sad, pottering about in her part of the kitchen, tidying up.

'What,' I said, 'are you so down about?'

She gave a despairing shrug.

'Semyon Yegorovich,' she said, 'I never thought that we lived in such poverty.'

I glanced over at the landlady's stuff: it was true, I thought, this was no palace: rotten, revolting, all kinds of rags. And all this was flooded with bright light, and you couldn't avoid seeing it.

I started to come home feeling depressed. I'd come home and head straight for bed without switching on the light.

Then I thought better of it, and after payday, I bought some white-wash, mixed it up and got to work. Tore off the wallpaper, got rid of the cobwebs, cleared out the sofa, painted everything: it gave me a great feeling inside.

But though everything was better, it wasn't really. I'd wasted my money: the landlady had the electricity cut off.

'All that light,' she said, 'makes everything look too squalid. Why bring poverty to light so glaringly?' she said.

I pleaded with her and presented the arguments, but it was no use.

'You can move out if you want,' she said. 'But I don't want to live under all that light. I haven't got the money to be redecorating the decor.'

But it's not exactly easy to move out comrades, when you've splashed out on redecorating. So I gave in.

So you see comrades, light's good, but even light has its problems. We've got to change every aspect of our lives. There must be cleanliness and order. We must decisively sweep away all that is rotten and revolting. What's good in the dark is bad in the light! Wouldn't you agree, comrades?

1924

Casual Work

The thing is my dad was a trader (said Ivan Ivanovich Gusev). Under the Tsarist regime he worked in the Deryabinsky market . . . And on account of this dad I'm completely done for. Because I can't get a job. Government institutions won't take me on. As for the free professions or some kind of casual or seasonal work, there's not a lot of that around either.

But the other day I came across a spot of work, sort of casual work, but I wasn't able to take advantage of the offer.

The offer was made by a girl. Kate by name. My neighbour. We live next door to one another.

So there's her room, and there's mine. But the dividing wall's very thin. You can hear everything through it: the girl coming home in the small hours, curling her hair with tongs, drinking beer, discussing financial issues with her male friends. You can hear every last detail, though you can't see the expression on their faces.

One morning the girl got up and banged on the wall with her fist.

'Oi,' she said, 'mon cher, have you got any matches?'

'Of course I have m'lady,' I answered through the wall. 'I,' I said, 'though I'm unemployed and live on God knows what,' I said, 'I've got some matches. Come on in.'

So in she came. In her peignoir, all *déshabillé*, with slippers on her bare feet, the flirt.

'Hello,' she said. 'I've got to curl my hair, but I haven't got any matches. I'll,' she said, 'give you your matches straight back.'

'Well,' I said, 'you'd better do just that. I,' I said, 'am unemployed and uneducated, I can't,' I said, 'just go round throwing matches away.'

Little by little we got talking.

'How do you make a living,' I asked, 'and how much are you charged per square yard for your room?'

She didn't answer the question directly, saying vaguely:

'Since you're unemployed and starving,' she said, 'out of the kindness of my heart, I can give you a job.'

'What as?' I asked.

'Well,' she said, 'as a pimp.'

'All right,' I said, 'in a word, tell me what it involves,' I said.

'It's perfectly simple,' she said. 'If I go to a restaurant alone, I can

charge one price, but if I'm with a man, and the man looks like my relative, then I can charge another, higher price. So,' she said, 'we go
around together. We arrive together, sit there for a while, and then you
have to sort of hurry off: oh, you'd say, Kate, my mum may be ill, I've
got to leave. And then you come back in an hour. Ah Kate, you say, here
I am, isn't it about time for us to set off home Kate?'

'Is that all?' I asked.

'Yes,' she said. 'Only dress as smart as you can. Put some pince-nez
glasses on your nose if you've got any. We'll start tonight.'

'All right,' I said, 'the job seems easy enough.'

And so when evening came, I got dressed up. Put on a jacket and a
sweater. Stuck some pince-nez on my nose, God knows where she got
hold of them. And off we went.

We entered the restaurant salon. We sat down at a table. I said:

'Can I take these glasses off? I'm not used to them and I can't see a
bloody thing. I might fall off my chair.'

But she said:

'No, grin and bear.'

We sat there. Grinning and bearing. I really felt like some grub. It
was unbearable: all around they were carrying roast chicken, the smell
was tingling in my nose.

Then she whispered in my ear:

'It's time,' she said, 'to go.'

I stood up, scraping my chair on purpose.

'Oh,' I said, 'Kate, I've got to hurry off, *voici-voilà,*my dear old mum
might have fallen ill,' I said. 'You sit here. I'll come back to get you.'

And she was nodding her head, as if to say: All right, clear off.

So I took off my glasses and went outside.

I walked about outside for half an hour, and was frozen stiff. Right to
the bone.

I went back in. I glanced over: my girl was sitting there at the table
with her little finger sticking in the air scoffing something. And next to
her some bourgeois bastard was leaning over to her and whispering
something in her inner ear.

I went up to them.

'Ah,' I said. 'Here I am. Isn't it about time for us to set off home
Kate?'

But she went:

'No,' she said, 'Pierre, I'll just sit here a little while longer with this
personal acquaintance of mine,' she said. 'You can go on home.'

'Well,' I said, 'if that's what you want. I'll go home alone then.'

I was standing there, about to leave, but I didn't feel like leaving. And what's more, I could have killed for some grub.

'I'll get going,' I said, 'in a minute. But I'll just,' I said, 'sit down for a moment, as a relative and a pimp. I'm frozen stiff.'

She was motioning to me with her eyes, but I didn't care.

I'll just sit here for a bit, I thought, and then I'll leave. It's not, I thought, as if I'm going to wear out their chairs.

I sat down, and went on sitting there. The bourgeois bastard got all embarrassed and stopped whispering.

I said:

'Take no notice of me . . . I'm her relative, you can whisper as much as you want.'

He replied:

'Excuse me,' he said, 'would you care for some porter?'

'All right,' I said. 'why shouldn't a relative,' I said, 'drink some porter. Yes please.'

I drank the porter, and it went straight to my head, probably on account of being hungry. I started eating someone's cutlet.

'If I wasn't a relative,' I said, 'I wouldn't have eaten this cutlet. But why shouldn't a relative eat something? A relative's got to keep his eyes peeled.'

'Excuse me,' said the bourgeois bastard. 'What are you hinting at?'

'Nothing,' I said. 'I'm not hinting at anything. But when it comes to ladies,' I said, 'everyone tries to swindle them. You've got to keep your eyes peeled.'

'What do you mean,' he said, 'swindle? What are you trying to say?'

'Work it out for yourself,' I said. 'I haven't got time to explain. I'd better be off. And you please make sure you pay her properly, no messing about.'

I put my pince-nez on my nose, politely bowed to everyone and left.

And now Kate is giving me ear-ache.

If that's the ear-ache you get in every job, I'm not sure I could stand it.

1924

Domestic Bliss

The other day I dropped in on someone I know, Yegorov. He's the time-keeper in our factory.

I arrived at his apartment.

He was sitting at the table looking very pleased with himself, reading the paper. His wife was sitting beside him doing some sewing.

My host's eyes lit up when he saw me.

'Ah,' he said, 'come on in my friend . . . Aren't you going to congratulate us then?'

'Congratulate you on what, Mitrofan Semyonych?' I asked.

'You mean you don't know?' he said. 'On our new life, on the changes we've made: we've built the new family.'

'How do you mean?' I said. 'You're not expecting an addition to the family are you?'

'Nope,' Yegorov laughed. 'That's not it. Missed by a mile . . . You can ask the wife yourself. It concerns her more . . . Look how happy she is sitting there sewing . . . Just like an angel . . . Let her tell you about her domestic bliss herself.'

I looked at Mitrofan Semyonych's spouse. But she gave a bit of a wry smile and said:

'Yes,' she said, 'you see, we don't cook at home any more . . . We're doing without a cooker. We go to the canteen now.'

'That's right!' exclaimed her husband, pleased with himself. 'We've had enough! We've started a new life. Out the window with the lot of it: the cooker, the saucepans, the washtub . . . Let the woman know freedom . . . She's got the same rights as me.'

My host talked about the unquestionable advantages of communal eating and then started to laugh.

'You can't imagine how much better off we are for this change. It's brought nothing but advantages, clear profit! When guests come, say. They sit there and wait. Constantly wondering if you're going to lay the table. But you announce to them, the freeloading bastards: By the way, you say, I'm afraid we dine in the canteen. You can come too if you like, but you don't have to, we're not forcing you.'

The husband started chuckling and glanced at his wife.

'Yes,' he said. 'It's a win-win situation. Time, for example. We've got so much free time on our hands! All the time in the world . . .

The way things used to be, the wife would get home from work and rush about, bang, crash, light the cooker . . . Think of the waste of matches alone! But now when she comes home, the stupid woman's got nothing to do. She can sew all day long if she wants. Let her enjoy her freedom.'

'Cooking,' I agreed, 'certainly does take up a lot of time.'

'You're not joking!' exclaimed my host with renewed enthusiasm.

'Now at least she comes home and she can sew, and when she's finished sewing, she can do some laundry. If there's no laundry to do, then she can knit some socks . . . She could even start taking orders for sewing, because she's got more free time than she knows what to do with.'

The husband fell silent, then continued, struck by the thought:

'That's a point. Why don't you start taking orders, Motya? You know, for sewing . . . The odd shirt, blouses, smocks . . .'

'Yes, all right,' said his wife, 'I suppose I could take some orders. I don't see why not . . .'

Clearly, the husband was upset by such a lukewarm response.

'I suppose I could,' he mimicked his wife. 'You, Motya, there's no pleasing you. Another woman in your place would be jumping for joy that she'd been emancipated, but you go round sulking like a mouse with a migraine, and don't say a word . . . Aren't you pleased you're not stuck in the kitchen all day? Come on, our guest is waiting for an answer!'

'Don't say that, of course I am,' the wife agreed in a despondent tone.

'As if you wouldn't be pleased! You used to slave over a hot stove all day long . . . The smoke, fumes, steam, flames, the smell . . . Yuch! Now you can sew to your heart's content, Motya. Enjoy your free time. Even you deserve a life.'

I looked at the husband. He was serious.

'Listen,' I said, 'a stone's no softer than a rock.'

'What do you mean?' Mitrofan Semyonych exclaimed in astonishment.

'I said: a stone's no softer than a rock. Cooking, sewing, what's the difference? Maybe your wife would like to read that paper of yours? Maybe she doesn't feel like sewing?'

'You what?' The husband took offence. 'What do you mean not sew? She's a woman.'

I stood up, said goodbye to my host and left. But as I was going, I heard the husband say to his wife:

'The bastard didn't like that. We didn't feed him, so he starts moaning and taking it out on other people . . . If he wants some dinner, he'd better go to the canteen and not hang around other people's houses . . . Come on, sew Motya, sew, pay attention to what you're doing.'

1924

What Generosity

In breweries they pay the workers two bottles of beer each to keep them in good health.

All right, so let them. We're not jealous. We're just a bit surprised by the way this is actually carried out. It turns out that in some Leningrad breweries they pay the workers with a special kind of beer – rejects. In this special beer you can find wood chips, hair, flies, bits of filth and other inedible items.

A curious picture is emerging.

Ivan Gusev, a brewery worker, received his two bottles of beer, stuffed them into his pocket, and whistling cheerfully, set off home.

'You can say what you like, but they haven't forgotten their brothers,' thought Gusev. 'They still care about the workers' health. If you're in a dangerous line of work, then it's there you go, have two free bottles of beer, it's good for your health. What generosity! That makes sixty kopecks a day . . . And in a month – fifteen roubles . . . And in a year – it comes to two hundred.'

Gusev didn't manage to work out how much it came to in ten years.

When he got home, Gusev was immediately surrounded by his relatives.

'Well, have you got it?' asked his wife.

'I've got it,' said Gusev. 'They pay us very regularly. They care about the workers' health. I'm grateful to them. It's just a shame that you can't drink the stuff, otherwise everything would be just perfect.'

'Maybe you can drink it?' asked his wife.

'I'm afraid not, there's something floating in it again.'

'What's floating in it today?' Gusev's son Petka asked excitedly. 'Let's have a look.'

Gusev opened the bottle and poured the beer into a clay mug. The whole household surrounded the table, peering at the beer.

'That looks like something,' said Gusev.

'There it is!' shouted Petka delighted. 'A fly!'

'That's right,' said Gusev, 'a fly. And there's something else floating there, apart from the fly. Is it a twig?'

'Just a bit of stick,' said his wife, disappointed.

'Yes, it's a stick,' Gusev confirmed. 'But what's that? It's not a cork is it?'

His wife walked away from the table, indignant.

'It's never anything useful round the house,' she said angrily. 'A bit of stick, a cork, a fly. If only it was a cheap thimble, or at least a button. I could do with some buttons.'

'I've got to have some pins,' said Aunt Marya venomously. 'You can wait with your buttons . . .'

'I want a trumpet,' Petka started whining. 'I want a trumpet in the bottle . . .'

'Shsh!' shouted Gusev, opening the second bottle.

The second bottle didn't contain anything substantial either: two small nails, a cockroach and the fairly well-worn sole of a shoe.

'A load of rubbish,' said Gusev, pouring the beer out of the window onto to the street.

'Ah well, maybe there'll be something tomorrow,' his wife comforted him.

'I want a piano,' snivelled Petka. 'I want a piano in the bottle . . .'

Gusev stroked his son's head and said:

'Now now, don't cry. It's not up to me, it's up to the management. Maybe tomorrow they'll get a bit more generous about the piano.'

Gusev stored the empty bottles behind the stove and sat down at the table, feeling disheartened.

Meanwhile, under the window, the passer-by who'd been covered with thick Bavarian beer was sobbing quietly.

1924

Monkey Language

This Russian's a hard language, my dear citizens. A disaster, it's so hard.

The main reason is there are so many foreign words in it. Just take French. Everything's fine and understandable. *Qu'est-ce que c'est*, *merçi*, *comme-çi* – they're all, if you look closely, completely French, natural, understandable words.

But now just go and try it with a Russian sentence: a disaster. The whole language is sprinkled with words with foreign, obscure meanings.

And that makes it difficult to speak, disturbs your breathing and wears out your nerves.

Just the other day I heard a conversation. It was at a meeting. The people next to me got into a discussion.

It was a very clever, intellectual conversation, but I, a person without higher education, could barely understand their conversation and sat there twiddling my thumbs, looking like a right idiot.

It started straightforwardly enough.

The man sitting next to me, a bearded man you couldn't call old, leant over to the man sitting on his left and asked politely:

'Comrade, will this session be plenary or what?'

'It'll be plenary,' his neighbour said casually.

'You don't say,' the first man was startled, 'I could see something was going on. It looked like it was going to be plenary.'

'Don't you worry about it,' the second man responded severely. 'It's going to be really plenary today, just wait till you see the quorum that's present.'

'Really?' asked his neighbour. 'Is a quorum really present?'

'Certainly is,' said the other.

'And what about it, this quorum?'

'Nothing particular,' answered his neighbour, slightly at a loss. 'It's present, and that's that.'

'Well, that's a fine state of affairs', the first man shook his head bitterly. 'Why did they have to go and do that then?'

The second man shrugged his shoulders and looked at him sternly, and then added with an indulgent smile:

'Well, I suppose you don't approve of these plenary sessions comrade . . . But I feel closer to them. You see everything in them is so sort of minimal and straight to the point . . . Although, I admit, recently I've felt rather permanent towards these meetings. I don't know, it's all industrial, a complete waste of time.'

'Not always,' the first retorted. 'If, of course, you see it from the point of view. If you get up there, as they say, onto the point of view and from there, from the point of view, well then it's concretely industrial.'

'Concretely actual,' the second corrected him sternly.

'All right,' the other agreed. 'I'll accept that too. Concretely actual. Although sometimes . . .'

'Always,' the second man cut him off sharply. 'Always, most-esteemed comrade. Particularly if, after the speeches, the subsection gets going minimally. Then there's no end of discussion and yelling . . .'

A man got up onto the platform and gestured for people to stop talking. Everyone fell silent. Only my neighbours, who were quite excited by their argument, didn't straight away. The first simply couldn't accept that subsections get going minimally. It seemed to him that subsections get going in some other way.

People shushed my neighbours. The neighbours shrugged their shoulders and fell silent. Then the first leant over to the second and asked quietly:

'Who's that then who's just come out?'

'That? Oh, that's the presidium who's just come out. A very astute man. And a first-class orator. He'll always say something astute and straight to the point.'

The orator spread his hands in front of him and started his speech.

And when he pronounced some arrogant words with an obscure, foreign meaning, my neighbours nodded their heads solemnly. And what's more, the second looked at the first sternly, to show him that he'd been right all along in the argument they'd just had.

Speaking Russian's hard, comrades.

1925

Firewood

This genuine incident occurred at Christmas. The newspapers squeezed it into the local news section, reporting that it happened in such and such a place at some time or other.

But for a restless and curious person like me, the dry lines of the newspaper weren't enough. I ran round to the address, found the culprit, wormed my way into his confidence and asked him to flesh out the whole story in detail.

He fleshed it out over a bottle of beer.

The reader is a suspicious creature. He'll think, there's a smooth-tongued liar if ever I've seen one.

But reader, I'm not lying. Even now, reader, I could look into your bright eyes and say, 'I'm not lying.' And as a rule I never lie and always try to write without making anything up. I haven't got a very good imagination. That's why I don't like wasting my precious life-blood on some non-existent made-up stuff. I know, dear reader, that life is much more important than literature.

So, let me tell you an almost Christmas story.

Firewood – said the man – is precious stuff. Especially when there's snow falling, and the frost's biting, then there's nothing on Earth you'd rather get your hands on than firewood.

You can even give firewood as a birthday present.

I gave my sister-in-law, Yelizaveta Ignatevna, a bundle of firewood for her birthday. But at the end of the party, Pyotr Semyonych, her husband, a bad-tempered and irritable man, beat me over the head with a log, the son of a bitch.

'You can't give people firewood as a birthday present, this isn't 1919, you know!'

But despite this, I haven't changed my opinion about firewood. Firewood is precious and sacred stuff.

And even when you're walking down the street and pass, let's say, a fence, and the frost is biting away at you, you can't help patting the wooden fence lovingly.

You get a special kind of thief going for firewood. Compared with him, your pickpocket is a minor social minnow.

A firewood thief is a desperate man. There's no telling what he'll do.

But we caught a thief by chance.

Our firewood was stacked in the yard. And this communal firewood started disappearing. Every day there'd be three or four logs missing.

Seryoga Pyostrikov from number four was kicking up the biggest fuss.

'We've got to stand guard,' he said, 'comrades, that's what we've got to do. Otherwise we haven't got a hope in hell of catching this thief.'

People agreed and started taking turns standing guard. There we were taking turns standing guard, but the firewood kept on disappearing.

A month passed. And then my nephew Mishka Bochkov came to see me:

'As you know uncle,' he said, 'I'm in the Chemists' Union. On the basis of our kinship ties, for a knock-down price I could lay my hands on a stick of dynamite for you. All you need to do,' he said, 'is put the dynamite in a log and wait. Up in Petrozavodsk,' he said, 'that's what we always do. It frightens the thieves and makes them think twice before stealing something. It's the perfect remedy,' he said. 'Go on, have some.'

'All right then, you son-of-a-chicken,' I said, 'bring the dynamite. We'll put it in today.'

He brought it.

I hollowed out a hole in a log and put the dynamite in. I sealed it up. And casually tossed the log back onto the pile. And began to wait to see what would happen.

That evening there was an explosion in our building.

People were frightened to death. They thought it was a flood, but I knew and my nephew Mishka Bochkov knew exactly what was up. What was up was that the dynamite had exploded in number four, in Seryoga Pyostrikov's stove.

I didn't say anything to Seryoga Pyostrikov about it, I just looked at his slimy face, the wreck of his apartment, the pile of bricks where his stove had been, and the broken doors, and left without saying anything.

One person died. Seryoga's lodger, the invalid Gusev, died from fright. A brick bashed his brains out.

Seryoga himself and his venerable mum are still living in the ruins. The whole family'll be going to court in the New Year for the theft and disappearance of firewood.

There's only one annoying and irritating thing: now Mishka Bochkov, the son-of-a-bitch, is taking all the credit.

But in court I'm going to say: how come he's getting all the credit when I hollowed out the log and put the dynamite in it?

Then the courts will give credit where it's due.

1925

The Actor

This story is based on a true incident. It happened in Astrakhan. It was told to me by an amateur actor.

This is what he said:

Citizens, you ask me whether I was ever an actor. Well, I was. I've played in a theatre. I've been entangled with that art. But it's a load of rubbish. There's nothing remarkable in it.

Though of course, if you think about it more deeply, this art has many good points.

When you go out onto the stage, say, and the audience is watching you. And you've got friends in the audience, relatives on your wife's side, or citizens from your own building. You look at them, they wink at you from the stalls – 'Don't be shy, Vasya,' they say, 'give it the lot.' And so you gesture to them, as if to say: Stop worrying citizens. I know what I'm doing. This isn't my first time you know.'

But if you think about it more deeply, there's nothing good about this profession. It's more worry than anything else.

So once we were putting on the play *Who is to Blame?* About life in the old days. It's a very powerful play. In one act, you see, thieves rob a merchant right in front of the audience's eyes. It looks very real. The merchant, you see, shouts and kicks out at them. But they rob him all the same. It's a terrifying play.

So there we were, putting on this play.

And just before the performance one amateur, who was playing the merchant, got drunk. The tension had shaken him up so badly that we could see he couldn't carry off the role of the merchant. And as he got near the footlights he crushed some as if on purpose.

The director, Ivan Palych, said to me:

'We can't let him go on for the second act, or the son-of-a-bitch will crush all the footlights. Why don't you,' he said, 'play the role instead of him? The public's stupid, they won't notice the difference.'

I said:

'Citizens,' I said, 'I can't go on stage. Don't even ask. I've just eaten two melons,' I said, 'I'm not thinking clearly.'

But he said, 'Do me a favour, as a friend. Just for one act. Maybe the other actor will come to in a while. Don't spoil our educational work.'

Eventually he persuaded me. I went out onto the stage.

And I went on in the middle of the play, as I was, in my jacket and trousers. The only thing I put on was someone else's beard.

And on I went. And though the public might be stupid, they recognized me straight away.

'Ah,' they said, 'that's Vasya who's just come on! Don't be shy,' they said, 'give it the lot . . .'

I said:

'This is no time to be shy, citizens, this is a critical moment. The actor,' I said, 'is completely pissed and can't come onstage. He's puking.'

The act began.

In the act I was playing the merchant. I was shouting and defending myself by kicking out at the robbers. And then I felt the hand of one of the amateurs really going into my pocket.

I wrapped my jacket closer around me. And moved away from the actors.

I was fighting them off. Smacking them right in the teeth. I really was.

'Don't come any closer you bastards,' I said, 'I'm warning you.'

But in accordance with the script they just kept on coming. They took my wallet off me (eighteen ten-rouble notes) and tried to get their hands on my watch.

I yelled:

'Help,' I said, 'citizens, they're robbing me for real!'

And this created the full effect. The public's stupid, they clapped rapturously. They shouted:

'Go on Vasya, go on. You can fight them off, son. Smash the evil bastards right in the head.'

I shouted:

'It's no use comrades!'

I went on whacking people right between the eyes.

I could see one amateur was covered in blood, but the others, the bastards, flew into a rage and came back at me.

'Comrades,' I shouted, 'what's going on? Why the hell should *I* have to suffer?'

Then the director stuck his head out from the wings.

'Well done,' he said, 'Vasya, you're playing the part,' he said, 'wonderfully. Keep it up.'

I could see that shouting wasn't going to do any good. Because whatever you shout, it all becomes part of the play.

I went down on my knees.

'Comrades,' I said, 'Director,' I said, 'Ivan Palych. I can't take any more! Lower the curtain. They really are nicking my last savings!' I said.

Then some of the theatrical specialists saw that these words weren't in the play, and came out from the wings. The prompter, thank God, came crawling out from his box.

'Citizens,' they said, 'it seems they really have swiped the merchant's wallet.'

The curtain came down. They brought me some water and I had a drink.

'Comrades,' I said. 'Director,' I said, 'Ivan Palych. What's going on?' I said. 'During the play,' I said, 'someone took my wallet off me.'

So they conducted a search of the amateurs. But they didn't find the money. Someone had dropped the empty wallet in the wings.

So the money had just disappeared. Vanished.

And you're talking about art? I know all about it! I've been an actor!

1925

The Match

At our factory the other day, comrades, an accident occurred. They almost stopped a meeting because of it.

Well, there was some guest lecturer giving a lecture. He was either from the Woodworkers' Union or from a match-makers' trust. It wasn't clear which. He didn't have it written on his face.

He gave a good long sort of speech. Said a lot of heart-felt, positive things. Productivity, he said, that foundation-stone of Soviet life, is improving. Total output, he said, is also bounding ahead. And the quality of goods too, he said, is becoming wonderful. I would even buy some things myself, he said, but I can't spare the cash.

He said some pretty upbeat stuff. The audience interrupted him about twenty times and clapped him. Well, you see, everyone likes it when productivity, that foundation-stone, is rising. You don't need me to tell you that.

Then the lecturer began quoting figures. To make his point clear.

He quoted two figures, then for some reason his voice went all hoarse.

He grabbed a glass of water and took a gulp. After a bit he said:

'For some reason, comrades,' he said, 'I'm feeling tired. I'll just have a smoke,' he said, 'and then I'll continue with the figures.'

And so he began to light up. Struck a match. But the match-head, the damned thing, sort of fizzed and shot off into the lecturer's eye.

The lecturer grabbed his eye with his hand, started howling at the top of his voice and fell to the floor. He was crushing up the matches against the floor. That would have been from the pain, wouldn't it?

After a while they'd bathed his eye and tied a handkerchief over it.

They brought him out onto the platform again.

He got up onto the platform and said:

'Why waste our time quoting figures and exposing ourselves to danger? Everything's already clear and straightforward. I declare the meeting closed.'

Then, well, people clapped the lecturer a bit and went off home.

But as I was leaving I picked up the matches that had shot into the lecturer's eye.

The matchbox was an ordinary yellow one. It had a drawing of an aeroplane on it. The sun and some clouds. And some other stuff that wasn't clear. And below that was written: ' "The Red October" Factory (formerly "Volkhov").'

I looked at the box and it made me think.

'What was that about productivity? Is it rising? Or is it falling?'

If it's rising though, it's probably on account of the spread of piece-work. That much is clear.

1925

A Bathhouse

They say, comrades, that the bathhouses in America are totally excellent.

A citizen just walks in, chucks his clothes in a special box and goes off to have his bath. He won't worry a bit about them getting stolen or lost, and they don't even bother with cloakroom tickets.

Well, some more anxious American might say to the attendant:

'Good-bye buddy,' he'd say, 'keep an eye on my stuff.'

And that'd be that.

Then this American would get washed and come back, and he'd be given clean clothes: washed and ironed. His foot-cloths would probably be whiter than snow. Drawers patched and darned. That's the life!

Our bathhouses are fine too. But worse. You can get washed in them though.

The only thing is there's a problem with the cloakroom tickets. Last Saturday I went to the bathhouse (I was hardly going to go to America, was I), and they gave me two tickets. One for my clothes, the other for my coat and hat.

But where's a naked man going to keep tickets? I'll tell you where, nowhere. He hasn't got any pockets. It's all stomach and legs. These tickets are hell itself. You can't tie them to your beard.

So well, I tied one to each foot so as not to lose them. And went off to the baths.

Now the tickets were flapping against my legs. It was no fun walking. But I had to walk. Because I needed a tub. What kind of bath can you get without a tub? Hell itself.

I looked for a tub. I saw one citizen washing in three tubs. Standing in one, getting his head into a lather in the second, and keeping hold of the third with his left hand so that no one swiped it.

I started pulling the third tub, trying, you know, to get it for myself, but the citizen wouldn't let go of it.

'What do you think you're doing,' he said, 'stealing other people's tubs? We'll see how you like it when I whack you in the face with this tub.'

I said:

'This isn't the tsarist régime. You can't just go round whacking people with tubs. What egoism,' I said. 'Other people have got to get washed too. This isn't a theatre, you know,' I said.

He turned his back on me and carried on washing.

There's no point standing here breathing down his neck, I thought. Now he's going to take three days washing on purpose.'

I walked on.

After an hour, I saw some bloke absent-mindedly take his hand off his tub. Whether he was looking for the soap or just lost in thought, I'm not sure. I just took the tub for myself.

Now I had a tub but nowhere to sit. And how can you wash standing up? That's not washing. That's hell itself.

All right then, so I stood there, standing holding my tub with one hand, and started washing.

And all around me, would you believe it, it was like a self-service laundry. One man was washing his trousers, another was scrubbing his drawers, and a third was slapping something else. I'd no sooner get washed and I'd be dirty again. The bastards were spraying me. And with the noise they made with their laundry, you didn't feel like washing. You couldn't even hear where you were rubbing the soap. Hell itself.

'Well,' I thought, 'damn the whole bloody lot of them. I'll finish washing at home.'

So I went to the changing room. Where they give back your clothes. They gave me my things, but the trousers weren't mine.

'Citizens,' I said, 'mine had a hole here. But these have one over there.'

But the attendant said:

'We're not here,' he said, 'to worry about holes. This isn't a theatre,' he said.

All right then. I put on these trousers and went to get my coat. They wouldn't give me back my coat, they wanted the ticket. But I'd left the ticket on my foot. I had to get undressed. I took off my trousers and looked for the ticket, but it wasn't there. The string was there, but the paper wasn't. The paper had washed off.

I gave the attendant the string, but he didn't want it.

'We can't give out clothes,' he said, 'on the strength of string. Otherwise,' he said, 'we'd have every citizen preparing pieces of string. We'd never have enough coats. Wait around,' he said, 'until the customers have gone, and we'll give you whatever's left.'

I said:

'Comrade, brother, what if there's only rubbish left? This isn't a theatre,' I said. 'Give it back on the strength of its distinguishing features. One pocket,' I said, 'is torn, the other's gone. As for buttons,' I said, 'the top one's there, but I'm not anticipating any lower ones.'

After all that he gave me back my coat. And he didn't take the string.

I put my coat on and went outside. I suddenly remembered I'd forgotten my soap.

I went back again. They wouldn't let me in with my coat on.

'Take your coat off,' they said.

I said:

'Citizens, I can't strip off for a third time. This isn't a theatre,' I said. 'At least give me the cost of the soap.'

They wouldn't.

They wouldn't and there was no point insisting. I left without my soap.

Of course, the reader used to formalities might be curious to know: What bathhouse was this? Where is it? What's the address?

What bathhouse? An ordinary bathhouse. Where they charge ten kopecks.

But I won't say what street it's on. I can't afford to. Because then when I next go there they'll bash my brains out with a tub, and that would be the end of a politically conscious, thoughtful citizen.

1925

Live-bait

On the tram, I always travel in the rear car.

You get a friendlier sort of person there.

In the front car it's dull and boring and you can't step on anyone's foot. But in the rear car, not to mention feet, it's a lot more easy-going and cheerful. Sometimes the passengers there chat to one another about abstract philosophical issues, about honesty or wages for example. Now and then you even get something unexpected happening.

The other day I was travelling on the Number 4.

There were two citizens sitting opposite me. One had a saw. The other had a beer bottle. It was empty. The man was holding the bottle in his hands and drumming on it with his fingers. Now and then he'd look at the other passengers through the green glass. You get a very interesting effect.

Next to me was a woman citizen in a warm shawl. She was sitting as if she was very tired or ill. From time to time she'd even close her eyes. And next to this woman was a package. Sort of wrapped up in newspaper and tied up with string.

And this package was placed not right next to the woman, but at a little distance from her. The woman occasionally glanced at it out of the corner of her eye.

'Oi, madam,' I said to the woman, 'watch out, or someone will nick your package. At least put it on your lap.'

The woman looked at me very angrily, made a mysterious sign with her hand, put her finger to her lips and closed her eyes again.

Then she looked at me a second time, extremely annoyed, and said:

'You've messed up my plan, you rotten meddling bastard . . .'

I was about to take offence, but the woman added sarcastically:

'And what if I didn't keep the package near me on purpose? What then? What if I wasn't sleeping, but could see everything as clear as day and was closing my eyes on purpose? Eh?'

'How do you mean?' I was taken aback.

'How do you mean? How do you mean?' the woman mimicked me. 'What if I wanted to catch a thief with this package . . .'

The other passengers started listening in on our conversation.

'So what's in the package then?' asked the man with the bottle in a businesslike way.

'That's what I'm saying,' said the woman. 'I might just have stuffed it with rags and bones, on purpose . . . Because a thief can't tell what's in it . . . He just snatches and grabs whatever he can lay his hands on . . . Don't try to argue with me, I know. I might just have been travelling like this for a week or so . . .'

'Well then, have you caught any?' asked some curious person.

'Are you joking,' the woman warmed to her subject, 'of course I've caught some . . . Just the other day a lady fell for it . . . Sort of young, good-looking. A dark-haired brunette . . . I glanced over and saw this woman loitering. After a while she snatched the package and was walking off . . . Ahah, I said, got you, you thieving bitch . . .'

'They ought to be thrown off the trams, these thieves,' said the man with the saw angrily.

'That's not going to do any good, throwing them off the trams,' someone interfered, 'They should be handed over to the militia.'

'That's right. The militia,' said the woman. 'They should definitely be handed over to the militia . . . And then there was another one fell for it . . . A man, a nice, good-natured sort of a bloke . . . He fell for it too . . . Took the package early in the journey and was holding it. Getting used to it. As if it was his. I kept quiet. Pretended to look the other way. And after a while he stood up and went meekly on his way . . . Hey, I said, comrade, got you, you snake . . .'

'So you catch them with live-bait, then?' grinned the man with the bottle. 'And do you catch many?'

'That's what I'm saying,' said the woman, 'I catch quite a few.'

She blinked, looked out of the window, got into a fluster and declared to the other passengers that she had missed her stop.

And as she was leaving the tram, she looked at me angrily and said once more:

'You messed up my plan, you rotten meddling bastard.'

And got off.

1925

Passenger

What I want to know is why they allow passengers to travel to Moscow on the top shelf. It's a baggage rack. Baggage should travel on baggage racks, not the public.

And people talk about civilization and education! For example, now they use these new diesel locomotives to pull trains. But then they allow totally uncivilized behaviour in the carriages.

You could knock your head off. If you fall. After all, you fall down, not up, don't you.

Maybe I didn't have to go to Moscow anyway. Maybe it was Vaska Bochkov, the son of a bitch, talked me into going.

'There's a free lunch going begging, have it,' he said. 'Go to Moscow if you like.'

'Comrade,' I said, 'why should I want to go to Moscow? I don't feel like going to Moscow.' I said, 'I haven't got house or home there. I, comrade,' I said, 'haven't even got anywhere to stay in that Moscow of yours.'

But he said:

'Go for the hell of it then. After all it's free. For once in your life,' he said, 'you've had a bit of luck come your way, and you, shit-for-brains, you don't want to take advantage of it.'

I went on the overnight train on Saturday evening.

I entered the carriage. I sat down on the edge of the seat. We left. We'd only gone three miles when I really felt like a bite to eat, but there wasn't even a bite to eat.

'Vaska Bochkov,' I thought, 'you son-of-a-bitch, what a long journey you've talked me into. I'd have preferred,' I thought, 'to have been sitting in comfort now, in a bar somewhere, rather than travelling backwards and forwards like this.'

In the meantime quite a lot of people had got on. By the window, for example, was a man with a beard. As luck would have it, next to him there was an old woman. We had one of those nasty, poisonous old women who are always elbowing everyone.

'He's spread himself out, the wicked bastard,' she said. 'Won't even give me enough space to breathe.'

I said:

'Old woman, you dear old thing, stop elbowing me. I didn't want to come,' I said, 'it was Vaska Bochkov talked me into it.'

She didn't sympathize.

It was becoming evening. Sparks from the diesel engine were falling like raindrops. We were surrounded by nature and beauty. But I didn't feel like looking at nature. If only, I thought, I could lie down and pull the covers over me.

But I could see there was nowhere to lie down. All the places were fully taken.

I appealed to the passengers:

'Citizens,' I said, 'at least let me sit in the middle. I,' I said, 'could fall off the edge here. I'm going to Moscow.'

'Everyone here's going to Moscow,' they replied. 'Anyway there are no reserved seats, so go back and just sit where you were.'

I sat there. Travelling. We went another three miles and my leg went numb. I got up. I looked up at the baggage rack. There was a basket travelling on it.

'Citizens,' I said, 'what's going on? There's a person here,' I said, 'who's got to travel all bent-double, with his legs going numb, and there are things up there . . . After all,' I said, 'a person's more important than things . . . Would the owner of that basket,' I said, 'come and take it away.'

The old woman got up, groaning. She climbed up to get her basket.

'You wicked bastards,' she said, 'won't give me a moment's peace, day or night. Go on then,' she said, 'you idiot, climb up in your crow's nest. Please God let him fall and break his head off before night comes.'

So I climbed up.

I climbed up, went three miles and fell into a sweet sleep.

Suddenly I felt myself being shoved sideways and somersaulting downwards. I could see I was falling. What's it like to fall when you're half-asleep, I thought.

And I could feel myself being bashed in the side, in the head, in the stomach and the arm . . . Down I fell.

And thankfully, as I was falling, I managed to catch my foot on the middle bunk: that softened the blow.

I was sitting on the floor feeling my head, to see if it was there. It was there.

Meanwhile in the carriage there was a fuss going on. It was the passengers, they thought their things might have been stolen in the commotion.

The train staff came to see what the fuss was about, with a torch.

The chief asked:

'Who fell down?'

I said:

'I fell down. From the baggage rack. I'm going to Moscow,' I said. 'Vaska Bochkov,' I said, 'the son-of-a-bitch talked me into the trip.'

The chief said:

'The passengers always fall down at Bologoye. There's a really sharp stop there.'

I said:

'It's pretty painful for a man who's just fallen down to hear this. Instead,' I said, 'the staff should stop people from travelling on the top racks. And if a passenger climbs up, they should push him off, or persuade him to come down, they should say: Don't climb up there citizen, you might fall off.'

Then the old woman started shouting too:

'He crushed my basket,' she said, 'with his head.'

I said:

'A person's more important than a basket. You can always buy a basket. But you've got to admit a head is priced less.'

We shouted and moaned and they bound up my head with a rag and the train carried on without stopping.

We got to Moscow. I got out. Sat around the station.

I drank four cups of water from a drinking-fountain. And got a train back.

And all the time my head was aching and buzzing. And I kept on having unprintable thoughts. 'Grr,' I thought, 'if I could get my hands on Vaska Bochkov now, I'd rearrange his rib-cage. What a trip,' I thought, 'that bastard talked me into.'

I got to Leningrad. I got out. Drank a cup of water from the drinking-fountain and walked off, swaying.

1925

Thieves

For some reason or other, citizens, a lot of thieves have appeared recently. Wherever you look, they're swiping anything they can lay their hands on.

You won't find anyone who hasn't had something pinched.

Take me. Only the other day they took my suitcase, just before we got into Zhmerinka.

So what can we do about this social epidemic then? Are we going to tear their arms off?

Well, they say that in Finland, in the old days they cut thieves' hands off. Your Finnish comrade would be, let's say, caught stealing and straight away it'd be chunk, and off you go you son-of-a-bitch without a hand. Mind you, people also got a lot more exemplary. Over there, they say, you don't have to lock your apartment. And if, for example, a citizen drops his wallet in the street, it gets left in the street. No one takes it they just put the wallet somewhere where everyone will see it, and it can lie there until the end of time . . . What a bunch of idiots.

I suppose they'd take the money in the wallet, they'd take that most likely. Fat chance it wouldn't be taken. If you wanted people to leave the money too, you wouldn't have to just cut off their hands, you'd have to chop their heads clean off, and even that wouldn't do it. The money? Well, you can always make some more. They left the wallet and you should be thankful for small mercies.

So then, just before we got to Zhmerinka, they snatched my suitcase. Would you believe it? Just like that. Lock, stock and barrel. Right down to the handle. There was a sponge in the suitcase, cost five kopecks, they took that too. I ask you, what do they want that for, the evil bastards, a sponge? They're bound to throw that away, the thieving bastards. But no. They swiped the lot, sponge and all.

But the thing was, earlier that evening some citizen had come and sat next to me.

'I hope,' he said, 'you'll travel carefully round here. Here,' he said, 'there are some really desperate thieves. They just pounce on passengers.'

'That,' I said, 'doesn't scare me. I,' I said, 'always sleep with my ear on the suitcase. I'll hear them.'

He said:

'Don't talk to me about your ear. This lot,' he said, 'are so crafty they'll even steal the boots off a man's feet. We're not talking ears here.'

'That doesn't scare me either,' I said, 'my boots are long and Russian. They won't be able to get them off.'

'Well then,' he said, 'suit yourself. All I can do is warn people. Have it your own way.'

At this point I dozed off.

Suddenly, just before we got into Zhmerinka, out of the blue someone started tugging at my foot. I swear he nearly pulled my leg off . . . I leapt up and smacked him in the shoulder. He jumped to one side. I went after him from the top bunk. But I couldn't run.

Because my boot had been half pulled off and my foot was flapping around in the top bit.

I started yelling. Woke the whole carriage up.

'What's the matter?' they asked.

'My boot, citizens,' I said, 'it nearly got filched.'

I started to pull my boot back on. Looked around, my suitcase had gone.

I started yelling again. I searched all the passengers, but no suitcase.

At the main station I went to the militia office to make a report.

Well, they were sympathetic, took a note of it.

I said:

'If you catch him, tear his bloody arms off.'

They laughed.

'All right,' they said, 'we'll tear them off. Only,' they said, 'put that pencil back where it was.'

And it was true, how it happened I just can't think. But I'd taken their indelible pencil from the table and stuffed it in my pocket.

The militiaman said:

'We might only be a small office,' he said, 'but in no time at all the passengers have stolen all our stationery. One son-of-a-bitch even carried off the inkpot. With ink in it.'

I made my apologies and left.

'Yes,' I thought, 'if we start cutting off hands, there'll be a hell of a lot of invalids.'

That'd be more trouble than it's worth.

1925

A Glass

Just recently, the decorator Ivan Antonovich Blokhin died from an illness. And his widow, Marya Vasilyevna Blokhina, a middle-aged lady, organized a bit of a picnic in the traditional way, after forty days.

And invited me.

'Come along,' she said, 'and we'll pay our respects to the dearly departed in our modest way. We won't have any chicken or roast duck,' she said, 'and don't expect any pâté either. But down as much tea as you like, don't stint yourself there, and you can even take some home with you if you like.'

I said:

'Although your tea doesn't interest me much, I'll come. Ivan Antonovich Blokhin was always pretty good to me, and even painted my ceiling for free.'

'All right then,' she said, 'all the more reason to come.'

On Thursday I went along.

Loads of people had turned up. All kinds of relatives. The brother-in-law of the deceased too, Pyotr Antonovich Blokhin. A poisonous sort of man with a moustache that pointed upwards. Sat in front of the melon. And would you believe it, all he did was slice up the melon with his pen-knife and eat it.

I had a glass of tea and didn't want any more. I just didn't feel like it. And anyway the tea wasn't very nice, it had a slight hint of floor-moppings. So I took my glass and put the bloody thing down, as far away from me as I could.

But I put it back slightly carelessly. There was a sugar-bowl there. I knocked the glass on this sugar bowl, against the handle. And the glass, the damned thing, cracked.

I thought they wouldn't notice. They noticed, the bastards.

The widow responded:

'You didn't just smash that glass did you sir?'

I said:

'It's nothing to worry about, Marya Vasilyevna Blokhina. You can still use it.'

But her brother-in-law finished stuffing himself with melon and said:

'What do you mean nothing to worry about? A fine load of nothing to worry about. The widow invites them over, and they go round smashing the widow's things.'

Marya Vasilyevna was inspecting the glass and getting more and more upset.

'It's sheer economic ruin, this breaking glasses. It's outrageous, all this breaking things. Somebody smashes a glass,' she said, 'somebody else pulls the tap off the samovar, and somebody else stuffs a napkin in their pocket. At this rate, what am I going to be left with?'

And the brother-in-law, the parasite, answered:

'What are you talking about? Guests like that,' he said, 'ought to get their faces smashed in with a melon.'

I didn't rise to that. I just went horribly pale and said:

'I find this talk of being smashed in the face pretty insulting, comrade brother-in-law. I,' I said, 'comrade brother-in-law, wouldn't even allow my own mother to smash my face in with a melon. And anyway,' I said, 'your tea smells of floor-moppings. Some party!' I said. 'You bastards, if I smashed three glasses and a tankard, it would be less than you deserve.'

Of course then the fuss really started, there was trouble.

The brother-in-law was the most worked up. Maybe all the melon he'd eaten had gone to his head.

The widow was also quivering in anger.

'I'm not in the habit,' she said, 'of putting floor-moppings in the tea. You're the one who probably does that at home, and then you try and put the blame on other people. Ivan Antonovich, the decorator,' she said, 'is probably turning in his grave with all these harsh words . . . You fish features,' she said, 'I'm not going to let you get away with this.'

I didn't respond to this, all I said was:

'Bollocks to you all, and bollocks to the brother-in-law,' I said.

And left as quickly as I could.

Two weeks after this incident, I received my court summons for the Blokhina case.

I turned up and was really surprised.

The People's Magistrate examined the case and said:

'These days,' he said, 'the courts are overloaded with cases like this, and would you believe it here's another one. Pay this citizen her twenty kopecks,' he said, 'and don't waste any more court time.'

I said:

'I agree to pay, just get them to give me the cracked glass. For the principle of it.'

The widow said:

'I hope you choke on the glass. Have it.'

The next day their concierge, Semyon, brought me the glass. They'd even deliberately cracked it in three more places.

I didn't comment on this, all I said was:

'Tell your bastards,' I said, 'that now I'm going to take them to court.'

Because, if my character's been insulted, then I seek legal redress.

1925

Crisis

The other day citizens, I saw a cartload of bricks going down the road. I'm not joking!

You know, my heart palpitated with joy. It must mean we're building something, citizens. They don't just transport bricks for no reason at all. They must be building a nice little house somewhere. They've started, touch wood.

In maybe twenty years' time, and who knows, even less, every citizen will probably have a whole room to themselves. And if the population doesn't grow too quickly and they allow everyone to have abortions, then two rooms. Or might even be three. With a bathroom.

What a life we'll lead then, eh citizens! In one room we'll sleep, say, in another receive guests, and in a third something else . . . Who knows? With all that freedom, we'll find something to be getting on with.

But just now things are a bit difficult with floor space. There's not a lot of it about on account of the housing crisis.

I was living in Moscow, comrades. I've only just returned from there. I myself have undergone this crisis.

So I arrived in Moscow, you see. I was walking around the streets with my stuff. And there was nowhere. Not just nowhere to stay, but nowhere even to put my stuff.

Can you imagine, two weeks I was walking around the streets with my stuff. I grew a beard and gradually lost my stuff. So there I was, you see, walking around light, without any stuff. Hunting for accommodation.

Finally, in one building, some man came down the stairs:

'For 30 roubles,' he said, 'I can fix you up in the bathroom. The apartment,' he said, 'is fit for royalty . . . Three toilets . . . A bath . . . You can live there in the bathroom to your heart's content,' he said. 'There's no windows, I'll grant you that, but there is a door. And running water's freely available. If you want,' he said, 'you can run yourself a bath full of water and dive around all day long.'

I said:

'Esteemed comrade, I'm not a fish,' I said. 'I don't require diving facilities. I'd rather,' I said, 'live on dry land. Knock a bit off,' I said, 'for the damp.'

He said:

'I can't comrade. I'd love to, but I can't. It doesn't depend on me alone. It's a communal apartment. And there's been a fixed price agreed for the bathroom.'

'What choice do I have then?' I said. 'All right. Extract,' I said, 'thirty from me then and let me get in there straight away,' I said. 'I've been walking the pavements for three weeks,' I said, 'and I might get tired otherwise.'

All right then. They let me in. I began living there.

And the bath really was fit for royalty. All over the place, wherever you put your foot, there was the marble bath, boiler and taps. Mind you, there was nowhere to sit. You could just about sit on the side of the bath, but you kept falling down, straight into the marble bath.

So I put down some planks as floor-boards, and went on living there.

After a month, though, I got married.

I met a young, kind-hearted wife. You know. Without a room of her own.

I thought she'd reject me on account of the bath, and I'd never know conjugal bliss and comfort, but not her, she didn't reject me. Just gave a little frown and answered:

'So what,' she said, 'living in a bath doesn't make you a bad person. If it comes to it,' she said, 'we can always put up a partition. Here for example,' she said, 'we could have my boudoir, and over there we'd have the dining room . . .'

I said:

'We could put up a partition, citizen. The only thing is the tenants,' I said, 'the bastards won't let us. That's what they keep on saying: no alterations.'

All right then. So we carried on living there as before.

In less than a year me and the wife had a tiny baby.

We called him Volodya and carried on with life. We could always give him a bath, and carry on living.

You know, it was even working out pretty well. The baby, you see, was getting a bath every day and never once caught a cold.

The only inconvenient thing was in the evenings the tenants of the communal apartment kept on barging into the bathroom to take baths.

While this went on the whole family had to be moved out into the corridor.

So I asked the tenants:

'Citizens,' I said, 'take your baths on a Saturday. Come on,' I said, 'you can't have a bath every day. When are we going to have a life?' I said. 'You've got to see it from our point of view.'

But the bastards, there were thirty-two of them, all swearing. And they threatened to smash my face in if I started making trouble.

Well, what can you do? You can't do anything. We carried on living there as before.

After a while, my wife's mum turned up in our bath from the provinces. She settled in behind the boiler.

'I've been dreaming for so long,' she said, 'of cradling my grandson in my arms. You can't,' she said, 'deny me that entertainment.'

I said:

'I'm not denying it. Go on granny,' I said, 'cradle away. You can even,' I said, 'fill up the bath and dive in with your grandson.'

So I said to my wife:

'Look citizen, if you've got any more relatives coming to stay with you, then tell me now, and put me out of my misery.'

She said:

'No, only my brother for Christmas . . .'

I left Moscow without waiting for her brother. I send my family money by post.

1925

Nervous People

The other day there was a fight in our communal apartment. Not so much a fight as a full-scale battle. On the corner of Glazovaya and Borovaya.

Of course, they were really putting everything into the fight. Gavrilov, the invalid, nearly got his head – all he had left – chopped off.

The main reason for it all is that people are very nervous. They get upset about minor trivialities. Tempers flare. And that makes them lash out like blind things.

Of course, they say that nerves are always shaken after a civil war. Maybe that's true, but all the same, this ideology won't make the invalid Gavrilov's head heal up any sooner.

So one of the tenants, Marya Vasilyevna Shchiptsova, went into the kitchen at nine o'clock in the evening, and lit the primus. She always, you see, lights the primus around this time. She drinks tea and applies a compress.

So she went into the kitchen. Stood the primus in front of her and lit it. But it wouldn't light, the stupid damned thing.

She thought:

'Why the hell's it not lighting? The stupid damned thing's not gone and got clogged up with soot has it?'

So she took a scourer in her left hand and was about to clean it.

She was about to clean it and took the scourer in her left hand, but another tenant, Darya Petrovna Kobylina, whose scourer it was, saw what had been taken and answered:

'By the way, most esteemed Marya Vasilyevna, would you mind putting that scourer back.'

Shchiptsova, of course, lost her temper at these words and answered:

'There you are Darya Petrovna, go and choke on your scourer. I can't even bear to touch it,' she said, 'let alone pick it up.'

So then of course, Darya Petrovna Kobylina lost her temper at these words. They started conversing. Then the noise started: crashing and banging.

The husband, Ivan Stepanych Kobylin, whose scourer it was, appeared on hearing all this noise. A healthy sort of man, even got a big paunch, but he too suffers from nerves.

So Ivan Stepanych appeared and said:

'I,' he said, 'work like an elephant for thirty-two roubles and a few kopecks in a cooperative, I smile to the customers,' he said, 'and weigh out their sausage for them, and out of this,' he said, 'with my hard-earned kopecks, I buy myself scourers, and there's no way I'm going to allow some passing personnel I hardly know to make use of these scourers.'

Then noise and discussions started up again on the subject of the scourer. So of course all the tenants came barging into the kitchen. Making a fuss. Even the invalid Gavrilov appeared.

'What's all the noise for,' they said, 'and where's the fight?'

Then straight after these words the fight was realized. It started.

But our kitchen's narrow, you see. Not suited to fighting. No room. Saucepans and primuses all over the place. Not even space to turn round. And now there were twelve people who'd shoved their way in. You want to smash some bastard in the face, say, and get three instead. And of course you bump into everything and fall over. An invalid with no legs hasn't a chance, even with three legs you haven't a hope in hell of staying standing.

But this invalid, the bloody dodderer, despite this pushed his way right into the thick of it. Ivan Stepanych, whose scourer it was, shouted at him:

'Get out of the way, Gavrilov. Look out or your other leg will get torn off.'

Gavrilov said:

'Then my leg's had it,' he said. 'But I can't get out now. My facial ambition's been beaten to a pulp,' he said.

And that moment someone really did give him one in the mouth. So he didn't get out, but kept on throwing himself about. Then someone hit the invalid across the skull with a saucepan.

The invalid just flopped onto the floor and lay there. Looking depressed.

Then some parasite ran off to get the militia.

The copper appeared. He shouted:

'Get the coffins ready you bastards, I'm going to shoot!'

Only after these fateful words did people come to a bit. They ran off to their rooms.

'Well, that's a strange thing,' they thought, 'however did we get into a fight, esteemed comrades?'

People ran off to their rooms, only Gavrilov the invalid didn't run off. He just lay there, looking depressed. And blood was trickling from his crown.

Two weeks after this incident the trial took place.

The People's Judge was a nervous sort of man too: he booked everyone.

1925

Connections

Vanyushka Ledentsov's got a job. Honestly. Now works in a trust.

Who'd have thought it! I mean the man didn't have any connections, no real contacts or Party cells, none of that. And he goes and gets a job!

And they say it's all favouritism and connections and it's tough to get in anywhere if you don't know anyone. Nonsense!

I mean in the whole trust, Ledentsov didn't know a single person. Never mind a bigwig or someone in charge, he didn't know anyone at all. Only a non-Party porter, and even he was a casual employee. And what can a casual porter do?

One day Vanyushka Ledentsov went to see this porter anyway. Stood him a couple of beers and said:

'The thing is, my friend, I don't have any connections, as you know. I'm not a member of any Party cell or anything. See what you can do.'

The porter said:

'I can't really do much, my friend. You see you can't just come wooshing in, without connections. You know how it is.'

But everything fell right into place. Last year the porter moved some furniture for the trust's accountant.

'Look here,' he said, 'respected comrade accountant. Not so long ago I moved a lot of furniture for you. Didn't break a thing, as such, except a table-leg and a basin. Get Vanyushka Ledentsov in somewhere would you? He's got no connections, the miserable bastard. None at all. Not a member of any cell. He's had it without connections.'

The accountant said:

'Can't do it, old son, not without connections I can't. I won't,' he said, 'promise anything.'

But then Vanyushka struck lucky. Fortune smiled on him, the fluky bastard.

The very next day, you see, the accountant took the commercial manager some papers to sign and said:

'You know comrade manager, nowadays without connections it's curtains.'

'What of it?'

'Well, it's just that,' said the accountant, 'there's this fellow here running around without connections, so he can't get in anywhere. And I don't reckon we'll be able to squeeze him in either.'

'You're right there,' said the manager, 'without contacts how can he be squeezed in, the awkward devil. He's in a fix without connections.'

And then the efficiency manager walked in.

'What were you two talking about?' he said.

'Yes, well,' they said, 'comrade efficency manager, there's a fellow here, Ledentsov's his name, hasn't got any connections, the stupid bastard, can't get in anywhere, he's running around like a headless chicken.'

The efficiency manager said:

'All right then, bring him along to our office. We'll see what we can do. It's not right, citizens, this doing everything by contacts. We've got to respect a man even if he hasn't got connections.'

And so they respected him.

And people say it's all favouritism and connections. I could tell them a thing or two . . .

1926

Economy Measures

Comrades, I don't know how the economy measures are working in other towns.

But in Borisov these measures have turned out very profitably.

In this one short winter, in our office alone we've saved fourteen yards of firewood. Not bad eh!

Ten years of those savings, that would be ten cubic metres. And in a hundred years we'll easily save three boat-loads. In a thousand years we'll even be able to trade firewood freely.

What were people thinking about earlier? Why didn't they introduce profitable measures like these earlier? That's the frustrating thing! You see, we started these economy measures back in autumn.

Our boss is one of us. He always consults us and talks to us like we're his own family. Even scrounges fags off us, the son-of-a-bitch.

So then one day this boss came along and declared:

'This is it lads, it's started . . . Tighten your belts! Economize on something or other . . .'

But just how we were to economize and what on wasn't clear. We started discussing what we could economize on. Maybe we could stop paying the accountant, the grey-haired bastard, or maybe something else.

The boss said:

'If you don't pay the accountant, lads, the grey-haired bastard will go straight round to the health and safety at work people. We can't have that. We'll have to think up something else.'

Then, thankfully, the cleaning woman Nyusha opened her women's question up for discussion.

'Considering,' she said, 'the international situation, and the general mess we're in, why don't we,' she said, 'for example, stop heating the toilets. What's the point in wasting fuel over there? After all, it's not a drawing room.'

'That's a point,' we said, 'let's just leave the toilets to get cold. We might save fourteen yards. And if it's a bit chilly, there's no harm in that. The public won't hang around if it's frosty. That will maybe even result in a net rise in productivity.'

So that's what we did. Stopped heating the toilets and started counting the savings.

And we really did save fourteen yards. We started to save a fifteenth, but then spring struck.

That was frustrating!

If, we thought, it wasn't for the bloody spring, we could have saved another half cubic metre.

In other words, spring messed up our plans. But well, the fourteen yards haven't gone to waste thank you very much.

And though some pipe turned out to be broken on account of the frost, we later found out that it had been installed under the tsarist régime. Pipes like that should be torn out root and branch.

We'll be perfectly fine without a pipe until autumn. And in autumn we'll install a cheap one. After all, it's not a drawing room!

1926

A Workshop for Health

The Crimea, it's a right little pearl. The state in which people come back from there, it's a miracle. I mean, some decrepit old intellectual goes there, and when he comes back you can barely recognize him. His features have filled out. All in all, he's full of energy and world-views.

In other words, the Crimea is simply a workshop for health.

A comrade from our yard, a certain Seryoga Pyostrikov, went to the Crimea.

He was an unstable personality. Those who knew him before will all confirm this. I mean, he didn't have the slightest passionate enthusiasm or world-view in him.

Other citizens from our building at least have a good time on public holidays. Play chase, drink, play dominoes. All in all, they live life to the full. Because they're healthy, the swines.

But this obscurantist would come home from work, say, plonk his belly on his windowsill and stick his nose into a book. Wouldn't even go out for a walk. His bone-structure wouldn't move, you see, it had got all shaken about during the day.

And need I say, he wouldn't drink or smoke and wasn't interested in female personnel. In a word, he would just lie in his window and rot away.

That's how unhealthy the man was!

His relations saw that something was wrong with the man. They started trying to get him a trip to the Crimea. He couldn't do it himself. They got one.

The man tried to say no, he wouldn't go, but he went.

They kept him there for a month and a half. Bathed him and injected some stuff or other in his leg.

Eventually he returned. Came on the train.

It was enough to make your jaw drop in astonishment. His face, of course, was pitch-black. It had filled out so much it was nearly bursting. His eyes were bright. His hair was standing on end. All his melancholy had gone.

Before, this man wouldn't harm a fly. But now he'd barely got back when, on the first day, he punched Fyodor the caretaker in the teeth. He hadn't kept an eye on the shed, all the firewood had been stolen.

He also wanted to shoot the Housing Manager with a pistol over some little thing. He threw aside all the tenants who tried to get involved.

So you see, you could hardly recognize the man. He'd completely recovered. They'd repaired the man. He'd had a full overhaul.

He'd even started drinking, he was so healthy. He wouldn't let a single girl pass him by. He caused no end of scandals.

The Crimea, it's a right workshop for the health, it changes a man.

The only drawback is at work, they want to sack Seryoga Pyostrikov. Because he hardly goes in any more.

It's a great thing, this health!

1926

Paris – Париж

The other day an old post-office specialist, Comrade Krylyshkin, got the sack.

For thirty years the man had been receiving foreign telegrams and recording them in a special little book. For thirty years the man had been serving to the best of his strengths and abilities. And that's the thanks he gets. His enemies conspired together, knocked him off his comfortable perch and got him booted out for not knowing foreign languages.

It's true that Comrade Krylyshkin didn't actually know these foreign languages. When it came to languages he, as they say, couldn't make head or tail of them. But, all the same, that didn't hurt the postal service or foreigners in the slightest.

So when some telegram came with a foreign name, Comrade Krylyshkin, without batting an eyelid, would go up to one of the desks, to one of the girls working there, to some Vera Ivanovna:

'Vera Ivanovna,' he'd say, 'I don't know what's come over me. I really need my eyes testing,' he'd say. 'You couldn't,' he'd say, 'tell me what's this they've scribbled here, could you?'

So, for example, she'd say: from London.

He'd take it back and record it.

Or he'd bring the telegram over to some worker who fancied himself as an intellectual.

'The handwriting you come across these days!' he'd say. 'Hens scratch better with their feet. Go on, guess what's marked there. Bet you can't.'

All right, they'd say: from some place like München.

'That's right,' he'd say, 'and I thought it was only specialists who could guess that kind of thing.'

Or another time, when he was in a hurry, Comrade Krylyshkin would just turn directly to the public:

'Psst . . . Young man, come over here to the counter, take a look, what's this someone's scribbled? There's a heated argument going on amongst the staff. Some say one thing, some say another.'

Thirty years he was at his post, a Hero of Labour, Comrade Krylyshkin, and then they just booted him out!

And it was on account of a stupid little thing that Pyotr Antonovich

Krylyshkin got in trouble. It was more like an accident, really. He just made a slight mistake when he was recording the name of the town the telegram had been sent from. The telegram had been sent from Paris. It had '*Paris*' marked on it in French. Pyotr Antonovich, without a second thought, took it and jotted down: from the town of Rachis.

Afterwards Pyotr Antonovich said:

'So I was wrong. It's just that the name seemed so Russian, "Rachis". No one's perfect, we all make mistakes.'

All the same, they went and booted Pyotr Antonovich Krylyshkin out.

I really feel sorry for him. Where can an old foreign-language specialist like him find work? Why couldn't they have just waited until he retired?

1926

The Benefits of Culture

I've always sympathized with the views of central government.

Back in the days of War Communism, when they brought in NEP, I didn't complain. If it's to be NEP, let it be NEP. You know best.

But all the same, when they brought in NEP I felt an uneasiness deep in my heart. I sort of sensed there'd be some sharp changes.

And there certainly were. Under War Communism it was as free as could be in the field of culture and civilization. In the theatre, for example, you were free to just sit there without taking your coat off, you could sit there in the clothes you came in. Now that really was an achievement.

And the question of culture. That really is a bloody tricky question. Even with regard to the old problem of taking your coat off in the theatre. Of course, I'm not denying that people look their best without their coats on, they're more beautiful and more elegant. But what's good in bourgeois countries sometimes comes out the wrong way round over here.

The other day Comrade Loktev and his lady, Nyusha Koshelkova, met me on the street. I was taking a stroll or was just on my way to moisten my throat, can't remember which.

We met and they tried to persuade me.

'Your throat,' he said, 'Vasily Mitrofanovich, isn't going anywhere. Your throat's always with you, you can always sprinkle it. Let's go to the theatre together now. There's a play on called *The Hot-Water Bottle*.'

So in other words, they persuaded me to go to the theatre, and spend the evening in a civilized manner.

So of course we arrived at the theatre. We bought tickets, of course. We went upstairs. Suddenly they called us back. Invited us to take our coats off.

'Take your coats off,' they said.

Of course Loktev and his lady had their coats off in a second. But of course I was standing there deep in thought. That evening I'd put my coat on straight over my nightshirt. I didn't have a jacket on. And I felt, comrades, kind of embarrassed to take it off. 'There could be,' I thought, 'a real scandal.' The thing was, my shirt wasn't really what you'd call dirty. The shirt was not particularly dirty. But of course it was a plain nightshirt. And of course it had a big greatcoat button sewn on the collar. 'I'll feel ashamed,' I thought, 'walking round the foyer with a big button like that.'

I said to my friends:

'I really don't know what to do comrades,' I said. 'I'm not very well dressed today. I feel a bit embarrassed to take my coat off. People will see my braces and my nightshirt's pretty plain.'

Comrade Loktev said:

'Show me then.'

I unbuttoned my coat. Displayed myself.

'Yes,' he said, 'you're right, you look . . .'

The lady looked too of course, and said:

'I'd better,' she said, 'go home. I can't take this,' she said. 'Hanging round with gentlemen only wearing their nightshirts. Why don't you just,' she said, 'put your drawers on over your trousers. Don't you feel embarrassed,' she said, 'going to the theatre in such an abstract state?'

I said:

'I didn't know I was going to the theatre, you stupid cow. What if I don't wear jackets very often. What if I'm trying to save them for best . . . what then, eh?'

We started to think what to do. Loktev, the evil swine, said:

'I know what. Vasily Mitrofanovich, I'll just,' he said, 'give you my waistcoat. Put the waistcoat on and walk round in it pretending you're too hot in your jacket.'

He undid his jacket and started feeling and fumbling inside.

'Oh,' he said, 'sh. . ., what a shame, I'm,' he said, 'not wearing a waistcoat myself today. I'd better,' he said, 'give you my tie, at least that'll look at bit better. Tie it round your neck and walk around pretending you feel too hot.'

The lady said:

'I think really it's better,' she said, 'if I just go home. I think I'd feel more relaxed at home. Otherwise,' she said, 'I've got one gentleman practically in his underwear, and the other with a tie instead of a jacket. Why,' she said, 'doesn't Vasily Mitrofanovich ask to be let in in his coat.'

We asked and pleaded, showed them our union cards, but they wouldn't let me in.

'This,' they said, 'isn't 1919, you can't just sit there in your great-coat.'

'Well,' I said, 'what action can I take? Looks like I'll have to go home comrades.'

But when I think that the money's already been paid, I can't leave, my legs just won't move towards the exit.

Loktev, the evil swine, said:

'I know what. You,' he said, 'take off your braces, let the lady carry them as she would a handbag. You can go in as you are: let them think you're wearing an open-necked summer shirt, in other words that you feel hot in it.'

The lady said:

'I don't care, I'm not carrying his braces. I,' she said, 'don't go to the theatre to carry male items around in my hands. Let Vasily Mitrofanovich carry them himself or stuff them in his pocket.'

I took off my coat. I was standing there in my shirt like a stupid bastard.

But it was pretty bitterly cold. I was shaking and my teeth were chattering. And all around me people were watching.

The lady responded:

'Come on you bastard, get those braces off. There are people around. Oh, really, I'd better go home now.'

But it wasn't easy to get my braces unfastened. I was cold. My fingers wouldn't obey me and unfasten them quickly. I was doing exercises with my hands.

Then we spruced ourselves up and sat down in our seats.

The first act went well. It was just a bit cold. I was doing gymnastics throughout the act.

Suddenly in the interval the people sitting behind me started making a scene. Called the management. Explained about me.

'The ladies,' they said, 'find it disgusting to see nightshirts. It shocks them,' they said. 'What's more,' they said, 'he's constantly bobbing about like a bastard.'

I said:

'I'm bobbing around from the cold. You try sitting there in your nightshirt. I'm not ecstatic about it myself, comrades. But what can I do?'

Of course they dragged me off to the office. Wrote everything down. Then they let me go.

'Now,' they said, 'you'll have to pay a three rouble fine.'

That's bloody outrageous! You just can't guess where the next blow's coming from . . .

1926

Lemonade

Of course, I'm not a drinker. If I do ever have a drink, then only very little, just a sip, out of politeness or to be sociable with a close friend.

I can't manage more than two bottles at a time no matter what. My health won't allow it. Once I remember on my ex-saint's day, I downed three litres.

But that was in my young strong years, when my heart beat desperately in my chest and I had all kinds of thoughts going through my head.

But now I'm getting old.

A veterinary assistant I know, Comrade Ptitsyn, examined me the other day and even, you know, got frightened. Started shaking.

'You,' he said, 'are in a state of total devaluation. There is no chance at all,' he said, 'of me identifying where your liver is,' he said, 'or where your bladder is. You,' he said, 'are totally burnt out.'

I wanted to beat up this vet's assistant, but I cooled down.

First, I thought, I'd better go to a good doctor and make sure.

The doctor didn't find any devaluation.

'Your organs,' he said, 'look quite tidy. Your bladder,' he said, 'is absolutely respectable and is not leaking. As for your heart, it is, as it happens, really excellent, even,' he said, 'bigger than it needs to be. But,' he said, 'stop drinking, otherwise it's quite likely death could occur.'

Well, I don't fancy dying of course. I like life. I'm still a young man, only just turned forty-three at the beginning of NEP. In the full flowering of health and strength, you could say. And a big heart in my chest. And what's more important, a bladder that isn't leaky. With that sort of bladder you can live and have a good time. I really must, I thought, stop drinking. So I went and stopped.

There I was not drinking. Not drinking at all. Not drinking for an hour. Not drinking for two hours. At five o'clock in the evening, naturally, I went to eat in a canteen.

I had some soup. Started to eat some cooked meat. Felt like a drink. Instead, I thought, of strong drink I'll order something a bit weaker, like mineral water or lemonade.

So I called the waiter:

'Oi,' I said, 'you who gave me the food, bring me some lemonade, you bird-brain.'

Of course they brought me some lemonade on a respectable tray. In a decanter. I poured it into the tiny glass.

I drank this tiny glass, and could feel something. Seemed like vodka. I poured myself some more: it really was vodka. What the devil was going on? I poured myself the rest: absolutely one hundred per cent genuine vodka.

'Bring me,' I yelled, 'some more!'

'There's,' I thought, 'a stroke of luck!'

The waiter brought some more.

I tried it again. There was no doubt about it: the real thing.

Afterwards, when I paid, I made a comment all the same.

'I asked,' I said, 'for lemonade, and what did you bring, you bird-brain?'

He said:

'We've always called it lemonade here. An entirely legal word. Even in the old days . . . As for natural lemonade, I'm sorry we don't have any, there's no demand for it.'

'Bring me,' I said, 'just one more.'

So I didn't give up. I really wanted to badly. Only circumstances prevented me. As they say, life dictates its own rules. You've just got to do what it says.

1926

A Hasty Business

This is a story about a Nepman.

Those proletarians who don't want to read about such things don't have to. We're not going to insist. But this fact really stands out. It simply cannot be passed by in complete silence.

It happened only just the other day.

Picture this. Nepman Yegor Gorbushkin was sitting in his apartment. Drinking his morning tea. With butter of course, cheese, and a mountain of sugar. Tea with strawberries.

His relations were tirelessly gobbling down these groceries. Nepman Gorbushkin wasn't exactly slacking himself, he was stuffing it down too.

The food went down with some light chatter. 'We'll just have a bite to eat,' they said, 'and then let's go and open up the stall. We've got to justify what we've eaten with a spot of trading.'

Suddenly, would you believe it, someone rang the bell. From the stairs.

The bell rang, and an ordinary-looking man came into the apartment and announced:

'I am an officer of the GPU. Don't be frightened. Whichever of you is Nepman Yegor Gorbushkin, he'd better get ready quickly and come with me. Here's the warrant and here's the summons.'

Nepman Gorbushkin turned desperately pale at this point. He started reading the summons. Yes, he really was being summoned for a criminal investigation.

The Nepman stood up from the table. Shaking desperately. Teeth chattering.

'As long as there's no capital punishment. Really, I'm not sure I could take capital punishment. The other stuff, with God's help I'll get through it somehow.'

The Nepman bade an emotional farewell to his relations, shed a few tears over the twists of fate, put a few uneaten groceries and three packets of cigarettes into a bundle, and departed to the sound of general weeping.

He departed and, as you can imagine, didn't reappear. It had already struck three in the afternoon, but there was no sign of the Nepman.

Then wailing and weeping took place in the apartment. The relations arrived to discuss what to do.

The Nepman's wife, Madame Gorbushkina, said through her sobbing:

She said, 'As yet, we don't know what my husband's got caught for. But one thing's for certain, they'll find something or other. Everyone's done something, and we're all skating on thin ice. But can they really give you capital punishment for that?'

The Nepman's brother, Pavel Gorbushkin, said:

'I wouldn't bank on capital punishment,' he said. 'But most likely, on grounds of his social status, for starters they'll confiscate his property. That,' he said, 'is as sure as can be. I propose, on account of this, that his property be liquidated, otherwise the widow won't have anything to live on.'

The relations began to shake everything out of the cupboards, at the double of course. They piled up all sorts of suits and clothes, and started to sell them. Tenants and traders gathered from all directions. The furniture was sold straight away, and they made a tidy sum on the piano.

By evening, in short, they'd sold the lot. People even started bidding for the apartment. The widow and her brother left themselves only a side room, having struck a deal on the rest of the apartment with some suitable prospective tenants.

Suddenly, at seven o'clock in the evening, Nepman Gorbushkin appeared. Cheerful and a little bit drunk.

'Phew,' he said, 'what a close shave. I,' he said, 'thought it was going to be capital punishment, but nothing of the sort. They'd summoned me to answer a few questions. Sort of like a witness. I,' he said, 'dear relatives, I was so happy, I spent the time in a restaurant. Sorry for the alarm and the worry.'

Then, of course, a silent tableau took place in the newly sold apartment.

But Nepman Gorbushkin wasn't the least bit upset.

'In fact,' he said, 'it's simply magnificent that we've sold everything. We're all skating on thin ice. And without property things are nobler and more peaceful.'

After a short foxtrot the relatives cautiously went home.

1926

Guests

There can certainly be no doubt about it. Something's got into guests these days. You've got to keep an eye on them all the time. Even to make sure it's their own overcoat they're putting on. And that they don't squeeze on an extra sheepskin hat.

Well of course, they can have food. But why do they have to go and fill their napkins with the stuff? That really is going too far. If you don't keep an eye on that sort of thing, after a couple of parties the guests will have walked off with everything you possess, even the beds and the sideboards. That's the sort of guests we've got these days!

On account of this, a little bit of an incident occurred to some people I know over the holidays just gone by.

There were about fifteen guests of every description invited for Christmas. There were ladies present as well as the not so ladylike. Drinkers and drunkards.

It was a magnificent party. On the grub alone they'd spent around seven roubles. As for the booze, the costs were shared. Two-fifty each on the door. Ladies free. Though that, I must say, is stupid. Some ladies will put away so much that any man would have a hard time keeping up with them, even if you gave him a head start. But let's not dwell on the details and get all upset. That's up to them. They should know what they're doing.

Now there were three of them throwing the party. The Zefirovs, man and wife, along with their elderly relative, Yevdokimych, the wife's dad.

Maybe the only reason he'd been invited was to keep tabs on the guests.

'With three of us,' they said, 'it'll be easy keeping a watch over the guests. We'll keep track of every guest.'

So they started watching.

Yevdokimych was the first to break ranks. The old bastard, may God grant him health and a happy old age, within the first five minutes had put away so much that he couldn't even say 'mummy'.

He just sat there, rolling his eyes and mooing certain things at the ladies.

The host himself, Zefirov, got really upset at his father's boozing and started walking around the apartment all worked up checking what was where and generally preventing any mischief.

But towards twelve, he got worked up into such a state that he too made a complete disgrace of himself. Then he fell asleep in front of everyone, on the windowsill in the dining room.

He later discovered his features had swollen up. He was walking around with a dental abcess for three weeks.

After stuffing their faces freely, the guests began to play and have fun. Blind man's buff, tag, *shchotochka*.

While they were playing *shchotochka*, the door opened and Madame Zefirova came in, pale as death, and said:

'This,' she said, 'it's an absolute disgrace! Someone has just unscrewed the 25-watt electric lightbulb in the toilet. There you go,' she said, 'you can't even let the guests into the toilet.'

There was noise and agitation. Old man Yevdokimych sobered up in an instant of course, and became anxious and started grabbing at the guests.

Needless to say the ladies screamed, they weren't going to stand for being groped.

'Grab the men, if you must, but not us.'

The men said:

'In that case search everyone.'

They took measures. Locked the doors. Started carrying out the search.

One by one, the guests themselves turned out their pockets, unbuttoned their shirts and trousers, and took off their boots. But nothing particularly incriminating was found, apart from a few sandwiches and half a bottle of madeira, two little shot glasses and a decanter.

The hostess, Madame Zefirova, began to beg passionately for forgiveness, saying that she'd got a bit upset and cast groundless aspersions on such distinguished company. She even suggested that a passer-by had gone into the toilet and unscrewed the lightbulb.

But the atmosphere had been ruined. No one wanted to play *shchotochka* any more, dancing to the balalaika had lost its appeal, and so the guests began to leave quietly.

In the morning though, when the host came to, everything finally became clear.

It turned out that the host, fearing that some of the most shameless guests might swipe the lightbulb, had unscrewed it and put it in his pocket.

That's where it got smashed.

Clearly the host had lain right on it when he fell asleep on the windowsill.

1927

Quality Merchandise

Some people I know, the Goosevs, had a German from Berlin living with them.

Rented a room. Lived there nearly two months.

And not one of your poxy Finns or other minorities, but a genuine German from Berlin. Couldn't speak a word of Russian. He'd nod his head and point to get by with the Goosevs.

Of course, his clothes were brilliant. Clean linen. Pressed trousers. Everything just right. Just like a print.

Now when this German went, he left a load of stuff for the landlords. A whole pile of foreign merchandise. All sorts of little bottles, collars and boxes. As well as all that, almost two pairs of long-johns. And a sweater that was virtually untorn. Loads of knick-knacks, everyday items for men and for ladies.

All this was simply thrown in a heap in a corner by the washbasin.

Madame Gooseva's an honest lady, you can't say anything much against her, and she indicated to the German as he was about to leave:

'*Bitte-dritte*, haven't you forgotten your foreign-made merchandise, in the rush?'

The German shook his head as if to say, '*Bitte-dritte*, please have it, it's yours and you're welcome.'

So the Goosevs threw themselves on this abandoned foreign merchandise. Goosev himself even drew up an inventory of the things. And needless to say, he immediately squeezed into the sweater and took the long-johns for himself.

Then he was walking around with the long-johns in his hands for weeks, showing everyone. Unbelievably proud of his genuine German long-johns, praising foreign workmanship.

All this stuff, to be fair, was pretty well worn, not to say barely holding together, but there was no denying it, it was genuine foreign goods, a pleasure to see.

Now amongst all the stuff that had been left behind was a sort of medicine bottle. Not so much a bottle as a sort of flattish jar type of thing full of powder. The powder was pinkish and fine. Nice enough smelling. Not quite like roses. But not quite like oregano either.

After the first days of joy and festivity at the German windfall, the Goosevs started trying to figure out what this powder could be. They sniffed it, chewed it with their teeth, and sprinkled some onto the fire, but couldn't work out what it was.

They went round the whole block asking the neighbours. Showed it to the students and other intellectuals, but nobody could make head or tail of it.

Many people claimed it was face-powder. Others declared it to be a fine German talc for sprinkling on new-born German babies.

But Goosev said:

'Fine German talc's no good to me, is it? I haven't got any new-born babies. Let's say it's face-powder, then I could sprinkle some on my face after I shave. You've got to live properly even if it's only once in your life.'

He started using the powder when he shaved. After each shave he'd be pink, radiant and even smelled good.

Of course there was envy wherever he went. Questions were asked.

Now Goosev became a champion of German industry. He was heated in his lavish praise of German merchandise.

'How long,' he said, 'have I been defacing my complexity with second-rate Russian rubbish? At last those days are over. I don't know what I'll do when this powder runs out! Just have to order another jar. What a wonderful product. I'm a changed man.'

A month later, as the face powder was running out, a friend of Goosev's, an intellectual, came round to tea. He managed to read the jar.

It turned out to be German flea powder.

Another, less cheerful person would have been deeply crushed by this situation. And maybe a less cheerful person's face would have broken out in spots and warts with all the hypochondria. But not Goosev, oh no, he wasn't like that.

'That's what I like about it,' he said. 'That's quality of production for you! What an achievement, you just can't beat it! You can powder your face or sprinkle it on fleas, does it all! What Russian rubbish can compare with that?'

After he had heaped praise on German industry again, he said:

'Now I get it. You see I'd been wondering. A whole month I've been powdering myself and not a single flea bite. They've been biting the wife, Madame Gooseva. And the boys have been scratching desperately for days. And Ninka the dog has been itching away too. Me? I haven't felt a thing. They may only be insects, the little bastards, but even fleas know genuine quality when they see it. That's really something . . .'

Now Goosev's powder has run out. He's probably covered with fleas again.

1927

Red Tape

We weren't frightened of bureaucracy. And the red tape you get in offices these days doesn't scare us either.

Recently one esteemed comrade, Fyodor Alekseyevich Kulkov, invented a method of fighting against bureaucracy. There's a political genius for you.

And his method is so effective, so cheap, that he should go abroad and get it patented. But the extremely unfortunate thing is that Fyodor Alekseyevich Kulkov can't travel abroad now: our dear friend got locked up for his experiment. A prophet is without honour in his own land.

And he thought up such a cunning method of fighting against bureaucracy.

You see, Kulkov had to keep on going to a certain much-esteemed office. Time after time. To get something sorted out. He went for a month, for two months. Every day he went. And still no results. Those bureaucrats wouldn't take any notice of him, no matter how loud he screamed.

They couldn't find his file. They sent him to another floor. They fobbed him off with the old 'Come back tomorrow.' Sometimes they simply blew their noses rudely when he asked something.

Their job's not much fun either, of course. These bureaucrats get maybe a hundred people a day coming up with all sorts of stupid questions. With the best will in the world, that makes you bad-tempered and nervous.

But Kulkov wasn't about to go into these intimate details. He just couldn't wait any longer.

He thought:

'If I don't get this business sorted out today, then that's definitely not on. This will drag on for another month. Right,' he thought, 'I'll take one of the office staff and I'll smash him in the face a bit. Maybe after this fact they'll take some notice of me and sort my file out favourably.'

Fyodor Kulkov went to the lowest basement level, just in case, saying, 'If they throw me out of the window, at least I won't completely shatter when I hit the ground.' He walked from room to room.

And suddenly he saw a totally disgraceful scene. Some middle-aged bureaucrat was sitting at a table on a bentwood chair. A clean collar.

Tie. Cuffs. Just sitting there and doing absolutely nothing. What's more, he was sitting there sprawled on a chair, whistling a bit through his lips and swinging his leg.

It was this last bit that simply drove Fyodor Kulkov spare.

'What?' he thought, 'here we are in the machinery of state! All over the place there are portraits hanging on the wall, tables and shelves full of books, and here, among all that, the swinging of legs and whistling: it's a downright insult!'

Fyodor Kulkov stared at the bureaucrat for a very long time and got totally worked up. Then he went up to him, turned him round, and naturally gave him a slight smack in the mouth.

The bureaucrat fell off his bentwood chair, of course.

And he stopped swinging his leg. Just yelped.

Then bureaucrats, as you can imagine, came running from all directions: they seized hold of Kulkov so that he couldn't get away.

The man who had been punched said:

'I,' he said, 'only came here to get my case sorted out, and I've been sitting here since this morning. And if I'm going to get smashed in the teeth in a government office on an empty stomach, then thank you very much, but I'd rather not, I can do without that sort of fact.'

Fyodor Kulkov was, so to speak, surprised in the extreme.

'I,' he said, 'simply, comrades, didn't know that he didn't work here, I thought it was just a bureaucrat sitting there. Otherwise I wouldn't have beaten him up.'

The managers were yelling:

'Find Kulkov's file!'

The punched person said:

'Excuse me, but in that case they should consider me too. Why should the puncher get so much priority? They should dig out my file too. Obrezkin's my name.'

'Find Obrezkin's file too!'

The punched person was desperately thanking Kulkov of course, shaking his hand:

'My face,' he said, 'that'll heal in time, but I'll be grateful to you as long as I live for your assistance against red tape.'

Then in no time at all they drew up a report, and as they were doing this Kulkov's file was brought out. They brought his file, entered a decision and gave it the complete go-ahead.

They said to the punched person:

'You,' they said, 'young man, have most likely come to the wrong institution. You,' they said, 'most likely need Social Security, and look,' they said, 'where you've ended up.'

The punched person said:

'Excuse me comrades! In that case, what have I been punched in the teeth for then? If that's the way it is, I should at least get some certificate saying on such and such a date Comrade Obrezkin really did get punched in the face.'

They refused to give Obrezkin a certificate, and so, of course, he tried to attack Kulkov. But they led him out and there the matter closed.

Kulkov himself got two weeks in gaol, but his case ended favourably and speedily without any red tape.

1927

Pushkin

Ninety years ago Alexander Sergeyevich Pushkin was killed in a duel.

All Russia, you could say, is grieving and shedding tears over this sombre anniversary. But it has to be said that Ivan Fyodorovich Golovkin is mourning and grieving more than anyone.

This mild-mannered man starts shaking terribly and stares off into the distance at the mere mention of the word Pushkin.

And I ask you, brothers, what else is he to do when he's discovered such a, what you might call sad side to the life of the poet of genius.

We'll begin our story in the distant past so as not to offend the memory of the great genius. We'll start around 1921. Then everything will be clearer.

In 1921, in the month of December, Ivan Fyodorovich Golovkin returned to his home town after he was demobbed from the army.

It was just around the time of the beginning of NEP. There was a flurry of activity. People were baking bread. Trade had got underway. In short, life was bubbling away.

But despite all this our friend Golovkin was walking around town, down on his luck. He didn't have accommodation. On Saturdays he would sleep round friends' houses. In the dog's bed. In the hall.

So of course on account of this, he was sceptically inclined:

'NEP,' he said, 'things are in a right welfare state. It's been six months now,' he said, 'and I still haven't found accommodation.'

In 1923 Golovkin sorted the problem out and found accommodation. Either he must have had to pay someone in order to move in, or fortune simply smiled in his general direction, anyhow, he found something.

It was a small room. Two windows. A floor, of course. A ceiling. It was all there. You can't argue with that.

And Golovkin settled in with real loving care. Ruined himself buying wallpaper, and put it up. Hammered in nails where needed, so that it looked a bit cosier. He was living like a Shah.

But of course time was passing. The eighty-seventh anniversary of the death of our beloved poet Pushkin passed, then the eighty-eighth.

On the eighty-ninth anniversary, rumours and talk began to spread in the apartment. Pushkin, people said. The writer. Once lived in this building, they said. Blessed this residential space with his irritable genius, they said. Wouldn't be a bad idea, in view of this, to stick up some sort of plaque with a full designation for the edification of posterity.

Ivan Fyodorovich Golovkin, without thinking what he was doing, heaven knows why, also took part in this plaque.

Then suddenly there was a bustle in the apartment. Ladies scuttled about. Cleaning pans. Mopping corners.

A five-man commission was coming. To inspect the accommodation.

The commission saw all the domestic mess in the apartment – pans and jackets – and they sighed bitterly.

'Here,' they said, 'Alexander Sergeyevich Pushkin once lived. And here, along with this, a right pigsty is being maintained. That broom over there. Those trousers hanging over there – those braces dangling from the wall. It's all an absolute insult to the memory of a genius!'

Well, in short, three weeks later they forced all the tenants to move out of the accommodation.

Golovkin, it's true, cursed a lot. Swore. Expressed his personal opinion openly, without fearing what the consequences might be.

'What,' he said, 'do you mean? All right, so he was a genius. All right, so he wrote poems: 'The bird hopped on the branch.' But why force average citizens to move out? I'm telling you, this country's got into a right welfare state. Forcing tenants to move out!'

Golovkin was even about to go to the Pushkin estate to swear some more, but started looking for accommodation instead.

He's still looking now. He's wasted away, he's turned grey. He's become very demanding too. Always asking questions, 'Who used to live in this accommodation?' There haven't been, heaven forbid, any Demyan Bednys or Meyerholds living here have there?' And if there have, then he, Golovkin, won't accept the accommodation even if you pay him.

He's got a point though: some of these immense geniuses act without thinking about it – they rush about from apartment to apartment, moving home. And then you get these unfortunate consequences.

You don't have to look far, in our own time our friend the poet Mitya Tsenzor, for example, Dmitry Mikhaylovich that is. In the last year he's lived in no less than seven rooms. He can't settle anywhere, you see. He doesn't pay his rent.

And who knows, he could be a genius!

In fifty years' time his name will be a dirty word for those seven rooms.

Although maybe the housing crisis will have eased off slightly by that time. That's our only hope.

1927

The Tsar's Boots

This year they were selling all sorts of second-hand tsarist stuff in the Winter Palace. I think it might have been the Museums Foundation that was running the sale. I'm not sure who it was.

Me and Katerina Fyodorovna Kolenkorova went along. She needed a samovar for ten persons.

They didn't have any samovars though. Either the Tsar drank out of a kettle, or they brought him some kind of glass from the kitchen, I'm not sure, but in any case, they didn't have any samovars for sale.

But they had loads of other things. And these things really were all magnificent. All kinds of tsarist embroidery, drapery, loads of glasses, spitoons, blouses and loads more tsarist gear. Your eyes were wandering all over the place, you didn't know what to grab and what item to acquire.

Then, with the money she had spare, instead of a samovar, Katerina Fyodorovna bought four blouses made of the finest Narsupur Indian cotton. Very luxurious. Tsarist.

Then I saw some boots listed. Tall and Russian, eighteen roubles.

I asked the co-op man who was selling the stuff:

'What sort of boots are these, my dear friend?'

He said:

'The normal sort, the Tsar's boots.'

'But,' I said, ' what guarantee do I have that these were the Tsar's? Maybe,' I said, 'some usher wore them, and you're trying to pass them off as the Tsar's. That's not very nice,' I said, 'that's bad.'

'Everything here's the property of the Tsar's family. We don't sell any old shit.'

'Show me,' I said, 'the goods.'

I took a look at the boots. I liked them really badly. And they were the right size. And they weren't too loose, but a tight fit, just right. They had heels, the toes were there. The boots were all in one piece. And hardly worn. Maybe the Tsar had worn them for three days in all. The soles hadn't come off yet.

'My God, Katerina Fyodorovna,' I said. 'Just think, in the old days, you wouldn't have even dared dream of the Tsar's footwear. Let alone walking down the street in the Tsar's boots. My God, Katerina Fyodorovna,' I said, 'how history changes!'

I felt no regrets as I gave him the eighteen roubles. After all, for the Tsar's boots it was a very, very reasonable price.

I forked out the eighteen roubles and took the Tsar's boots off home.

It was a real job putting them on though. I could hardly fit them on over a sock, let alone a foot-cloth. 'It'll be all right,' I thought, 'I'll wear them in.'

I wore them in for three days. Suddenly, on the fourth day, the sole came unstuck. Not so much just the sole as sort of the lot, along with the heel, the whole ground floor fell off. My foot was even poking through.

And the bloody thing happened outside, on Boulevard of the Soviets, just before I got to the Palace of Labour. So I just traipsed all the way back to Vasilyevsky Island without a sole.

What really got to me was the money. Eighteen roubles after all. And there was no one to complain to. If the boots had come from the Sprinter factory, or some other factory, then it would have been another matter. You could have taken legal action or got a red director sacked for this type of technical deficiency. But these were tsarist boots.

The next day, of course, I went to the Museums Foundation. But they'd already stopped trading there, everything was closed.

I wanted to pop round to the Hermitage Museum or somewhere else, but then I gave up. It was Katerina Fyodorovna who stopped me.

'It's not only the Tsar's,' she said, 'but any royal boot would be rotten after that many years. You can say what you like, but after all it's been ten years since the Revolution. The stitching could have moulded away in all that time. That's what you've got to bear in mind.'

And it's true comrades, ten tears have passed. Time flies! Even merchandise like that has started falling apart.

But though Katerina Fyodorovna calmed me down, all the same, when those tsarist lady's blouses of hers fell to pieces after the first wash, she cursed the tsarist regime bitterly.

But it's true, really, ten years have passed, there's no point in getting upset.

Time's passing so quickly now comrades!

1927

The Galosh

Losing a galosh on the tram isn't exactly hard.

Especially if you're being squeezed from one side and some thug behind you treads on your heel, and that's your galosh gone.

Losing a galosh is very easily done.

My galosh came off in the blinking of an eye. Before I knew what was happening, you could say.

I got on the tram, with my galoshes all present and correct. I got off the tram, looked, one galosh was there, on my foot, and the other wasn't. My boot was there. And my sock, I could see, was there. And my long-johns were where they should be. But there was no galosh.

Well, you're hardly going to run after a tram.

I took off the remaining galosh, wrapped it up in newspaper, and went on my way just as I was.

After work, I thought, I'll make some inquiries. I'm damned if I'm going to let good merchandise slip through my fingers just like that. I'll dig it up somewhere.

After work I went to look for it. First of all I thought I'd have a word with a tram-driver I know.

He got my hopes up straight away.

'You can thank your lucky stars,' he said, 'that you lost it on a tram. In some other public place I wouldn't be so sure, but losing something on a tram, nothing to worry about. We've got this Lost Property Office. You go along, you collect it. There's nothing to it.'

'Right,' I said, 'Thanks. Well, that's a weight off my mind. You see that galosh is nearly new. I've only been wearing it a couple of years.'

The next day I went to the Lost Property Office.

'Would there be any chance lads,' I said, 'of getting my galosh back? It came off on the tram.'

'There would,' they said. 'What kind of galosh is it?'

'It's an ordinary galosh,' I said. 'Size number 12.'

'We've got,' they said, 'maybe twelve thousand size 12s. Describe it.'

'It's like any other,' I said. 'The back is frayed of course, there's no cloth inside, the cloth has worn away.'

'We've got,' they said, 'more than a thousand of that sort of galosh. Doesn't it have any special distinguishing marks?'

'It does have,' I said, 'some special distinguishing marks. The toe has kind of been completely torn off. It's barely holding together. And it has very nearly no heel,' I said. 'The heel's worn away. But the sides,' I said, 'they're still all right, for the time being they're holding firm.'

'Sit down over here,' they said. 'We'll take a look.'

Suddenly, they brought out my galosh.

So I started rejoicing. I was genuinely moved.

There you are, I thought, the machinery of state works wonderfully. And what people of principle, I thought, personally taking so much trouble over a single galosh.

I said to them:

'I'll be grateful to you my dear friends,' I said, 'for as long as I live. Hand it over. Quick. I'll put it on straight away. Thank you.'

'No way,' they said, 'most esteemed comrade, we can't give it to you. We can't tell, they said, if it's really you that lost this galosh.'

'It was me that lost it,' I said. 'I can give you my word of honour.'

They said:

'We believe you and sympathize with you entirely, and it's very likely that it was you that lost this very galosh. But we simply can't give it to you. Bring in some certification that you really did lose a galosh. Why don't you get the House Committee to confirm it, and then we'll redistribute to you, without unnecessary red tape, that which you lawfully lost.'

I said:

'My brothers,' I said, 'my dear, dear comrades, they don't know anything about this in my block. What if they won't write me a confirmation?'

They replied:

'They'll write it,' they said, 'it's their job to. What do you think they're there for?'

I stared at my galosh once more and left.

The next day I went to the Chairman of our block, and said to him;

'Write me a piece of paper. Or my galosh is lost forever.'

'Ah,' he said, 'but did you really lose it? Or are you trying it on? Maybe you just want to get your hands on an extra item of mass consumption?'

'I swear to you,' I said, 'I lost it.'

He said:

'The thing is, I can't just take your word for it. But if you got me some certification from the tram depot saying you had lost a galosh, then I could give you the piece of paper. But not just like that.'

I said:

'But they've just sent me to you.'

He said:

'Well in that case write a statement.'

I said:

'What should I write, then?'

He said:

'Write: "On the morning of such and such date, my galosh went missing. And so on." Then you write: "I hereby give you a written undertaking not to move house until the matter is cleared up." '

I wrote the statement. The next day I received the proper certification.

I went to the Lost Property Office with this certification. And there, can you imagine it, without fuss or red tape they gave me back my galosh.

Only when I put the galosh on my foot did I feel genuine emotion. Those people, I thought, really know what work is! In other places, would they really have spent so much time on my galosh? They'd have thrown it straight out and that would've been the end of it. Whereas here I've barely spent a week on it, and I get it back.

The only shame is that during this week, in all the fuss, I lost the other galosh. I was carrying it around under my arm in a paper bag, and I couldn't remember where I left it. It wasn't on a tram, that's for sure. That's what makes it worse, that it wasn't on a tram. Well, where do you look?

But then I've got the other galosh. I've put it on the chest of drawers.

If ever you feel depressed, you just take one look at the galosh and you feel a little better and not so upset.

There you are, I think, that's how marvellously our official machinery works!

I'll keep that galosh to remind me. For my descendants to admire.

1927

Does a Man Need Much?

Recently we've been travelling all round the Union. We were particularly trying to see how people live.

They're not living badly. They're doing their best.

In every town new houses and homes are springing up noticeably. There are more and more of those little shacks people call cottages these days.

And because of this, the housing crisis has started to just ease off a little bit. We never saw more than seventeen people in a single room.

And only in one town did we see twenty-three persons in a room. Cab-drivers. With their families. But that was in Rostov. After all, it's a southern town, it's climatic. I've heard you can even grow peaches there. And the sea-shore's not all that far away. The sea down there, you know, never freezes over, all year round. With record-breaking climatic conditions like those there isn't really any dire need for covered accommodation.

And if you look at the North, it's easier.

In Leningrad itself there's a whole host of apartments.

It wasn't all that long ago that a good friend of mine, a certain Ivan Andreyevich, found himself an apartment. In this very same city of Leningrad. And he wasn't looking long. Just went round the Apartment Bureau a couple of times. There they just said:

'OK. How many rooms? Five, six?'

'Three, please,' he said.

'OK.'

And they gave him the address.

And just think, there are panicky people, who used up all their courage and bravery in the Civil War, saying: crisis!

This certain Ivan Andreyevich went round to the address: yes, there really were three rooms and everything you could ask for.

And he didn't have to do any particularly major building work. Put in front doors and partitions. Oh yes, and finish off building the staircase up to his floor.

And as for resetting the chimney, that was his choice. The chimney had been laid under tsarism. It did give off fumes, of course, but only as far as the hall. It's just that Ivan Andreyevich has got a weak chest. He can't bear smoke. He's always gasping.

Another healthier fellow would have lived with the chimney. If it got bad he'd have stuck his head out the window, and he'd have lived with it.

But in this case the chimney had to be relaid.

And Ivan Andreyevich didn't have to spend all that much money. Of course, he had to spend a fair amount. You could say the son-of-a-bitch sold himself outright, down to his last kopeck. And even got into debt. But he didn't lose heart.

'If it comes to it,' he said, 'I can always sell the apartment.'

And with these thoughts, he didn't worry in the slightest, but calmly finished off the building jobs.

'That's why I'm not completely trapped yet. Any idiot will buy a fresh apartment like this from me.'

And it's certainly true that when he had to pay his debts, Ivan Andreyevich went and sold the apartment without much trouble or expense.

And the whole business didn't lose him more than forty roubles. But for an apartment like that there's no shame in losing a hundred.

And with the money he got, Ivan Andreyevich bought back all the things he'd sold and paid off his debts.

And now he's apparently found another suitable apartment and has started doing some building jobs again.

And they say it's a dire crisis. Not particularly. You can live.

1927

Fantasy Shirt

Last Saturday after work I dropped by the shops. I had to buy a shirt.

On Sunday there was going to be a party at our place. I felt like dressing up a bit. I fancied buying some kind of a shirt that was a bit special. Some kind of fantasy shirt.

I chose one. A sort of sky-blue colour, with two detachable collars. Well, it was every bit as good as imported goods.

I headed off home as fast as I could. Tried it on. Luxury. A lovely sight. A joy to behold!

At the party, I thought, the ladies would be throwing themselves at me.

I should admit, I'm fanatical about cleanliness. There I was trying on the shirt, and somehow I felt uncomfortable. God only knows, I thought. You never know how many people have had their hands all over it. Wouldn't be a bad idea to get it laundered. We're only talking about twenty kopecks. Then I could wear it with pleasure.

I ran over to the laundry woman. She lives in the same yard as me. Lukerya Petrovna.

'My dear Lukerya Petrovna,' I said, 'please do your best. The party's tomorrow. I've got to have it for tomorrow. Can I rely on you?'

'You can rely on me,' she said. 'Come round,' she said, 'just before the party and you can put your shirt on. It will be washed and pressed, with the two detachable collars.'

The next day, before the party, I popped round to the laundry woman.

I took the shirt from her. I ran off to get changed.

I put the shirt on. But what on earth was this? Some kind of tiny shirt: the collar wouldn't fit and the cuffs were where the elbows had been. What the hell was going on?

I quickly hurried back to the laundry woman.

The laundry woman said:

'That's nothing unusual. It's only to be expected. New shirts these days always shrink. Either it's the material they're made from or the manufacturers don't wash the fabric. That's nothing.'

'What do you mean nothing! It won't fit round my neck. It used to be,' I said, 'size 38, and now it's probably a 32.'

The laundry woman said:

'And you can thank your lucky stars for that,' she said. 'The other day I washed one for the accountant, started off size 40 and now he'll be lucky if it's a five. The accountant threatened to smash my face in for that, but it's not my fault.'

Damn it! What, I thought, can I do?

And I didn't have much time. It was time to go to the party.

I put the shirt on, and over it, to hide it, I squeezed on my old shirt, so as not to cause offence, and hurried off to the party.

It went well. No one noticed. It was OK.

1927

Hard Labour

Owning a bicycle these days, now that really is hard labour.

It's quite true you can get a great deal of pleasure from them, physical recreation and the rest of it. You can also run down dogs. Or frighten chickens.

But, despite all this, I repudiate bicycles. My machine made me seriously ill, my very own vehicle.

I overstrained myself. Now I'm getting treatment as an outpatient. I ruptured myself. I might even be an invalid for the rest of my life. My very own vehicle crippled me.

It's true, the situation's got so bad you can't take your eyes off your vehicle for two minutes, or they'll swipe it. So on account of this, I had to carry the vehicle myself in my time off from riding it. On my shoulders.

I'd take the bike into a shop, and the wheels would drive the other customers over the counter. Or I'd have to climb up different floors to see friends. Or to report for work. Or to see relatives.

What's more, even when you're at your relatives', you have to sit there holding the handlebars. You can never tell what might get into them. I don't know. You can't see into someone else's consciousness. They'll unscrew the back wheel or pull out the inner-tube. Then they'll say it was like that when they found it.

All in all, I had a hard time of it.

I'm not even sure who rode who the most. Me the bicycle or it me.

Some prewar cyclists tried to leave their bicycles outside, of course. Chained and padlocked. But it didn't work, someone made off with them.

So I too was forced to take the world-view of these other citizens into account. I had to carry the vehicle myself.

For a man with a healthy mentality, it's not hard to carry a vehicle around, of course. But in my case there was a messy set of circumstances.

I needed one rouble in a hurry. I was dry and desperate.

'I've got to,' I thought, 'get hold of it somewhere.'

Since I had the vehicle, I jumped on it and rode off. I dropped in on one friend, but he wasn't at home. I went round to another's house, the money wasn't at home but the friend was.

The first friend only lives on the second floor, but the other one lives on the sixth. I dashed up and down carrying the vehicle – my tongue was hanging out.

Then I went to a relative's house. On Simbirskaya Street. My dear old aunt.

But just to be a pain in the neck, she lives on the fifth floor.

So I climbed up to the fifth floor with my machine. I saw there was a note on the door saying she'd be back in half-an-hour.

'She's out doddering,' I thought, 'the wrinkly old bag.'

That was a real blow, and in the heat of the moment I went downstairs. I should have waited for her upstairs with my vehicle, but I went downstairs because of the blow to my feelings. I started to wait for my aunt downstairs.

It wasn't long before she arrived, and she took offence at my not wanting to go upstairs with her.

'I've only got about ten kopecks on me,' she said. 'The rest of my money's in the apartment.'

I lifted my vehicle up onto my shoulders and followed my aunt. I could feel hiccups coming and my tongue starting to hang out. But I got there. Received my money in full. Had a bit of grub to strengthen the organism. Pumped up the tyres and went downstairs.

I'd just got to the bottom of the stairs when I saw that the front door was closed. It closes in these apartments at seven o'clock.

I didn't say anything then, just started grinding my teeth really badly, picked up the bicycle and started to climb up the stairs with it again.

How long it took me, I can't remember. It was just as if I was sleepwalking.

My aunt started letting me out the back way. She was laughing, the pain in the neck.

'You should have left your vehicle upstairs,' she said, 'if you're afraid to leave it downstairs.'

After a bit she stopped laughing, she could see the terrible paleness spreading across my face. I was holding onto the handlebars and swaying.

All the same, I got outside. But was too weak to ride.

And now I'm suffering the after-effects, this hard labour has made me ill.

The only consolation is that it's even worse for motorcyclists. They must really suffer!

And what's more, it's a good thing we haven't managed to build any skyscrapers here yet. Just think how many people would be driven to their beds!

1927

Green Merchandise

So autumn's here again. So you could say the building season is coming to a close.

I don't know how it is in other buildings, but in our building they did manage to do some redecorating. They painted the banisters on the stairs.

It wasn't done with the rent money of course, we aren't that rich round here. The money came from one of the tenants. He, the son-of-a-chicken, won five hundred roubles in savings bonds. Out of sheer fright he forked out fifty roubles towards the upkeep of the building. Later, when he came to his senses, he regretted it sorely. But it was too late. The banisters had already been painted.

They painted the banisters green. It turned out very nice. A noble sort of dark-green colour. It even seemed to have a touch of red about it. Or was that the rust showing through the paint? Hard to tell.

But anyway it turned out quite nice. To put it plainly, not an eyesore. You didn't instinctively shudder in pain.

So as I was saying, they painted them. People were admiring the banisters. The Chairman even made a short speech about the advantages of painted banisters. But after a while, after three days, the tenants started getting upset: why were the banisters taking so long to dry? The children in the apartments were getting paint all over them and were going round like zebras.

The Chairman made a good point:

'Comrades, we can't make unreasonable demands of this paint. Give it time, and it'll dry, and then it might not come off anymore.'

The tenants waited patiently.

Two weeks passed, and it still hadn't dried.

A painter was called in. The painter tried the paint on his tongue, went white and said:

'The paint,' he said, 'is the normal sort, it's oil paint. As for it not drying, I'll tell you why that is. It definitely has added linseed oil instead of olive oil. And linseed oil isn't in the business of drying quickly. But,' he said, 'there's nothing to panic about. In a month's time, with a bit of luck, it'll slowly, not exactly dry out, more sort of evaporate. Mind you,' he said, 'the banisters aren't likely to be green. They're much more likely to be blue. Or maybe they're more likely still to be grey with streaks.'

The Chairman said:

'You know, that's worked out well then. If it's grey with streaks, the dirt won't be so noticeable.'

The tenants started admiring the banisters again. They'd been admiring them for a month or two, and then they noticed that they were starting to dry out a bit. Though, to be honest, there wasn't much left to dry out. Nearly all the paint had come off on the children who lived in the apartments and inexperienced visitors.

But you've got to be an optimist, and find a good side to all the sad things that happen.

I'd say that the paint was still quite good and reasonably priced. It came off suits without any trouble at all. You didn't even have to wash it off. It disappeared of its own accord.

God only knows what it was made of. I dare say some down-and-out inventor is keeping his invention a closely-guarded secret. He's probably scared he'll get beaten up.

1927

A Fight

Yesterday, comrades, I was walking to the station. I wanted to catch the train and go into town. I was still at my dacha. Near Leningrad.

I was just coming up to the station and I saw, in the station, on the platform itself, just across from the railway official's office, a fight was occurring. In a word, there was a punch-up.

I ought to say that where our dacha is, the village is as quiet as the grave. There's simply no drunkenness, no noise especially, no scandals. Day after day. There's nothing like that at all. Just silence. Sometimes you even get a ringing in your ears from the complete silence.

For intellectual labour or shop-workers, or, let's say, the clergy, our blessed neck of the woods is just the right place for a break.

Of course, you don't get this silence for the whole of the month. It goes without saying that some days of the week can be ruled out. Well, you can rule out, say, Saturday, and Sunday, clearly. And Monday. Oh yes, and Tuesday too. Well, holidays of course. And then there's pay-days. On paydays, there's really no point in denying it, the trouble, as such, does reach boiling-point. On those days, it really is sort of not a good idea to go outside. Your ears ring with shouts and all manner of possibilities.

So, as I was saying, on one of these normal days I arrived at the station. I wanted to catch a train to go into town. I was still at my dacha. Near Leningrad.

So I came to the station and I saw . . . a fight.

Two citizens were setting about each other. One was swinging a bottle about and the other was defending himself with a balalaika. Though he was defending himself, he was also trying to hit his opponent with the sharp corners of the musical instrument.

There was also a third citizen. Their friend. The most sober of the three. He was separating them. He was pushing right in between them and trying to stop them fighting. And of course, he was taking all the blows himself. From both the bottle and the balalaika.

And when this third citizen started swaying, and had clearly been weakened from the frequent blows to the vital organs of his body, then I decided to call a militiaman so as to put a stop to the destruction of this noble organism.

And suddenly I saw: right there by the station, on the crossing, a militiaman was standing and munching sunflower seeds.

I shouted and waved at him to come over.

A member of the public said:

'He won't move an inch. He lives round here. You're wasting your breath.'

'Why's that,' I said, 'why doesn't he come and do something?'

'He just won't. If he gets involved, he'll get funny looks from the locals afterwards. They'll say he's trying to pretend he's the boss. And then they'll cast aspersions when they sober up. We've already had cases like that. This is not Leningrad. Here everyone knows everyone else.'

The militiaman stood at his post and looked towards us with a bored expression. Chewing sunflower seeds. Then he sighed and turned away.

The fight was gradually petering out.

And soon the three brawlers left the station embracing each other.

1927

Of Lamp-shades

In our communal apartment the lamp-shade in the hall got smashed. The one on the electric light.

One of the tenants, the son-of-a-bitch, came in one evening stewed as a newt, and tried to do something with the table. I think he was playing a game or trying to throw it in the air. And he broke the lamp-shade. It was a nice smooth frosted-glass lamp-shade.

Afterwards he moved out of the apartment, because he didn't want to pay for the lamp-shade.

It took the tenants a whole year to collect the money for a new lamp-shade. And when they'd collected it, they unanimously nominated me to acquire the thing.

Yesterday I went to try and buy it. But have you tried buying anything recently? It's an ordeal!

I went to one shop: no lamp-shades.

I went to another: they had lamp-shades, but for street-lamps. With lamp-posts.

In the third shop the sales assistant gave me a small lamp-shade that didn't really look suitable, but announced in a tired voice that this lamp-shade was from the window-display, and so it wasn't for sale.

In the fifth shop they said:

'What do you want a lamp-shade for, comrade? Buy a switch. Or this chandelier over here. If it comes to the worst, you can always hang yourself from it . . .'

In the seventh shop, the manager waved his hands at me angrily when I forced my way in. He said there would be no selling undertaken today on account of a stock-take of all the goods stolen during the current calendar month.

The ninth and tenth shops were closed for their annual stock-take.

In the thirteenth shop, the following historic conversation took place:

I said:

'Do you have any . . .'

The manager blew his nose on his sleeve cheerlessly and said:

'We haven't got any . . .'

'Excuse me,' I said, 'I haven't told you what I wanted yet.'

'Well, we haven't got any,' said the manager. 'What's wrong with you, are you a baby or something?'

Then, without even entering a fourteenth shop, I went straight to WoodTrust and with the money we'd collected, bought a little stand for walking-sticks and umbrellas.

It turned out the tenants were quite pleased.

'It's just as well,' they said. 'Otherwise someone would only get pissed and knock the fragile object down again.'

And if you think about it from a deeper, philosophical point of view, why the hell does man need lamp-shades anyway?

1927

Three Men and a Cat

My stove's no good. My whole family is constantly being poisoned by the fumes from it. And the bloody Housing Committee refuses to do the repairs. They're economizing. So they can embezzle it all again.

The other day they inspected my stove. Took a look at the dampers in the flue. Poked their heads inside.

'No, there's nothing wrong,' they said. 'It won't kill you.'

'Comrades,' I said, 'you should feel pretty ashamed pronouncing words like: "it won't kill you." We're constantly being poisoned by the fumes from this stove of yours. Even the cat's been poisoned. Only the other day she was sick over by the bucket. And you say "it won't kill you."'

The Chairman of the Housing Committee said:

'All right then,' he said, 'we'll conduct an experiment to see whether your stove's leaking. We'll heat up the stove, and if we're poisoned by the fumes, then your luck's in, we'll reset your stove. If we aren't poisoned, then we apologize, but that's just the way your heating system is.'

They lit the stove. We all gathered around it.

We sat there sniffing.

The Chairman was sitting right over by the dampers, Secretary Griboyedov was sitting over here, and the Treasurer was sitting on my bed.

Soon, of course, the fumes started wafting through the room.

The Chairman sniffed the air and said:

'No, there's nothing wrong. Can't smell anything. There's warm air circulating and that's all.'

The Treasurer, the toad, said:

'The atmosphere's perfect. You can even sniff it. It doesn't make your head feel weak. In my apartment,' he said, 'the atmosphere stinks far worse, but I,' he said, 'don't go round whining about it. But the air here's perfectly fine.'

I said:

'What do you mean perfectly fine, for Christ's sake. The gas is streaming out over there.'

The Chairman said:

'Call the cat. If the cat sits here calmly, that means there's not a bloody thing wrong. An animal is always disinterested. It's not a human being. You can trust it.'

In came the cat. Sat down on the bed. Sat there calmly. She was bound to sit there calmly, she'd pretty much got used to it.

'No, there's nothing wrong,' said the Chairman, 'we'd better be off.'

Suddenly the Treasurer started swaying on the bed and said:

'I'm afraid I've got to get on with some urgent business.'

And he went over to the window and breathed through a slit.

And he was standing there looking green and literally swaying on his feet.

The Chairman said:

'We'll all be off now.'

I pulled him away from the window.

'That's no way,' I said, 'to conduct an examination.'

He said:

'All right. I can move away from the window. I find your air really wholesome. Natural air, good for your health. We can't do any repairs for you. The stove's fine.'

But half an hour later, when this same Chairman was put on a stretcher and they were taking the stretcher to the ambulance, I talked to him again.

I said:

'Well?'

'No,' he said, 'we won't repair it. It won't kill you.'

And so they didn't repair it.

What can I do? I'm starting to get used to it. Human beings are not fleas, they can get used to anything.

1927

The Cross

Yesterday I had to pop into an extremely important institution. On personal business.

Just before setting off I had a solid breakfast of course, to keep my spirits up. And off I went.

I arrived at this institution. I opened the door. Wiped my feet. Went up the stairs. Suddenly, behind me some citizen in a double-breasted jacket called me back. Told me to come back down the stairs.

I came back down the stairs.

'Where do you think you're going,' he said, 'goat-head?'

'Oh, I'm just,' I said, 'on official business.'

'Well if,' he said, 'you're on official business, then first of all, you might just need a pass. Then you can go poking your nose in upstairs. This isn't Andreyevsky Market here you know,' he said. 'The eleventh year of the Revolution, it's about time people understood these things. What a lack of consciousness!'

'What if I didn't know,' I said. 'Where,' I said, 'do I get one of these passes?'

'Over there on the right,' he said, 'at the window.'

I went up to the little window. I tapped on it with my finger. A voice sort of rang out:

'What d'you want?'

'Oh, just a pass,' I said.

'All right.'

In some other institution, in another country, this kind of thing would lead to loads of red tape, they'd have asked for your papers and photoed your features for an ID card. But here they didn't even look at my face. A bare arm was stuck out, waved about and simply gave out a pass.

God almighty, I thought. How free and easy it is for us to live and go about our business in this country! And to think they talk about red tape. Many rootless intellectuals even construct decadent theories based on that. So much for them! They couldn't be more wrong.

They gave me a pass.

The man in the double-breasted jacket said:

'All right then, now you can go in. Trying to go barging in without a pass. If we allowed that kind of thing, an unwanted element could get in. They could blow the institution sky-high. This isn't Andreyevsky Market you know. Now you can go in.'

I dashed upstairs with this pass.

'Where,' I said, 'can I find Comrade Shchukin?'

The person behind the desk said to me suspiciously:

'Have you got a pass?'

'Here you are, here's my pass,' I said. 'I came in legally. I didn't climb in the window.'

He looked at my pass and said more politely:

'The thing is, Comrade Shchukin is in a meeting right now. Better come back next week. You see he's in a meeting all this week.'

'Fine,' I said. 'It can wait. I look forward to seeing you then.'

'Wait a second,' he said, 'give me your pass, I'll put a cross on it so you can come back again.'

I went back down the stairs. The man in the double-breasted jacket said:

'Where do you think you're going? Stop right there!'

I said:

'My dear comrade, I'm going home. I'd like to leave this institution and go outside.'

'Show me your pass.'

'Here you are,' I said, 'here it is.'

'Does it have a cross on it?'

'It certainly does,' I said.

'All right then,' he said, 'now you can leave.'

I went outside, ate a French loaf to strengthen my shattered organism, and set off for another institution on personal business.

1927

Rostov

By the way, Rostov's a nice town. I went there this autumn. Passed through.

A wonderfully peaceful town. And the climate's quite mild. And what's more, there's a complete absence of hooliganism. It's pretty amazing really, how they manage it.

A young girl can freely walk the streets at night alone. No one will lay a finger on her.

Well, that is, alone, I don't know about that of course. I can't guarantee that. But if she's in a two or a small group she can walk around in complete freedom. There's no particularly excessive raising of voices. They even allow you to walk on the pavement. They don't jostle you unless provoked. As for swearing, they swear of course. But among themselves. Not at passers-by.

This phenomenon, that is the complete absence of hooliganism, is produced, I think, on account of physical exercise. Physical exercise always distracts citizens from hooliganism. And physical exercise in this southern town has been raised to the highest level. Football, relay races, diving and swimming are all over the place. It's an amazing town in that respect.

I myself was witness to such a sporting incident.

I was sitting in the town gardens. I was reading, as I now recall, the newspaper. The debates section.

Everywhere around me was the mild autumn weather. The sun was shining. People were sitting on the benches. One of those silent autumn wordless scenes.

There was a lad strolling through the park. Holding a box. Clean your boots for five kopecks.

This little lad started on me too. Began to spit all over my boots for a five-kopeck piece.

He cleaned one. And he'd just started on the other when suddenly behind me someone sort of grabbed me by the shoulders from behind. I looked: some man I didn't know jumped over me in his underpants.

I was just about to curse him, the son-of-a-bitch, what on earth did he think he was doing jumping over people he didn't know, when suddenly, *boing*, another man jumped over me from behind. In all, there were four of them jumped over me. There you are, I thought, there's hooliganism in the flesh.

Suddenly I took another look, and there was no hooliganism. It was pure physical exercise. Leap-frog. The young people were playing leap-frog. It was wonderful, the way they were jumping over people who were sitting down.

The lad who was cleaning my boots said:

'There's nothing to be scared of. They're always practising leap-frog here. I'll just finish polishing your other boot. Sit down!'

Fair enough, I thought, better leap-frog than hooliganism.

All the same, I didn't let him finish cleaning the other boot. Gave the lad five kopecks and set off for the exit as quick as I could. Otherwise, I thought, they'll jump over me while I'm moving and knock me over, the bastards. And getting up after that would be no joke.

I got out onto the street, peace again. Clean, wonderful. No excessive raising of voices. No jostling you off the pavement.

Not so much a town, more a water-colour painting.

1927

No Hanging Matter

Something slightly unpleasant occurred in our building. A man was stabbed.

Mind you, to be fair, it all happened in a very civilized way.

In a more petit-bourgeois building, this fact would have set off all sorts of rowing, fights and punch-ups. Just for the hell of it, they would have smashed a few windows, vandalized the handrails on the stairs and so on.

But here two private traders quietly and peacefully got into a bit of an argument about a family matter and one slightly stabbed the other. And thankfully, on account of the cold weather, the man was wearing a quilted jacket, a waistcoat and three shirts. Otherwise he would have died writhing in agony.

As you might have guessed, they then called the ambulance. The militia. And each went their separate way. Or was carried off. And that was that.

Having said that . . .

The tenants started expressing their first impressions about the assault – who, they said, was going to get the room now? They were saying that private trader Kostya Ponomarev, God help him, had been arrested, and had thereby vacated his accommodation. So who should it go to? There was no shortage of candidates. All of them impatient. Apparently some had even been members of the Party since 1917.

And then the assaulted man himself poked his nose in the matter. Sent a medical orderly from the hospital. Asking for Kostya's room to be reserved for him.

As if that wasn't enough, next he reappeared on our horizon himself. They'd patched up his hole down at the hospital, and so, having summoned up his strength, there he was again. Staking all kinds of unthinkable demands. Saying the man who'd been stabbed should get the room. There's a decree about it, he said.

The Chairman of the Housing Committee said:

'Although that's pure demogoguery and there's definitely no decree of that description whatsoever, but,' he said, 'I'm sorry to say, you've got to see things from the point of view of the injured object. All the more so because the son-of-a-bitch is living in the kitchen and breathing all kinds of noxious fumes, and after all, he's the one who was stabbed, and nobody else.'

The cunning bastard was walking round all hunched-up on purpose, groaning and constantly holding his stabbed place, saying the pain was too much for him.

So the other tenants sort of gave in. They could see that the assaulted man was completely hell-bent on getting his hands on the property.

OK then, forget about it. Let him have it, they said. To hell with it. Good luck to him.

Having said that . . . The luck didn't turn out to be all that good anyway. Kostya Ponamarev only got six months.

And the assaulted man got all upset about it. He was a pitiful sight. Even the other candidates began to comfort him.

'Cheer up young man,' they said. 'Don't get yourself in such a state. Just ask yourself, why *should* they give him more? It's not as if he spent state funds or smashed you in the face as part of his job.'

The assaulted man said:

'True. You've got a point there. It's no hanging matter. But I just think that six months doesn't seem all that much. It's barely enough for me to settle into his room.'

They said:

'Mind you, he might come back and stab you again. He might see that you're there in his room and do you in. Then they might give him a bit longer. They might even give him eighteen months.'

The assaulted man said:

'No comrades. I can see that there was no point in me getting stabbed. What if he comes back some day soon? What if he's suddenly included in an amnesty and turns up tomorrow? What am I meant to do, sit there and wait for him?'

So the assaulted man didn't move into Kostya's room.

He's probably done the right thing there.

1928

Sobering Thoughts

I'm not saying we've got a lot of drunks in this country. There aren't all that many drunks. In the whole of May I only came across a single drunk who was lying flat on his face.

He was lying on the pavement. I nearly trod on him in the dark, the stupid bastard.

I looked down, and there was a drunken man lying there sobbing and wiping his miserable face with his fur hat.

'Come on,' I said to him, 'get up mister. Think you're tucked up in bed, do you?' I tried to get him to his feet, but he didn't want to. He was sobbing.

'What,' I said, 'are you sobbing about mister? You stupid bastard.'

'You see,' he said, 'it really upsets me.'

'What,' I asked, 'really upsets you?'

'It's people,' he said, 'you see. They're such a bunch of bastards.'

'How are they bastards?'

'You see, they just walk by . . . They barge past without giving you a second thought . . . They can't look a man in the face, to see why he's lying on the ground: is he drunk or has there been an accident . . .'

'But you're drunk,' I said.

'Well yes,' he said, 'of course I'm drunk. But I could have fallen over even if I wasn't drunk. You never know . . . Let's say, my foot, I wasn't drunk, and I happened to put my foot down carelessly . . . Or I just got out of breath . . . Or I might've been stripped bare by thieves . . . in that case it'd be go on, walk all over me, over someone who wasn't drunk, off you go, barging on, skulking about your affairs . . .'

'Wait a minute,' I said, 'But you *are* drunk.'

'Yes,' he said, ' I know I'm not sober. But I've sobered up a bit now. I've been lying here two hours on purpose . . . And in two hours not so much as a single dog's come up to me, you could die of humiliation. They'll just let someone who isn't drunk croak there, under the feet of passers-by. What's wrong? I'll tell you what's wrong, people have no heart anymore. When you used to fall down, they'd be flocking around you. They'd thrust eau-de-Cologne under your nose. Give you heart massage. Until, of course, they realized what the problem was. When they realized, they'd turn away. But now what do they do?'

I helped my drunk up onto his feet. Gave him a gentle push forward, to get him moving. It worked, he walked off.

He'd only gone about five paces when he sat down on a step.

'No,' he said, 'I can't walk. It still hurts thinking about it. The tears,' he said, 'are getting in my eyes. People are so heartless.'

1928

Foreigners

I'd always be able to tell a foreigner from one us Soviet citizens. All of them, all of those bourgeois foreigners, they've got something different in those ugly faces of theirs. Their faces, how can I put it, are more stiff and snooty than ours. It's as if, say, they'd taken a single facial expression, and they had to use this facial expression to look at the rest of the world.

Some foreigners put a monocle in their eye, to show total self-control. As if to say, we'll not drop this bit of glass and we won't bat an eyelid, whatever happens.

You've got to give it to them, they carry it off pretty well.

But foreigners can't help it. Their bourgeois life over there is pretty chaotic. Their bourgeois morality won't let them live naturally. Without that kind of self-control, they could disgrace themselves outrageously.

Like, for instance, when one foreigner choked on a bone. He was eating chicken, you see, and swallowed something. The whole thing happened at a banquet. A friend of mine, who works at the Trade Delegation, told me about it.

As I was saying, the whole thing happened at a banquet. Millionaires must have come from everywhere. Ford sitting on one chair. And all sorts of others too.

And then, with all this going on, someone swallowed a bone.

Of course, from our free perspective, there's no shame in this fact. So he swallowed it, so what? Over here everything's pretty quick in that respect. Ambulance. Hospital. Graveyard.

But they couldn't have that happening there. They were a very exclusively select company. There were millionaires all over the place. Ford sitting on one chair. Other frock-coated gents. Ladies. In electricity alone they were probably burning two hundred candlepower.

And then someone swallowed a bone. You'd think he'd immediately start blowing his nose. Hacking. Grabbing his throat. Heaven forbid! That's *mauvais ton* and God knows what.

And as for getting down from the table and running to the toilet as fast as you can, no, that's not right either, that's impolite. 'Aha,' they'd say, 'he's gone for a piss.' And that's absolutely forbidden.

But this Frenchman who'd swallowed a bone, at first of course, he was frightened to death. He tried to poke around inside his throat. Then he went a terrible pale colour. Started writhing around on his chair. But got a grip on himself straight away. And a minute later started smiling. Started blowing the ladies all kinds of kisses. Maybe even stared patting the host's dog under the table.

The host addressed him in French:

'I'm terribly sorry,' he said, 'have you really swallowed something inedible? You will tell me,' he said, 'won't you, if there's anything I can do.'

The Frenchman said:

'*Comment?* What's the fuss about? What are you talking about? I'm sorry, I don't know about yours, but my throat's perfectly all right.'

And he started blowing kisses again. Then he got stuck into the blancmange. Ate a portion.

To cut a long story short, he sat there until the end of the dinner and didn't let on to anyone.

Only as everyone got up from the table, he swayed slightly and grabbed hold of his stomach, he probably had a sudden pain there. And then he was all right again.

He sat in the lounge for three minutes or so out of petty-bourgeois politeness and went off to the hall.

Even in the hall he didn't particularly hurry, chatted with the hostess, took her hand, even though he had a bone in his throat he still managed to fish around under the table for his galoshes. And left.

When he was on the stairs of course, he started speeding up.

Ran to his carriage.

'Oi, chicken-face,' he shouted, 'take me to casualty.'

Whether this Frenchman died or survived, I can't tell you, I don't know. Probably survived. They're a pretty lively nation.

1928

An Unpleasant Story

This happened long ago. I think it was 1924. In a word, when NEP had expanded to its full magnificent size.

NEP, you could say, is beside the point. But what I'm going to tell you is just a funny Moscow story.

The story unfolded out of the fear of certain circumstances. Well, you'll see what it's all about for yourself.

So, this event occurred in Moscow. In fact it was in Zusev's apartment, Yegor Mitrofanych Zusev, maybe you know him, this comrade from Moscow. He works in one of the free professions.

Anyway, he had a party at his place one Saturday. No particular reason. Just felt like having a bit of a good time.

So of course people gathered. Mostly young, passionate. All with young, what they call beginners' brains.

And they'd hardly even arrived, really, before energetic arguments immediately broke out. Conversations. Discussions.

And somehow or other, the conversation soon turned to major political events.

One of the guests said something about Comrade Trotsky's book. Another supported him. A third said:

'That's sheer trotskyism.'

A fourth said:

'Yes,' he said, 'maybe that is the case, but, maybe it isn't the case. Anyway,' he said, ' we don't yet know what Trotsky understands by the word trotskyism.'

Suddenly one of the guests, a woman, Comrade Anna Sidorova, went all white and said:

'Comrades! You know what, why don't we call Comrade Trotsky. Let's ask him.'

The guests fell silent. For a moment everyone was looking at the phone.

Comrade Sidorova went even whiter and said:

'Why don't we phone the Kremlin, say . . . We'll ask for Comrade Lev Trotsky and ask him . . .'

There was a shouting and mumuring.

'That's right!' they said, 'why not . . . Good idea! . . . We'll call and ask him . . . We'll say, blah, blah, blah, Lev Davydovich . . .'

Then one energetic comrade, Mitrokhin, walked confidently over to the phone and said:

'I'll just get him.'

He picked up the handset and said:

'Please get me . . . the Kremlin . . .'

The guests held their breath and stood around the phone in a semi-circle. Comrade Anna Sidorova turned completely white, like a sheet of paper, and went to the kitchen to bring herself round.

Tenants gathered in the room from the whole apartment of course. The landlady also appeared, Darya Vasilyevna Pilatova – the apartment was registered in her name. She stopped by the door and watched events unfold, looking sick with worry.

And events were unfolding with a terrible speed.

Energetic Comrade Mitrokhin said:

'Please get me Comrade Trotsky on the telephone . . . What ? . . .'

And suddenly the guests saw that Comrade Mitrokhin's face had changed, he glanced around at all the people who'd gathered, jammed the handset between his knees so that they wouldn't hear anything at the other end, and whispered:

'What should I say ? . . . They're asking – What's it about? Who am I calling from? . . . It must be his secretary . . .'

At this everyone started away from the phone slightly. Someone said:

'Say you're from the editorial board . . . from *Pravda* . . . Go on, say it, you stupid bastard . . .'

'From *Pravda*,' mumbled Miktrokhin. 'What's that sir? Oh, just about the article.'

Someone said:

'Now you've done it. You're really in trouble now. Just wait, something unpleasant's going to happen.'

The landlady of the apartment, Darya Vasilyevna Pilatova, in whose noble name the apartment was registered, started swaying from side to side and said:

'Oh, I feel sick! You've landed me right in it, you bastards. What's going to happen now? Put the phone down! This is my apartment, put the phone down! I won't have people talking with leaders in my apartment . . .'

Comrade Mitrokhin cast an anguished glance over the whole company and hung up.

Another awful silence fell over the room.

Some of the guests quietly stood up and made their way home.

Those left sat in complete immobility for five minutes.

Suddenly the phone started ringing.

Zusev, the host, went over to the telephone himself and with gloomy determination picked up the handset.

He began to listen. And suddenly his eyes grew wide and his forehead became covered in sweat. And the handset began to tap against his ear.

A voice thundered in the handset:

'Who called Comrade Trotsky? What did they want him for?'

'There must be some mistake sir,' said Zusev . . . 'No one here called him. Sorry . . .'

'We haven't made any mistake. Someone called us from your number.'

The guests began to go out into the hall. And trying not to look at one another, they silently put on their coats and left the apartment.

No one guessed that the call was a hoax.

They only found out about it the next day. One of the guests confessed. He had left the room straight after the first conversation and called from a public phone-box.

Comrade Zusev got into an argument with him. He even wanted to smash his face in.

1928

Pawning

It's really terrible, the red tape you get at pawnbrokers' these days. Any citizens wanting to pawn something urgently, they can forget it. It's definitely not quick. You have to wait for hours. And while you're queueing you get crushed from all sides. And that's not all.

The other day a bloke we know thought he'd pawn his overcoat. He desperately needed three roubles. A one-off. So he took his overcoat and went off to queue. And waited there patiently.

There he was waiting, and after a bit he thought:

'While I'm waiting, comrades,' he thought, 'Autumn could occur. It's pointless me pawning my autumn coat. Just to be on the safe side, I'll pawn my winter one.'

So he ran home, got his winter coat and put on his autumn coat. And there he was waiting patiently.

After a bit, he thought:

'This is no good. In the time it takes for the queue to get to me, winter could set in. I'd be better off,' he thought, 'putting my winter coat on and pawning my autumn one.'

So then that's what he did. He put on the winter coat and carried the autumn one, and waited there patiently.

He's still waiting there now. Puts on one coat and then the other. Sometimes he takes them both off. Depending on the season. He doesn't know which one to pawn.

Don't ask us what should be done. Come on, for five kopecks you can't expect us to do the drawings and give out free advice as well.

1928

A Summer Break

You can say what you like of course, but having your own individual apartment, that really is petit-bourgeois.

We've got to live as friends, as a collective family, and not lock ourselves up in our domestic castles.

We've got to live in communal apartments. There everything's out in the open. There's always someone to talk to. To ask for advice. To fight.

Of course, there are drawbacks.

The electricity causes trouble, for example.

You don't know how to work out the bill. Who should pay what.

Of course, in the long run, when our production has turned around, then if we want we can have two meters per tenant fitted in every corner. And then we can let the meters determine the amount of energy expended. And then, of course, life in our apartments will shine like the sun.

But in the meantime, it's true, we're in a really tricky situation.

For example, we're nine families. One supply. One meter. And you've got to prepare for the bill at the end of the month. And then, of course, the bitterest misunderstandings occur and sometimes even punch-ups.

OK, so you're going to say, count the number of light-bulbs.

OK then, the number of light-bulbs. One class-conscious tenant only switches on the light for five minutes to get dressed or catch a flea. But another tenant is munching away until twelve o'clock at night with the light on. And doesn't want to switch the electricity off. Though it's not as if he's got to have enough light to draw patterns by.

You'll probably find a third tenant, an intellectual no doubt, who'll be poring over his books until one o'clock at night and beyond, with no regard for the collective environment.

And he might even unscrew the bulb and put in a brighter one. And read his algebra as if it's the middle of the day.

And having shut himself up in his lair, this same intellectual might even be using an electric element to boil water or make macaroni. That's what you've got to realize!

We had one tenant, a porter, he was literally driven nuts on account of all this. He couldn't sleep properly any more and was constantly trying to find out who was reading algebra at night and who was warming groceries with their electric element. And that was the end of him. He went nuts.

And after he'd gone nuts, a relative of his took over the room. And then there was a regular bacchanalia.

Every month we ran up no less than twelve roubles on the meter. And in the most degenerate month, all right, it was thirteen. But of course, that was with the tenant who went nuts checking up. He was very good at checking up. Like I was saying, he literally wouldn't sleep at night and hardly a minute passed without him carrying out an inspection. He'd go into one place, then another, and was always threatening to chop people up with an axe if he found any excesses. In fact, it's a wonder this way of life didn't drive the other tenants themselves nuts.

So anyway, we were on no more than twelve roubles a month.

And suddenly we got a bill for sixteen. Sorry, what's going on? What bastard has rung up that quantity? It's got to be an element or a heater or something like that.

People cursed and cursed, but paid up.

A month later we were on sixteen again.

The honest tenants said straight out:

'What's the point of living. We live like bastards, always saving, and others don't give a damn about the current. If that's how it is, we won't give a damn either. We're going to switch on elements and make macaroni.'

Next month we had nineteen on the meter.

The tenants groaned, but they paid up all the same. Then they began to really ring it up. No one switched any lights off. They were reading novels. Using elements.

A month later we were on twenty-six.

And that's when the bacchanalia really started.

To cut a long story short, when we'd rung up thirty-eight roubles on the meter, they had to cut off the energy. Everyone had refused to pay. Though there was an intellectual who was begging and grabbing hold of the cable, but no one took any notice of him. They disconnected us.

Of course this is only temporary. No one's against electrification. At the general meeting people declared as much: no one's against it, they said, and in the long run we'll get connected. But for the moment that's the way it is. Especially since it's nearly spring. It's light. And then it'll be summer. The birds'll be singing. And what do you need lighting for then? You're hardly going to be drawing patterns. But then in winter, we'll have to see. Maybe in winter we'll get reconnected to electric power. Or we'll start checking up or something.

In the meantime, we're having a summer break. All this stuff with the apartment, it's exhausting.

1929

Loose Packaging

These days there's no bribery. Before though, you couldn't go any-where without giving or taking something.

But now people's morality has changed significantly for the better.

There really isn't any bribery these days.

Recently we had to send a parcel from a goods station.

Our aunt had died from the flu and in her will had asked us to send her sheets and other petit-bourgeois stuff off to the countryside, to rela-tions on my wife's side.

So there we stood at the station and saw a scene straight out of Raphael.

There was a booth for the receiving of parcels. A queue, of course. Metric decimal scales. A weight-checker standing by them. The weight-checker was one of those white-collar workers who are decent through and through. He was saying the figures very quickly, writing things down, putting weights on the scales, sticking on labels and explaining things.

All you could hear was his pleasant voice:

'Forty. One-hundred-and-twenty. Fifty. Lift it off. Take it away. Don't put it there you idiot, put it over here.'

It was a pleasant picture of labour and fast work-rate.

Only then we suddenly noticed that despite all the beauty of his work, the weight-checker was a very demanding stickler. He really was defending the interests of citizens and the state. All right, so it wasn't every single one, but after every second or third person he'd definitely refuse to take the parcel. If the packaging was the slightest bit loose, then he wouldn't take it. Though you could see that it pained him to do so.

Of course, those who had loose packaging were moaning and groan-ing and agonizing.

The weight-checker was telling them:

'Instead of moaning, make your packaging secure. Somewhere around here there's a man with some nails hanging about. Get him to secure it. Get him to bang a couple of nails in here and tighten the wire. And then when you come back, you won't have to queue, I'll take it.'

And he was right: there was a man standing behind the booth. He had a hammer and nails in his hands. He was toiling away and securing the loose packaging for those who wanted him to. Those who had been refused looked at him pleadingly and offered him their friendship and money to do it.

But then one citizen came to the front of the queue. He was fair-haired, wearing glasses. He wasn't an intellectual, just short-sighted. He probably had trachoma in his eyes. And so he'd started wearing glasses so that people wouldn't notice. Or maybe he worked at an optics factory and they gave out glasses there for free.

And so he put his six boxes on the metric decimal scales.

The weight-checker inspected his six boxes and said:

'The packaging's loose. We can't accept it. Take it back.'

The man wearing glasses, when he heard these words, totally lost heart. But before he lost heart, he went for the weight-checker so badly that he almost gave him some unsolicited dental treatment. The man wearing glasses shouted:

'You dog, what the hell are you up to! I'm,' he said, 'not sending my own boxes. I'm,' he said, 'sending state boxes from an optics factory. What am I going to do with these boxes now? Where am I going to find a cart? Where am I going to find a hundred roubles to take it back? Answer me you dog, or I'll make mincemeat of you!'

The weight-checker said:

'How should I know?' And at the same time gestured to one side with his hand.

The other man, owing to his short-sighted vision and his steamed-up lenses, took this gesture for something else. He blushed, remembered something that he had forgotten a long time ago, rummaged around in his pockets and unearthed eight roubles of money from them, all in one-rouble bills. And he tried to give them to the weight-checker.

Then the weight-checker turned crimson at the spectacle of this money.

He shouted:

'What do you think you're doing? You're not trying to bribe me are you, four-eyes?'

Of course, the man in glasses immediately understood the full disgrace of his position.

'No,' he said, 'I just took my money out. I just wanted you to hold it while I took my boxes off the scales.'

He became all flustered and began spouting complete nonsense and apologizing, and it even seemed he was willing to be punched in the mouth.

The weight-checker said:

'You should be ashamed of yourself. Take your six boxes off the scales, they're literally making my blood run cold. But, since they're state boxes, you can go and see that worker over there and he'll secure the packaging for you. And as for the money, you can thank your lucky stars that I haven't got time to pursue your case.'

All the same, he called another colleague over and told him, in the voice of someone who has just suffered an insult:

'You know, someone just tried to bribe me. Would you believe it, it's absurd. It's a shame I was in a hurry and didn't pretend to take the money, because now it's hard to prove it.'

His colleague answered:

'Yes, that's a pity. The matter should be exposed. People shouldn't be allowed to think that we've got our fingers in the till, like in the old days.'

The man wearing glasses, covered in sweat, was struggling with his boxes. He got them strengthened, given an air of respectability and dragged back to the scales.

Then it started to seem to me that my parcel's packaging was loose too.

And before it got to my turn in the queue, I went over to the worker and asked him to secure my doubtful packaging just in case. He asked me for eight roubles.

I said:

'What, have you gone mad, eight roubles for three nails?'

He said to me in a confidential tone of voice:

'I know, I'd do it for you for three roubles, but,' he said, 'you've got to see it from my awkward point of view, I've got to split it with that crocodile over there.'

Then I started to understand how the whole system worked.

'So you mean,' I said, 'you share it with the weight-checker?'

Then he got a bit embarrassed that he'd said something he should-n't have, and started mumbling all kinds of nonsense and rubbish, moaning about his tiny salary and the cost of living, gave me a big dis-count and got to work.

Then it was my turn.

I put my box on the scales and admired its secure packaging.

The weight-checker said:

'Your packaging's a bit loose. I can't accept this one.'

I said:

'Really? I've only just had it secured. Him over there with the pincers secured it.'

'Oh sorry, I'm sorry. I do beg your pardon. Now your packaging's secure, but it was loose. I can always tell that. I'm sorry, I'm very sorry.'

He accepted my box and wrote the invoice.

I read the invoice, it said:

'Loose packaging.'

'What are you trying to do to me, you thieving Arabs?' I said. 'With that written on it, it's bound to be stolen on the way. And that would make it impossible for me to demand compensation. Now,' I said, 'I understand your thieving tricks.'

The weight-checker said:

'I'm sorry, I'm very sorry. I do beg your pardon.'

He crossed out what he'd written, and I went home, thinking on the way about the complex mental structure of my fellow citizens, about our efforts to construct a new morality, about cunning and the reluctance of my esteemed fellow citizens to abandon their entrenched positions.

I'm sorry, I'm very sorry.

1932

A Trap

A friend of mine, he's a poet by the way, went abroad this year.

He travelled all over Italy and Germany so as to acquaint himself with bourgeois culture and to fill in a few gaps in his wardrobe.

He saw a lot of interesting things.

He said there's an enormous crisis, of course. Unemployment, contradictions all over the place. Loads of food and consumer durables, but nothing to buy it with.

And he even had dinner with a duchess.

He was sitting in a restaurant with a friend of his, and the friend said to him:

'If you want I can call a duchess, for a laugh. A genuine duchess, with five houses, a skyscraper, vineyards and so on.'

Well, he was overdoing it a bit of course.

And so he rang her up on the telephone. And soon a beautiful woman of about twenty came in. Wonderfully dressed. Etiquette. A world-weary way of speaking. Three pocket handkerchieves. Shoes on her bare feet.

She ordered herself some meat-balls and said in the course of conversation:

'Yes, I haven't eaten any meat for the best part of a week you know.'

Well, with a word or two of French and some Russian the poet replied, excuse me, he said, but you've got so many houses *à la maison* you must be lying,' he said, 'aren't you laying it on a bit thick, pretending to be poor, and trying to imply something.'

She said:

'You know, it's already been a year since the tenants of those houses last paid me any rent. People don't have any money.'

I didn't tell you this little fact for any particular reason, more out of general interest. To set the scene. To describe the bourgeois crisis. They've got a really desperate crisis over there all over the place. But you've got to admit, their streets are clean.

My friend the poet really praised, by the way, their European cleanliness and civilized behaviour. Particularly, he said, in Germany, despite the enormous crisis, they maintain amazing, fantastic levels of cleanliness and tidiness.

The streets, God almighty, they wash them with soapy water. In blocks of apartments they scrub the staircases every morning. Cats are not permitted on the stairs or on windowsills like they are over here.

Cat ladies take their cats out for a walk on little leads. Can you believe it?

Everything's dazzlingly clean, of course. There's nowhere to spit.

Even second-string places, like – I don't mean to be rude – but toilets, even they shine with a heavenly cleanliness. It's a pleasure, it's in no way insulting to human dignity to go to one.

He went, by the way, to one of these second-string institutions. Just for fun. To have a look and see if there's really a difference, between how it is over there and over here.

It turned out there was. It would make you catch your breath, he said, with delight and astonishment. Spellbinding cleanliness, light-blue walls, and there's a bunch of violets. You don't feel like leaving. It's better than in a café.

'What,' he thought, 'the hell is this. Our country leads the world when it comes to political tendencies, but when it comes to cleanliness, we're lagging a long way behind. It's not good enough,' he thought. 'When I get back to Moscow I'll write an article about it and hold Europe up as an example to follow. There's certainly a lot of people back home who are hypocritical about these questions. You see, they're embarrassed to write and read about such vulgar things. But,' he thought, 'I'll shake that complacency out of them. Wait till I get home, I'll write a poem saying we shouldn't put up with a lot of dirtiness, comrades. Especially as there's a campaign for cleanliness on now, I shall respond to society's literary requirements.'

So there was our poet shut in his cubicle. Thinking, admiring the violets, dreaming of the poem he'd rattle off. Some rhymes and lines even came to him. Something like this:

> Over there even this place is charming -
> They've got violets blooming.
> Is it because Atilla passed us by
> That we live in such a pig-sty?

After a while, whistling the latest German foxtrot, 'Auf Wiedersehen, Madame', he was ready to leave.

He tried to open the door, but it wouldn't open. He pulled the door-handle, but nothing happened. He put his shoulder against it, but no, it wouldn't open.

At first he pretty much lost his cool. That's it, he thought, I've fallen into a trap.

After a while, he was slapping himself.

'What a fool I am,' he thought, 'I forgot that I'm in the capitalist world. Over here you've probably got to pay a pfennig to blow your nose. Probably,' he thought, 'you've got to put a coin in somewhere, then the door will open all by itself. Mechanics. Bastards. Bloodsuckers. Fleece you seven times over. Luckily,' he thought, 'I've got some change in my pocket. I'd be in a right mess without this bit of change.'

He took some coins out of his pocket. 'I'll pay off the capitalist sharks. I'll stuff a coin or two down their throats.'

But he looked around, there wasn't anywhere. There weren't any boxes with slots. There was some kind of notice, but it didn't have any figures indicated on it. And where to shove change and how much to shove, you couldn't tell.

Then our friend sort of went a bit mad. Started off by banging on the door lightly. No one came over. So he started to kick the door.

He could hear people gathering. Germans were coming over to him. Mumbling in that dialect of theirs.

The poet said:

'Let me out, please help me.'

The Germans whispered something, but clearly they didn't understand the full poignancy of the situation.

The poet said:

'*Genosse, Genosse, der Tür*, the bastard, won't open. *Comprenezschen*. Please let me out. I've been sitting here for two hours.'

The Germans said:

'*Sprechen Sie Deutsch?*'

Now the poet begged them:

'*Der Tür*, he said, open *der Tür*, damn you!'

Suddenly a Russian voice rang out from behind the door:

'What's up with you in there? Can't you open the door?'

'No, I can't,' he said. 'I've been banging on it for over an hour.'

The Russian voice said:

'The bastards, they've come up with a mechanical door. You,' he said, 'have probably forgotten to pull the chain. Flush the toilet and the door will open by itself. They deliberately made it like that for forgetful people.'

My friend did as he was told, and suddenly, as if in a fairy-tale, the door opened. Our friend came staggering out to faint smiles and German whispering.

The Russian said:

'Though I'm an émigré, all these German schemes and sausagery stick in my throat too. In my opinion it's an insult to humanity . . .'

My friend didn't want to strike up a conversation with an émigré of course, and pulling up his jacket collar he quickly made for the exit.

At the exit the caretaker brushed him down, took a small quantity of money and let him go on his way.

Only when he got outside did my friend draw breath and calm down.

'Ah,' he thought, 'so the much-praised German cleanliness doesn't come of its own accord. That's why the Germans use coercion to instill it and think up all sorts of cunning devices to uphold civilization. If only they thought up things like that back home.'

With this thought my friend calmed down and, whistling 'Auf Wiedersehen, Madame', went round to someone's house for dinner as if nothing had happened.

1933

How Much Does A Man Need?

Of course, payment really limits a man in his fantasies. It works against excesses and the expression of all kinds of dark sides of people's characters. In this sense, it has its positive sides. It gives life a polish.

If you imagine that, starting tomorrow, the trams will be free, then you can bet your life that many citizens will simply be denied access to this cheap means of transportation. Of course even now, to put it mildly, it's not all that pleasant travelling on the trams, but if they were free it would have long ago become unthinkable. They wouldn't just be travelling on the steps, but, believe me, they'd even be hanging from the electric pick-up.

Some people don't have to travel at all, they only live a few paces away. The walk would do them good, but they'd definitely have to take the tram. They'd definitely have to display their repressed ambitions. They'd push their way right into the thick of the human bodies to get on, even though they could get crushed to death. They wouldn't care. They'd just want to take the tram. And they wouldn't give a damn how.

And I bet they'd go right to the end of the line, even if they didn't need to. And if it was the circle line, then I reckon they'd go all the way round, and even do a second round, before they'd willingly get off at their own stop. That's what some people are like. There are even some who'd go round three times. And some you'd never get out of the tram. They'd probably even sleep there. They'd get into a frenzy if you announced it was free.

In my opinion we've got to change people's characters. In my opinion it's a hangover from bourgeois culture. And we've got to fight it with all our strength and renovate our minds.

Just the other day, I myself, having not yet wholly renovated my mind, ate something like, I think, ten bowls of ice-cream at a banquet. Even after two weeks I couldn't straighten my body.

So what I am stating here I've personally thought through and experienced.

I once saw a free merry-go-round on a square somewhere. They'd put it right opposite a church. Probably so that believers could amuse themselves and unbelievers could spend their time in a civilized manner, without entering the church.

There was something really serious going on there. Many didn't realize, of course, that the merry-go-round was free. And so they were too shy to get on. But those that did realize simply couldn't control themselves.

I saw one man they tried to drag off, but he wouldn't move.

Once he'd got on the wooden horse, it was like he'd been glued to it and he whizzed around on it for three hours or so. Only when he was completely senseless and had turned a chalky pale colour did he allow himself to be taken off by his friends. And even then he was kicking out, trying to stop them taking him off.

So of course, when they laid him down on the ground he was panting like a fish, and staring at the sky, hardly understanding a thing. But then when he felt better he climbed back on the horse and went round until he felt ill again. Even then he wouldn't get off straight away. He only got off after he'd puked up.

Then, whether he wanted to or not, he had to get off. People started to get upset, saying that with the turning of the merry-go-round it creates an unpleasant effect. Otherwise he wouldn't have got off. But the attendant dragged him off, and I think he even gave him a kick in the teeth for his unacceptable disgusting behaviour.

After which the man lay there on his stomach for a long time, hoping to have another little go when he'd had a rest. But then, probably after he'd failed to get a grip on his shaken health, he went off home.

So on the whole, it's hard to say how much a man really does need in all. Probably more than however much he needs and not less than however much he wants.

So everything's OK then. There's a 'ceiling'. Warmest regards to all those young people who are reconstructing their characters.

As for old people, we won't mention them. They were brought up on the old monetary ways, and don't know when to stop and at the slightest excuse reach into their pockets. And at the same time they don't know where to stop when it comes to getting hold of money. That's where they're capable of all kinds of disgusting behaviour.

1934–5

An Incident on the Volga

To start with, we wanted to tell you about an amusing little piece of bad luck.

The precise nature of this bad luck was that a group of holiday-makers received a profound shock on account of a misunderstanding.

This is how it happened. It's a true story.

In the first years after the Revolution, when life was settling down and wonderful ships with first-class cabins and serving passengers hot meals started sailing down the Volga again, a group of holiday-makers – six office-workers, including myself – went to have a holiday on the Volga.

Everyone had been advising us to take a trip down the Volga. Because you can have a really wonderful holiday there. The nature. The shores. The water, the food and the cabins.

So the group of office-workers, having got tired, so to speak, of the thunder of Revolution, went off to revive themselves.

We got a wonderful first-class steamer, *Comrade Penkin* was her name.

We wondered who this Penkin was, and were told that apparently he worked in water-born transportation.

We couldn't care less really, and so of course, we took a trip on this unknown comrade.

We arrived at Samara.

We got out in our group and went to look round the town. We looked round. Suddenly we heard a whistle.

People said:

'The timetable's unreliable these days. Our *Penkin* could suddenly decide to leave. Let's go back.'

And so having just about managed to look round the town, back we went.

As we approached the jetty we could see that our steamer wasn't there anymore. She had gone.

People started shouting and wailing.

One of our group shouted:

'I left my documents there in my trousers.'

Others shouted:

'And we've left our luggage and our money. What are we going to do now? . . . This is terrible!'

I said:

'Let's get on this steamer that's going the other way and go home.'

We saw that there really was a Volga steamer at the jetty, named *Thunderstorm*.

We asked people in mournful tones whether the *Penkin* had left long ago. Maybe we could catch up with her by land.

People said:

'What do you want to catch up with her for? That's the *Penkin* over there. It's just that she's now *Thunderstorm*. It's the former *Penkin*. They've painted over the name.'

We were extremely pleased to hear this. We all made for our steamer and didn't get off until we got all the way to Saratov. We were afraid to.

We asked the captain, incidentally, what was the reason for this amusing incident and for the hurry.

The captain said:

'You see, we gave this steamer that name by a sort of mistake. Penkin does work in water-born transport, only he was sort of not quite up to the job. At the moment he's being prosecuted for exceeding his authority. So we received a telegram telling us to get rid of his name. And we renamed her *Thunderstorm*.

Then we said:

'Ah, so that's why!' and laughed hollowly.

We arrived at Saratov. We got out in our group and went to look round the town.

We didn't exactly hang around there for long either. But we went to a stall and bought some cigarettes. And looked at a couple of buildings.

We returned, and again we saw that our steamer *Thunderstorm* had gone. We saw another steamer standing there in her place.

We weren't as scared as we had been in Samara, of course. We thought we might have a chance. Maybe they'd painted over the name again. But all the same, some of us got very frightened again.

We ran up close. We asked people:

'Where's *Thunderstorm*?'

The people said:

'That's *Thunderstorm* over there. Formerly *Penkin*. Now, starting from Saratov, they're calling her *Korolenko*.'

We said:

'Why are they doing all this repainting?'

The people said:

'We don't know. Ask the boatswain.'

The boatswain said:

'These names are a real pain. They called us *Penkin* by mistake. And as for *Thunderstorm*, that was an irrelevant name. It sort of lacked a principled position. It's a natural phenomenon. It's no benefit to heart or brain. And so the captain got it in the neck. So that's why we did the repainting.'

We all cheered up then and said:

'Oh, so that's it!' We got on this *Korolenko* and off we went.

Then the boatswain said:

'Remember, at Astrakhan don't be afraid if you come back to find another name.'

But we said:

'Well, that's hardly likely, since this Korolenko is a famous writer.'

Anyway, we got to Astrakhan. And from there we set off on dry land. So we don't know the subsequent fate of the steamer.

But you can rest assured that she kept this last name. For ever and ever. Especially since Korolenko's dead. Penkin was alive, you see, and that was his main stroke of bad luck, which led to his being renamed.

So bad luck most probably consists in the simple fact that people are sometimes alive then, does it? No, I'm sorry, I really can't understand what the essence of misfortune is. On the one hand, sometimes it seems we're better off dead. But on the other, as they say, thanks all the same. A funny kind of good fortune. I'd rather not. At the same time, being alive is in that respect a sort of relative misfortune.

So, you could say, unpleasant things are coming at people from two directions at once.

And that is why we have put this little piece of nonsense about a kind of misunderstanding with our stories about misfortune.

1934–5

Water Sports

A cinema worker from Moscow visited Leningrad on business.

He stayed at the Europa Hotel.

Had a wonderfully comfortable room. Two beds. A bath. Carpets. Paintings. All this sort of put our new arrival in the mood for meeting people and passing time pleasantly.

So friends and acquaintances started coming round to see him.

And as always, some of his friends came by and took a bath. You see, many of them lived in apartments where there was no bath. And many people don't really like going to the steam baths, and in fact people are tending to forget about this everyday procedure. And so here was a perfect opportunity: you go round to see a friend, chat, philosophize and take a bath at the same time. Especially since there's hot water. And free government-supplied towels and so on.

This is why many people like it when a friend visits from out of town.

To cut a long story short, in five days our visiting Muscovite had even become a bit exhausted with this undeviating line of friends.

But of course he held out until the very last moment, when finally a catastrophe unfolded.

One way or another, that evening six friends had come round more or less all at once.

After a brief chat, the guests immediately formed a small queue for the bathroom.

Three washed quickly and, once they'd had a cup of tea, left.

But the fourth was an old lady. A relative of our visitor. She was an exceptionally long time taking a bath. It seems she was even washing something from her wardrobe.

She was fussing about in there for so long that the Muscovite and his waiting friends got pretty depressed. She was in the bathroom for an hour and a quarter.

But seeing as she was our Muscovite's dear old aunt, he wouldn't allow his friends any excesses towards her.

In short, by the time she came out it was well past midnight.

One of the friends couldn't wait any longer, and left. But the other was completely shameless, and just wouldn't give up. Come what may, he wanted a bath that very day, so that he would be clean for something or other in the morning.

And so he waited for the aunt to leave. Cleaned the bath. And turned on the hot water tap. Then he lay down on the couch and began to wait for the bath to fill up.

But somehow or other he must have fallen asleep because he was so tired. And what's more, the Muscovite himself was dozing on the sofa.

So the water filled the bath and then overflowed, and in a short while flooded the hotel room and even seeped through to the next floor. But since the floor below was the lounge, which was empty, at first no one noticed the catastrophe.

In short, the intense heat and steam woke our two friends up. The visiting Muscovite, as he told people afterwards, even dreamed he was in Gagry.

But when he woke up, he saw that the whole room was filled with water and there were slippers, newspapers and all sorts of wooden items floating around.

The hot water, of course, made it impossible for them to stop the flood immediately because they couldn't reach the bath to turn the tap off. They sat on the sofas, not daring to put their feet into the steaming water.

But then, by managing to move chairs and hopping from one chair to another, the Muscovite's frightened friend made it to the bath and turned the tap off.

They'd only just turned the tap off, and water had just started to flow away, when the management ran in with pale faces.

When they'd inspected the bathroom and the floor below, the management began to debate something with an engineer who'd just appeared.

Our friends got into a bitter argument: who was guilty and who should pay for the damage.

The visiting Muscovite's friend, breathless with fear, said that he'd pay off the first 40 roubles, but that anything above that should be paid by the guest himself, who had been so thoughtless as to let his bath be used by people from outside the hotel.

Then they got into an argument that could have ended unfortunately if the management had not been there.

The Muscovite, in a shaky voice, said to the management:

'What do you think the cost of the damage will be?'

The management said:

'Well, you see, downstairs, in the lounge, the stucco's been washed away: one large classical figure and three cherubs. So that raises the cost quite a bit.'

When he heard about the classical figure and the cherubs, the Muscovite's friend started literally shaking.

The Muscovite, giving the management a look full of anguish, whispered:

'And what will this washing away of cherubs cost?'

The engineer said:

'We reckon the operation's going to cost about seven or eight thousand . . .'

This sum completely knocked the Muscovite's last bit of strength out of him, and he lay down on the sofa, not understanding what was going on.

Meanwhile his friend displayed an unpleasant side to his character. Like a complete bastard, he tried, as they say, to suffer an eclipse. But was caught by the weak but honest hand of the visitor.

The Muscovite, only just managing to move his tongue, said to the management:

'Couldn't you make it two thousand? If it comes to it, don't bother with the cherubs. We're in the Second Five-year Plan, this is no time to be paying for cherubs . . .'

The management said:

'There's no need to get worked up and start to haggle. It's not as if we're asking you to pay for the damage.'

When he heard these words, the Muscovite's friend closed his eyes, thinking it was a dream.

But the management said:

'We don't blame you at all. It was our technical deficiency. We'd not calculated water drainage properly and that's our technical fault.'

The engineer then gave a scientific explanation. He said, pointing to the bath:

'See there inside the bath, near the top, there's a small hole, water has to flow into it depending on how full the bath is. Where the calculation is scientifically correct, the water cannot flow over the sides. But here we were to some extent at fault, and the hole, as you yourselves saw, couldn't absorb the flow of liquid. We're very sorry for the disturbance this has caused. This will not happen again. We'll put it right. These are the sort of technical shortcomings that have no place in this glorious society of ours.'

When he heard these words, the Muscovite's friend wanted to fall down on his knees to offer his thanks to the management and to fate, but his host wouldn't let him to do this.

He said to the engineer:

'That's what I thought, of course that's what it was. But tell me, who's going to pay for the damage to my things: my slippers are ruined and my suitcase got wet, and there may be other things ruined on account of your technical failings.'

The management said:

'Make a claim, we'll pay for the damage.'

The next day, the Muscovite received 46 roubles for the suitcase that had got wet.

The Muscovite's friend also tried to take advantage of the situation to extract a small sum on account of the technical deficiency, but didn't succeed because he had no right to be in someone else's hotel room in the middle of the night.

But the next day he still came to the hotel and took a bath, even though the Muscovite was extremely unhappy about it and even got angry.

1935

The Story of an Illness

Frankly, I prefer to stay at home when I'm ill. All right, I'm not disputing that in hospital it's probably more civilized, more radiant. And they take more care over the calories in the food. But, as they say, there's no place like home.

I was taken to hospital with typhoid fever. My family thought that this would relieve my incredible sufferings.

The only thing is they didn't achieve their goal, because I was put in an unusual hospital, where I wasn't happy with a number of things.

I mean, a patient's only just been brought in, they register him in a book, and suddenly he reads a sign on the wall:

'corpses to be retrieved between 3 pm and 4 pm'

I don't know how it is in other hospitals, but I just came over all weak when I read this appeal. The thing is, I have a high temperature, and in general life in my organism barely keeps ticking, it could even be hanging by a thread, and then I have to read words like that.

I said to the man who registered me:

'What do you think you're doing,' I said, 'comrade porter, hanging up vulgar inscriptions like that? It doesn't exactly,' I said, 'make interesting reading for patients.'

The porter, or what do they call them, Healthcare Operative, was surprised that I spoke to him like that, and said:

'Look what we've got here: a patient, he can hardly walk, he's nearly steaming at the mouth with fever, and he's,' he said, 'casting self-criticism all over the place. If,' he said, 'you get better, which is hardly likely, then you can criticize, and if not, then you really will be left for retrieval between three and four in the state that's written here, and that'll teach you.'

I wanted to give this Healthcare Operative a good beating, but seeing as I had a high temperature, 39.8, I decided not to start an argument. I just said to him:

'Just you wait, Mr Stethoscope, when I get better I'll make you pay for your rudeness. Is it right that patients should have to listen to speeches like that? It,' I said, 'poleaxes their inner strength.'

The porter was surprised that a gravely ill person was able to remonstrate with him so fluently, and changed the subject at once. Then a nurse came along.

'Come on patient,' she said, 'We're going to the cleaning point.'

But these words also convulsed me with pain.

'It would be better,' I said, 'if you called it the bath and not the cleaning point. It sounds nicer,' I said, 'and elevates the patient. And I'm not a floor,' I said, 'to be cleaned.'

The nurse said:

'He might be ill, but,' she said, 'he still notices all kinds of subtleties. You aren't likely,' she said, 'to get better, sticking your nose into everything.'

Then she brought me to the bath and told me to get undressed.

So I started undressing and then I saw that in the bath a head was sticking out of the water. And suddenly I saw that an old woman seemed to be sitting in the bath, probably one of the patients.

I said to the nurse:

'Where the hell have you taken me you evil dogs, you've taken me to the ladies' baths. There's someone,' I said, 'already having a bath over there.'

The nurse said:

'It's only an old woman sitting there. She's ill, don't pay any attention to her. She's got a high temperature and doesn't react to anything. So don't be embarrassed, just go ahead and undress. In the meantime we'll pull the old woman out of the bath and fill it right up to the brim with fresh water for you.'

I said:

'The old woman might not react, but maybe I still do react. And I,' I said, 'definitely don't enjoy seeing what you've got floating in your baths.'

Then the Healthcare Operative came back.

'This is the first time,' he said, 'that I've come across such a fussy patient. He doesn't like this, the piss-taker, and that's not good enough for him. A dying old woman is taking a bath, and he's still expressing complaints. But she's probably got a temperature of about 40 and doesn't take anything in and sees everything as if through a sieve. And in any case, the sight of you is hardly likely to keep her in this world for an extra five minutes. No,' he said, 'I prefer it when the patients come to us in a state of unconsciousness. Then at least everything suits them, they're happy with everything, and they don't try and start arguments with us about professional matters.'

Then the old woman in the bath suddenly said something.

'Take me out of the water,' she said, 'or,' she said, 'I'll get out myself in a minute and I'll get you for this.'

So they took care of the old woman and told me to get undressed.

And while I was getting undressed, they immediately filled up the bath with hot water and told me to get in.

And, knowing my character, they didn't argue with me anymore and tried to just say yes to everything. Only after the bath they gave me some huge clothes that were not my size. I thought they had deliberately given me this wrong-sized set of clothes out of spite, but then I saw that it was a normal occurrence here. The small patients, as a rule, had big night-shirts on, and the big patients, small ones.

Mine in fact turned out to be better than the others. On my shirt the name of the hospital was on the sleeve and didn't spoil the general appearance, but with the other patients, the name was either on the back or on the front of their shirts, and that lowered their human dignity and morale.

But seeing as my temperature was constantly rising, I decided not to argue about these things.

So they put me in a small ward where there were about thirty assorted patients. Some, by the look of them, were seriously ill. Whereas others were quite the opposite, they'd got better. Some were whistling. Others were playing draughts. A third group were wandering through the wards reading out what was written above the bedheads word by word.

I said to the nurse:

'If I've been put into a hospital for the mentally ill, just tell me. Every year,' I said, 'I spend time in hospitals, but I've never seen anything like this. Everywhere else it's quiet and orderly, but here it's like a street market.'

She said:

'Maybe the gentleman would like to be put in a separate ward and have a sentry posted to keep flies and bedbugs off him?'

I started shouting, to get the chief doctor to come, but instead of him I got the same porter as before. By this time I was in a weakened state. Just the sight of him made me totally lose consciousness.

I must have only come to, I think, about three days later.

The nurse said to me:

'Well,' she said, 'you've got an iron constitution. You've,' she said, 'come through all kinds of ordeals. We even accidentally put you in front of an open window, and surprisingly, you started getting better. Now,' she said, 'if you don't catch anything off one of the other patients around you, then,' she said, 'we'll be able congratulate you on your recovery.'

Although my organism didn't give in to any other illnesses, only just before I was due to leave I did catch a kid's disease: whooping-cough.

The nurse said:

'You've probably caught the infection from the next wing. That's our children's section. You've probably been careless enough to eat with a knife and fork that a child with whooping-cough must have eaten with. And that's why you're feeling unwell.'

Soon, my organism eventually won through, and I started getting better again. But just as they were about to discharge me, I suffered a lot and fell sick again, this time with a nervous complaint. On account of my nerves, I got loads of little spots on my skin, a sort of rash. And the doctor said:

'Stop getting nervous, and this will go in time.'

But I was feeling nervous simply because they wouldn't discharge me. They forgot, or there was something missing, or someone hadn't come and they couldn't sign. Then finally a patients' wives movement started up, and the whole staff were run off their feet. The porter said:

'We're so overcrowded that we can't even get round to discharging patients. You're only eight days overdue, and you're whingeing! We've got some patients who aren't discharged for three weeks after they're better, and they don't make a fuss.'

But soon they did discharge me, and I returned home.

My wife said:

'Petya, a week ago we thought that you'd gone off to meet your maker, because a notice came from the hospital which said:

'On receipt of this notice, present yourself immediately for the retrieval of your husband's body.'

It turned out that my wife had gone straight over to the hospital, but they'd apologized for the error, which had occurred in the accounts department. Someone else had died, but for some reason they'd thought it was me. In fact at that time I was perfectly well. I'd just become covered in spots because of nerves. For some reason this episode gave me an unpleasant feeling, and I wanted to go straight over to the hospital, to shout at someone there, but when I remembered the sort of things that go on there, well, you'll understand why I didn't go after all.

Now I stay at home when I'm ill.

1936

Go On, Sleep!

Frankly, I don't like travelling. What puts me off is the problem of finding somewhere to spend the night.

I've only ever managed to get hold of a room in a hotel twice, in a hundred attempts.

And even then, the last time I got a room partly by accident. They mistook me for someone else. Then, the next day of course, they suddenly realized their mistake and invited me to vacate the room, but I was already going.

At first I was surprised how polite they were.

Just as he was sniffing the roses, the porter said:

'I feel I should warn you, your room has a defect. Your window's broken. So if, let's say, a cat jumps into your room during the night, don't be frightened.'

I said:

'Why should a cat jump into my room? I don't quite understand.'

The porter said:

'You see, you're at exactly the same level as the rubbish dump, so the animals can't tell which is which, and jump in thinking it's the other thing.'

Of course, when I entered the room I could completely understand the psychology of the cats. They could well be unable to tell the difference.

On the whole, I don't need a luxury room. But this dirty little broom-cupboard with a rickety chair got to me slightly.

What really surprised me was the puddle in the room.

I started to call someone to get rid of it, but no one came. So I spoke to the porter.

He said:

'If you have a puddle in your room, then I think that probably means that someone spilt some water there. I haven't got any spare staff today, but I'll order the puddle to be wiped away tomorrow – anyway, it'll probably have dried out on its own by morning. The climate's warm down here.'

I said:

'And then the room's totally terrifying. It's dark, and the only furniture's a chair, a bed and some kind of box. I realize, I said, there are all sorts of hotels. The other day, I said, I was in the Donbass, in Konstantinovka to be precise, and instead of a blanket I had to use a table-cloth . . .'

'We haven't got as far as tablecloths yet,' said the porter, 'but we do offer short lengths of material instead of blanket covers. And as for the dark, well, you haven't got to draw intricate patterns, have you? Go on, sleep citizen, and don't bother the administration with your unnecessary chat.'

I didn't bother arguing with him because I was already feeling sleepy, and when I got back to the room I undressed and dived straight into bed.

But for a moment I couldn't quite understand what was happening to me. It was as if I was sliding down a hillside.

I tried to get up to see what kind of bed this was that was so comfortable to slide down. But then my feet got tangled up in the sheet, which was full of holes. Extricating myself from them, I put on the light and examined what I was lying on.

It turned out that starting from the bed-head, the crushed wire base of the bed sloped downwards, making it impossible for someone sleeping to remain in a horizontal position.

Then I put the pillow at the foot of the bed, shoved my suitcase in under it and lay the other way round.

But then it was more like I was sitting than lying down.

So I shoved my overcoat and briefcase in the middle, and lay down on this construction, with the intention, as the saying goes, of sleeping like the dead.

And so I was already snoozing, when suddenly I started getting bitten by bedbugs.

Two or three bedbugs wouldn't have scared me, but here there was, you could say, a whole huge infantry divison of them, acting in coordination with the hopping cavalry.

I succumbed to panic, but then conducted a well-planned struggle.

But when the struggle was at its height, the light suddenly went out.

Completely defenceless, I started nervously walking around the room, sighing and lamenting, when suddenly a knocking resounded on the plywood wall, and a rough female voice pronounced:

'What the hell are you doing, spinning around in there like a nutter!'

I was stunned at first, but then I started a verbal battle with my neighbour, which I'm even ashamed to relate, because in the heat of the moment and with our nerves on edge, we said a whole load of the most highly insulting words to each other.

'If I ever meet you, damn you,' my neighbour said to me as a finale, 'then I'll definitely give you a slap, just bear that in mind.'

I wanted so badly to say something to her in response to this, I was almost in tears, but I sensibly kept quiet and just chucked the box at her wall, so that she'd think I was trying to shoot her. After this she was silent.

Then, moving the bed away from the wall, I took the water carafe and made a circle of water around the bed, so that extraneous bedbugs couldn't get to me. After which I went to bed again, committing, as the saying goes, my mortal remains to the will of the Lord.

Despite the hellish bites, I'd just started to drift off when suddenly a terrible woman's shriek rang out from the other side of the wall.

I shouted to my neighbour:

'If you deliberately screamed to wake me up, then tomorrow I'll make you pay for your hooliganism.'

Then we had another verbal battle, from which it became clear that a cat had jumped onto her bed from the yard, and this had frightened her.

The stupid porter had probably got the rooms mixed up. He'd promised me a cat, but my window was intact. Hers wasn't.

Anyway, I drifted off again. But being of a nervous disposition, I kept on twitching. And every time I twitched I was woken up by the bed-springs. They gave off a sinister sound, a squealing and a grating.

Morning had already come. I took the mattress off the bed and laid it down on the floor. As I lay down on this wonderful pallet, I could feel myself being enveloped by utter bliss.

'Go on, sleep, others need your pillow,' I said to myself, remembering a poster that had been hanging in the House of the Peasantry in the town of Feodosiya last year.

At that moment the wail of an electric saw sounded in the yard.

Anyway, weakened and grey-faced, I left this unhappy hotel.

I decided I would never set foot in this hotel or this town ever again. But fate took a different decision.

In the train, after I'd gone a hundred kilometres, I discovered that they'd given me back the wrong passport. And since it was a lady's passport, travelling any further was not a possibility.

The next day, I was back at the hotel.

Naturally I felt painfully embarrassed to meet my neighbour from the next room. She herself, it turned out, had left and now returned with my passport.

She turned out to be a really nice girl, a swimming instructor. Later we got to know each other well and forgot about all the drama the previous night. So the stay in that hotel did have certain plus points after all. In that respect it's true, you sometimes meet interesting people when you're travelling.

1936

The Pushkin Centenary Celebrations

First Speech About Pushkin

'It is with a feeling of pride that I'd like to remark that during these Centenary celebrations our building is not lagging behind events. First of all, we've acquired a one-volume collection of Pushkin's works at 6 roubles 50 for universal utilization. Secondly, we've erected a plaster bust of the distinguished poet in the Housing Committee office, which should also help remind all those behind on their rent instalments to pay up.

'What's more, in the gateway of our building we have hung an artistic portrait of Pushkin with fir wreaths round it.

'And finally, the present meeting speaks for itself.

'All right, maybe it's not much, but frankly, our Housing Committee office didn't expect there'd be such a fuss. We thought, OK, they'll mention it in the press as usual: he was a poet of genius, they'll say, who lived in the bleak time of Tsar Nicholas I. And then, well, there'll be all kinds of shows with artistic readings of extracts, or they'll sing something from *Eugene Onegin*.

'But what's been going on this time, frankly, it's made our Housing Committee office sit up and take notice and take a long hard look at our position in the field of the literary art, so as to be sure that afterwards there'll be no slinging accusations at us that we haven't been valuing poems properly and so on.

'Also, let me tell you, it's lucky that, as far as poets are concerned, our building, as they say, has been spared. Though we do have one tenant, Tsaplin, who writes poems, but he's an accountant, and what's more he's such a troublemaking bastard I don't even know if I should speak about the likes of him during the Pushkin Celebrations. The day before yesterday he came to the Housing Committee office, making threats and so on. "You spindly bastard," he shouted, "I'll have you buried alive if you don't get my stove repaired before the Pushkin Celebrations. The fumes are choking me," he said, "and I can't write poems." I said, "For all my sensitive attitude to poets, at the present moment I cannot have your stove repaired, on account of the stove repair man being drunk." The way he was shouting! And he started chasing after me.

'We can count ourselves lucky that our register of residents doesn't contain any of your trained writers and so on. Or they'd probably harp on about their stoves just like this Tsaplin.

'All right, so he can write poems, so what? If that's how it is, then excuse me, but my little Kolya who's seven can start lodging claims at the Housing Committee: he can write too. And some of his poems are pretty decent:

> We children like it when birdies are caged in.
> We don't like enemies of the five-year plan.

'The little rascal's all of seven but he can already turn out stirring stuff like that! But that doesn't necessarily mean that I want to compare him with Pushkin. Pushkin is one thing, and Comrade Resident-choking-from-fumes Tsaplin is quite another. What a loud-mouthed bastard! The worst thing was that my wife was just arriving as he was chasing after me. "I'm," he shouted, "gonna stick your head up that stove." Well, I ask you! The Pushkin Celebrations are now taking place, and he's got me all worked up.

'Pushkin writes so well that every line is beyond perfection. For a resident who was that much of a genius, we'd have repaired his stove in autumn. But do *his* repairs, Tsaplin's that is – you must be joking.

'A hundred years have passed, and Pushkin's poems still amaze people. But what, pardon me for asking, will Tsaplin be in a hundred years' time? The troublemaking bastard! Or if Tsaplin had lived a hundred years ago, I bet I know what would have become of him, and what would have remained of him until our times!

'Frankly, if I'd been in d'Anthès's shoes I would have riddled that Tsaplin with bullets. The second would have said: 'Fire one shot at him,' but I'd have emptied all five into him, because I don't like troublemaking bastards.

'Poets of genius and distinction die before their time, but that troublemaking bastard Tsaplin will remain, and he'll probably even wear *us* out.'

(*Voices*: 'Tell us about Pushkin.')

'I *am* talking about Pushkin, I'm hardly talking about Lermontov, am I? Pushkin's poems, I was saying, still amaze people. Every line is popular. Even people who haven't read him, they know him too. Personally, I like his lyrical verse in *Eugene Onegin*: "Why aren't you dancing, Lensky?" and *The Queen of Spades*: "I'd like to be a little branch."'

(*Voices*: 'That's an opera libretto, not by Pushkin.')

'How d'you mean not by Pushkin? You're having me on . . . Though flicking through our one-volume collection of Pushkin I see that there really isn't any verse in *The Queen of Spades* . . . Well, if the lines: "If only pretty girls could all fly like the birds" aren't by Pushkin, then I'm not sure what to think about these Celebrations. I'll tell you one thing, I'm not going to repair Tsaplin's stove. Pushkin's one thing, Tsaplin's another thing altogether. The troublemaking bastard!'

1937

Second Speech About Pushkin

'Well, dear comrades, I'm no literary historian, of course. I'll just take the liberty of approaching this great date in a simple, as they say, in a human way.

'This frank approach, I suggest, will bring this great poet even closer to us.

'So then, a hundred years separate us from him! Time really does fly faster than ever!

'The war with Germany, as we all remember, started twenty-three years ago. That means when it started it wasn't a hundred years to Pushkin's time, but only seventy-seven.

'And just think, I was born in 1879. So I was even nearer the great poet. It wasn't as if I could have met him, but as they say, we were only about forty years apart.

'What's more, my very own grandmother was born in 1836. So Pushkin could have met her and even held her in his arms. He could have cradled her on his lap, and she could have, perish the thought, cried not realizing who was holding her.

'Though it's not very likely that Pushkin would have cradled her, especially since she lived in Kaluga, and Pushkin doesn't seem to have gone there, but all the same we can admit that exciting possibility, especially since for all we know he might just have gone to Kaluga to see some friends.

'What's more, my father was born in 1850. But by that time Pushkin was unfortunately no longer with us, or otherwise he could have cradled my father too.

'But my great-grandmother, he could probably have held her in his arms. Just imagine, she was born in 1763, so the great poet could have just gone round to her parents' house and demanded that they let him hold her in his arms and cradle her . . . Although, I suppose in 1837 she would have been about sixty or so years old, so frankly, I don't really know how they would have got on and how they would have done these things . . . Maybe it would even have been her cradling him . . . But what for us is hidden in a cloud of ignorance, they probably didn't find a problem, and knew perfectly well who to cradle and who to rock. And if the old bat really was about sixty back then, it's plainly stupid even to think of someone cradling her. It was her, more likely, that would be doing the cradling.

'And who knows, rocking him in her arms and singing lyric songs to him, without knowing it, she herself might have awakened poetic feelings in him, and maybe, along with the better-known nanny Arina Rodionovna, she inspired him to write certain individual poems.

'As for Gogol and Turgenev, they could have been cradled by any of my relations, since there's even less time separating them. As I always say: children are the joy of our lives, and a happy childhood is a problem which, as they say, is very, very much of no small importance, which we've now resolved. Nurseries, children's homes, mother and baby rooms at railway stations, all these are worthy signs of this very same thing . . . Um, what was I talking about?'

(*Voice from the audience*: 'Pushkin . . .')

'Oh yes . . . Well, as I was saying, Pushkin . . . The one-hundredth anniversary. And it looks like we'll soon be landed with other glorious centenaries: Turgenev, Lermontov, Tolstoy, Maykov and so on and so forth. We'll be rushed off our feet.

'Mind you, between you and me, sometimes you find it a bit strange that there's this respect for poets. Take singers, it's not that we give them a hard time, but no one goes on about them like they do with that other lot. But they're artists too, you know. They can touch your heart as well. And your emotions. And the rest of it.

'Of course I'm not denying that Pushkin's a great genius, and every line he wrote merits widespread attention. Some people, for example, even respect Pushkin for his minor poetry. But personally I wouldn't go that far. A minor poem is just what they say it is, minor and not really a major work. It's not that anyone could have written it, but, as they say, when you look at it you definitely won't see anything particularly original or artistic. Would you believe for example, this load of what I would call simple, not-very-highly-artistic words:

> A serf-boy takes his dog out sleighing,
> Himself transformed into a horse;
> One finger's frostbitten, of course . . .

(*Voice from the audience*: 'That's *Eugene Onegin* . . . That's not a minor poem.')

'Are you sure? When I was a kid we did it as an individual poem. Well, all right then, that's fine by me. *Eugene Onegin* really is an epic poem of genius . . . But, of course, in any epic there may be isolated artistic shortcomings. On the whole though, I'd say for children he's a very interesting poet. In his own time they maybe even thought of him just as a children's poet. But he's come down to us in a somewhat different way. Especially when you think how fast our children have been growing up. They're no longer satisfied with children's verse like:

> Choo-choo goes the train,
> Chuga-chuga go the wheels,
> Gosizdat, hip-hurra
> Away with the writers, ha ha ha . . .

'I remember in our school they made us learn a minor, stupid little poem by Pushkin. I can't remember whether it was about a switch or a bird, I think it was about a branch. About how a branch was growing, and the poet says to it, artistically: "Tell me, branch of Palestine . . .""

(*Voice from the audience*: 'That's Lermontov . . .')

'Is it? Well, you see I normally get them mixed up . . . For me it's as if Pushkin and Lermontov are one and the same. I don't distinguish between them.'

(*Noise in the hall. Voices*: 'Say something about Pushkin's poetic art.')

'I'm just coming to that, comrades. With Pushkin, his poetic art is astonishing. He was paid ten roubles a line of poetry. What's more, he was constantly being reprinted. But he still went on writing more and more. There was no stopping him.

'Of course, court life was constantly getting in the way of his poem-writing. If it wasn't balls it was something else. As the poet himself said:

> Whence comes the noise, the furious cries?
> Whither and whom call the timbrel and bells . . .

'The timbrel! Just think, fancy him coming up with that . . .

'We're not going to waste time over the poet's biographical details, of course: everyone is familiar with them. But as they say, on the one hand there's his private life, a seven-room apartment, a coach and horses, and on the other hand the Tsar himself, Nick-the-Stick, court life, the lycée, d'Anthès and so on. And between you and me, Tamara wasn't exactly faithful to him . . .'

(*Noise in the hall. Shouts*: 'Natalya, not Tamara.')

'Are you sure? Oh yes, Natalya. Tamara, that's Lermontov . . . As I was saying. But Nick-the-Stick himself, of course, couldn't write poetry. And so of course he couldn't help getting upset and envying the poet . . .'

(*Noise in the hall. Individual exclamations turning into shouts. Some people stand up*: 'That's enough! Get him off!')

'All right then, I'm just finishing comrades . . . Pushkin's influence on us is enormous. He was a great poet of genius. And we should regret that he is not living now, with us. We would have treated him like a king and arranged a fairy-tale life for the poet, that is, of course, if we knew that he would actually turn out to be Pushkin. Otherwise, what happens is that contemporaries place their hopes in their own man, and organize a decent life for him, give him cars and apartments, and then it turns out that he's not all that good. And, as they say, no one returns a bribe . . . It's a dodgy profession on the whole, the whole lot of them can go to heaven for all I care. As far as I'm concerned, singers cheer you up more. As soon as they burst into song you can see what kind of voice they've got.'

'And so, before I finish my lecture about our poet of genius, I'd like to point out that after the celebratory part of the programme there will be an artistic concert.'

(*Appreciative applause. Everyone stands up and goes to the buffet.*)

1937

In Praise of Transport

The other day an engineer friend of mine invited me round for dinner.

What makes this engineer different from many other engineers is that he owns his own automobile, a GAZ.

I don't know how having your own automobile affects other people, but getting an automobile has had a distressing effect on this friend of mine.

He used to be a nice man, and it was quite interesting to go round to his place. But now it's as if he's become an entirely different person. All he can think about is the automobile industry. He won't talk about anything else, only about that.

And at this dinner, our host was personally insulted if a guest was rude enough to try and talk about anything else.

So, having endured conversations about the particularities of this or that make of automobile until three o'clock, the guests started getting ready to go home.

The host, smiling sweetly, said:

'Had you been anywhere else, my dear guests, you'd now be starting to hobble your way home on foot, or, as they say, you'd be taking the old number 11. But since you're at my place, you're all going to go home by automobile. What do you think of that then, eh?'

The guests expressed delight.

The host said:

'I don't know about you, but now I literally feel like a separate human individual and all the planets revolve around me . . . I'll just phone my chauffeur and get him to bring my automobile round to the entrance.'

The host went over to the phone and made a call. Then he returned to his guests, sighed and said:

'He's just bringing the automobile round . . . There's only one inconvenient thing, you see our garage is in one district, and we're in another, and the chauffeur, would you believe it, lives beyond Nevskaya Zastava. But I've told the chauffeur to get to the garage as fast as he can. After all, he doesn't really live that far away: fifteen or twenty minutes' walk.'

The engineer's wife said:

'Oh Kolya, what a shame you didn't tell the chauffeur to take a taxi.

He could have taken a taxi and got to the garage in an instant.'

'Oh yes, that's a point,' said the host, and his face lit up, 'I forget about that little trick every single time. I'll just phone the chauffeur, he probably hasn't left yet.'

It so happened that the chauffeur hadn't left yet. So the host instructed him to take a taxi, to get to the garage more quickly.

One of the guests said:

'Look, maybe we should all simply go home in the taxi the chauffeur is going to get?'

This thought astonished and even scared the host a bit. He said:

'But what do you mean, travel in a taxi when you own your own automobile! No, I can't let you do that.'

We began waiting.

After about twenty minutes the telephone rang. It was the chauffeur.

I don't know what he said exactly, but turning to us, looking disheartened, the host said:

'The chauffeur says that he can't get a taxi. Would you believe it, he got as far as the station, found a taxi, but it wouldn't take him because it was going in the other direction. I'll just tell my chauffeur to walk to the centre and take a taxi from there.'

One of the guests half-asked:

'Maybe we really should just take the taxi that the chauffeur is going to get?'

'That's an idea,' said the host, 'I'll just tell my chauffeur to come here in the taxi. Then it'll only take a moment to take you to the garage. And from then on you'll be fine. We just need to get as far as the garage.'

Having given the chauffeur the corresponding orders, the host started to converse with the guests about the advantages of transport.

In twenty minutes' time or so, the taxi was standing outside.

The guests and the hosts went outside.

One of the guests sighed and said:

'It really does seem a shame to have got hold of a taxi but to end up going to the middle of nowhere. For God's sake, let's just get in and go home in this taxi. It'd be great if we were home in just a few moments. Otherwise we'll have to go all the way to the garage.'

The host said quietly:

'Please don't . . . You'll put me in a terrible position . . . I've woken the chauffeur up now. He's been trudging around the streets for more than an hour . . . Please go to the garage.'

The guests began to get into the car.

But since one of the seats had been already taken by the taxi-driver and the other by our host's chauffeur, there were only three places left.

There were five guests.

The host counted the guests and said:

'It's a pity my chauffeur didn't grab two taxis. Now I don't know what I'm going to do. Here's what, why don't three guests get in the back and the other two can wait for my car here, by the front entrance . . .'

The guests stood there in embarrassed silence. The host said:

'That's not it. I know: one guest and the chauffeur wait here and the others can get off to the garage.'

The engineer's wife said:

'No, that won't work, because then there'll be no one to drive our car back here. Both groups will be just left waiting.'

The host said:

'That's true. It's a pity we've got five guests instead of three. We could have dealt with three in no time . . . All right then, here's what you can do: three of you get in the car, and the chauffeur and one of the guests can follow on foot at their own pace.'

One of the guests, scared that he'd have to walk, slipped away unnoticed, like an Englishman, without saying goodbye.

There were four guests left.

The host counted the guests and said:

'That makes it a bit easier. Here's what you can do now: three guests and the chauffeur can take the taxi. The fourth guest can choose, either he waits here, or if that doesn't suit him, he can make his own way to the garage on foot.'

One of the guests said:

'Look, there's a freight tram. I'll just hop on the rear car. Bye!'

The guest jumped up onto the rear car and soon disappeared into the misty distance.

The host said:

'He's only got himself to blame if he didn't want to wait for the car to come. Now you can all get in and off you go.'

The chauffeur asked our host dejectedly:

'One thing, Nikolay Petrovich, don't forget to give me some money to pay for the taxi. I've already paid twelve roubles of my own money for this morning's taxi.'

The host rummaged in his wallet and, giving the chauffeur the money, said sadly:

'Yes, this taxi business is costing me an arm and a leg.'

The engineer's wife said:

'By my reckoning these taxis are costing you at least thirty roubles a day. If it wasn't for the taxis, we'd have traded in our GAZ for an M-1 long ago.'

At last we set off.

On the way the guests started trying to convince the driver to take them all home without going to the garage.

The host's chauffeur unexpectedly agreed and was even happy at the idea. He said:

'That's the most sensible thing to do. Otherwise, it could end up like the time when I took the guests to the garage, and we had to hang around there for an hour and a half. By the time we'd woken up the security guard, filled up the tank and with one thing and another, we looked round and the trams were already running. So the guests all took the tram.'

The taxi was taking us to our respective homes when the host's chauffeur said:

'The only thing is, I'm worried that I won't have enough to pay for the taxi. After all, we're making a large detour, and then there's the waiting . . .'

We each gave the chauffeur five roubles. And he told us that he thought he had enough now, and if it came to it he could always walk the rest of the way to Nevskaya Zastava.

1938

The Photograph

Earlier this year I had to get a photograph for a pass. I don't know how it works in other towns, but here in the middle of nowhere it's no simple run-of-the-mill matter to get your photo taken for an ID card.

We've only got one photographic studio. But as well as individual citizens they also photograph groups and events. So maybe that's why you have to wait so damn long to get your order back.

So since I am more of an individual person than a group or an event, I started to get worried and had my photograph taken two months before the actual date.

When they gave me my photographs, I was shocked how I'd come out looking completely unlike myself. Before me was a really old specimen of totally unattractive appearance.

I said to the woman who issued me the photo:

'Why do you photograph people like that? Look at the lines and wrinkles all over my face.'

She said:

'It's a normal photo. Though you should realize that the retoucher is on sick-leave. We haven't got anyone to paint over the defects of your unphotogenic appearance.'

The photographer, who was behind the curtain in the room next door, said:

'What's that piss-taker complaining about now?'

I said:

'You've photographed me badly. You've mutilated me. Do I look like that?'

The photographer said:

'I photograph operetta artistes, and even they don't get this offended. And now we've got some bloke with too many wrinkles . . . "The lense is too sharp, and there is too much contrast . . ." You don't know anything about it, but you try to stick your oar in playing the critic.'

I said:

'What do I need contrast for on my face: you've got to see it from my point of view. I just want,' I said, 'to get photographed as I am. So that there's something to look at.'

The photographer said:

'Huh, he even wants something to look at. He's had his photo taken, but he still wants to look at it. There's a war going on, and he's making a fuss over nothing. He sees defects . . . I regret taking such a reasonable photograph of you. Next time I take your photograph, it'll come out so you won't even be able to look at it without wincing.'

But I didn't start arguing with him. It doesn't matter, I thought, what the photo looks like. Everyone can see what I look like anyway.

And with these thoughts I went to the militia station. The militia sergeant started to stick the photo onto the pass. Then he said:

'That doesn't look like you in the photo.'

'What do you mean,' I said, 'not me. I can assure you it's me. Ask the photographer. He'll confirm it.'

The sergeant said:

'We can't allow that, constantly having to ask the photographer. No, when I look at a photo I want to see the person's face, without having to call the photographer. But what can I observe here? That's not you. It's someone with typhus. He hasn't got any cheeks. Go and get another one done.'

'Comrade,' I said, 'Station Commander, try and see it from my point of view . . .'

'No, no,' he said, 'I don't want to hear it. Get another one done.'

I ran off to the photographic studio. I said to the photographer:

'See how terrible your pictures are. They won't even accept your work.'

The photographer said:

'The work's perfectly fine. Though you've got to remember that we didn't use all the lighting for you. We only had one lamp on. That's why there are shadows on your face, darkening it, so that you can't see anything. Look how well your ears have come out.'

'Yes, OK,' I said, 'the ears. But my cheeks,' I said, 'where are they? I should definitely have cheeks as part and parcel of the human face.'

The photographer said:

'I don't know about that. We didn't touch your cheeks. We've got our own.'

'In that case,' I said, 'where are they? Where are my cheeks? I've just spent,' I said, 'two weeks on holiday. I put on four kilograms. But then with one photo you've done God only knows what to me.'

The photographer said:

'What, do you think I've got your cheeks? I've already explained to you: they were in the dark. And that's why they haven't come out well.'

I said:

'What am I going to do without cheeks?'

'You can do what you like,' he said. 'But I'm not taking another photograph. If I did that with everyone, I'd lose my bonus and not fulfill the plan. And the plan's more important to me than your unphotogenic appearance.'

The other customers said to me:

'Don't annoy the photographer, or he'll take even worse photographs.'

One of the other customers said to me:

'Run over to the market, comrade. There's a man there taking photographs with a Pushka camera.'

I ran over to the market. There I found the photographer. He said:

'No, I only take photographs if you've got your own photographic paper. If you haven't got any photographic paper, you'd better not come and see me, because I won't take your photo. But if you've got paper I will. And if you've got a feather-bed, I'll also take your photo. My aunt's just arrived from Barnaul, she hasn't got anything to sleep on.'

I was about to go when I heard a shopkeeper calling me over to him. He said:

'Come to my shop. I've got the finished product.'

I saw that he had all kinds of finished photos spread out on a newspaper. There were about three hundred of the things.

The shopkeeper said:

'Choose any one you want and do what you want with it. You can stick it on your forehead for all I care. Wait a second, I'll choose one for you myself. What's more important, to find one the right size or one that looks like you?'

'One that looks like me,' I said. 'Only choose one with cheeks.'

He said:

'You can have one with cheeks if you want. Only they're five roubles more. Here, take this photo. You won't find a better one. It's got cheeks, and you can't say that it looks absolutely nothing like you at all.'

I paid thirty roubles for two photographs and went to the militia station.

The sergeant started gluing in the photograph. Then he said:

'But this is a woman.'

'What do you mean a woman,' I said. 'It's a man wearing a jacket.'

The sergeant said:

'Rubbish! That's not a man, he's got a brooch on his chest. And it's from this brooch that I can see it's a woman.'

I looked at the photo, and could see that it really was a woman. She had a voile blouse on under the jacket. And a brooch with a picture of a landscape on her chest. But a male haircut. And my cheeks.

The sergeant said:

'Come back with genuine photographs. But if you show me photos of women or children once more, you aren't likely to make it out of here, because I'm beginning to have suspicions that you're trying to hide under someone else's appearance.'

I spent a whole week in a haze. I went round trying to find somewhere to get my photo taken. On the eighth day, as I was in discussion with the photographer, I suddenly felt ill. They carried me out into the garden and laid me down on the grass so that I would be fanned by fresh air. When I came round, I went to the militia station. I put my first photographs, the ones without any cheeks, on the table and said to the sergeant:

'That's all I have Comrade Station Commander. And there won't be any more.'

The sergeant looked at the photos, and then at me, and said:

'Now they're OK, they've come out well. They look like you.'

I was about to say that I hadn't had another photograph done at all. Then I looked at myself in the mirror, and I could see it was true, now there was a certain resemblance. They'd come out well.

The sergeant said:

'Although you look even shabbier in the photograph than you do in reality. But,' he said, 'I think that in a year you'll catch up with it.'

I said:

'I'll catch up with it sooner than that, since I've still got to have my photo taken for my season ticket, for my membership card and so I can send some photos to my relatives.'

Then the sergeant stuck the photo in and warmly congratulated me on receiving my new ID card.

1945

Glossary

communal apartment Multi-roomed apartments that had been broken up into a number of bedsit-type single rooms. The inhabitants shared a kitchen, toilet and, if there was one, a bathroom. These shared facilities, along with the fact that the conversion of the apartment into single rooms was often crude, so that walls were thin, meant that there was little privacy and many potential causes for rows.

dacha A Russian summer house. Zoshchenko himself rented the same dacha every year in the seaside town of Sestroretsk, north of St Petersburg Though it no longer stands, he was buried in Sestroretsk graveyard, where there is now a life-sized statue of him.

House (Management) Committee (*domoupravleniye*) In conditions where the state owned and managed all housing, the House Committee was a powerful body. It was represented by a **Housing Manager** (*upravdom*), or **Chairman of the Housing Co-op** or **Committee** (*predsedatel´ tovarishch-estva*), positions that attracted the meddling, the officious and the corrupt. The *upravdom* was universally loathed. Zoshchenko's contemporary, Mikhail Bulgakov, memorably satirized this figure in his play *Ivan Vasilyevich* and his novel *The Master and Margarita*.

militia (*militsiya*) The Soviet police force.

NEP New Economic Policy (*Novaya ekonomicheskaya politika*, 1921–28). This introduced a partial restoration of the free market, with the aim of revitalizing the economy after the period of War Communism (1918–21). NEP ended with the first Five-Year Plan.

Nepman (*nepman*) Entrepreneur who flourished under NEP. In Party circles in particular, such people were regarded as a bad influence, and their trading was seen as tantamount to theft.

specialists (*spetsy*) Skilled people whose class and political views were suspect, but whose abilities the Soviet government felt were indispensable in the NEP period, and therefore continued to employ them. The Party and workers in the enterprises where specialists were employed scrutinized them closely, and 1920s newspapers contain many complaints about them.

trust (*trest*) In the Soviet Union in the 1920s, an agglomeration of several related industrial enterprises. Despite the capitalist-sounding name, it was a completely state-owned form of production.

yard; mile Imperial weights and measures have been employed to translate the traditional Russian units, the *sazhen* (equivalent to 2.13 metres or approximately 7 feet) and the *verst* (1.06 kilometres or almost two-thirds of a mile). Metric measures also appear in the stories because the Bolshevik government introduced the metric system soon after coming to power, though the population took some time getting used to it. Hence the characters' use of traditional units is a sign of their political backwardness.

Notes

1923

A Thief

Page 27: *Tyapkin*. *Tyapat´* means to pinch or steal. This character is presumably related to the corrupt judge in Gogol's *The Government Inspector*, Lyapkin-Tyapkin, the name implying poor-quality work (*lyap-tyap*).

Page 27: *Pargolovo*. A northern suburb of St Petersburg, which became filled with dachas after the construction of the railway in 1870.

A Speech about Bribery

Pages 31–32: *his ugly, thieving face*. Nepmen's trading was seen as morally equivalent to theft. See Glossary.

A Crime Report

Page 34: *former title*. Position in Tsarist society.

An Anonymous Friend

Page 36: *Malaya Okhta*. A well-known district in St Petersburg on the right (eastern) bank of the River Neva.

A Victim of the Revolution

Page 39: *meshchanin.* A member of the petty-bourgeoisie: a town-dweller with a little property. Especially after the Revolution the term implied a striving after individual material advancement rather than a social class; hence it is sometimes translated as 'philistine,' as in the title of Maxim Gorky's play *Philistines* (*Meshchane*).

1924

Love

Page 45: *Vasya Chesnokov*. Another instance of Zoshchenko's use of character-revealing names. 'Chesnokov' is from *chesnok*, garlic; 'Vasya' is a rustic, unsophisticated name. Both contrast with the character's apparently gallant behaviour at the beginning of the story, and suggest that it is a veneer.

Host Accountancy

The Russian title *Khozraschot* is a pun on *khozyaystvennyy raschot* which literally means economic accounting, but could mean household accounting or home accounting. *Khozraschot* was an NEP policy whereby enterprises were to keep proper accounts of their expenses and strive towards being self-financing rather than rely on subsidies, as they had during the Civil War period.

Page 49: *new money*. In 1924 the Soviet government introduced a new gold rouble, the *chervonets*, which replaced the old 'money sign', millions of which were required to buy even a loaf of bread.

A Forgotten Slogan

Page 55: *club*. This means an officially-sponsored political club, at which there would be no alcohol, where lectures, debates and film-screenings would be the primary forms of entertainment.

Page 56: *ogress*. In Russian *kikimora*, a female hobgoblin.

A Bad Habit

In February 1924 the Soviet government, or People's Commissariat as it was then called, introduced a decree declaring tipping an illegal activity, to be treated in the same way as bribery.

Page 58: *civilized*. The Russian word *intelligentnyy* is a vague term meaning well-mannered, possessing the correct cultural values, and bears a relation to the term *intelligent* (a member of the *intelligentsiya*).

Electrification

Electrification was a symbol of modernization and efficiency in revolutionary Russia. The most famous example is Lenin's slogan: 'Communism is Soviet power plus electrification of the whole country.' The literal-minded narrator associates the introduction of electric lighting with moral 'enlightenment'.

Domestic Bliss

Page 65: *host*. It should be noted that the Russian word *khozyain* means boss, owner (in which senses it is always masculine) and host. In this story it is masculine throughout.

Page 65: *canteen*. In an attempt to collectivize domestic work and emancipate women, the Soviet government established a number of canteens. The most famous example was probably the state-run canteen in what is now the Praga restaurant building in Moscow.

1925

Firewood

Page 72: *as a birthday present*. The Russian term *imeniny* in fact refers to a person's name-day, the day of the saint after whom the person is named, traditionally a more important cause for celebration in Russia than a birthday.

Page 73: *Up in Petrozavodsk*. Town on the Karelian Peninsula 300 km north of St Petersburg, famous for its armaments factory.

Page 73: *flood*. In St Petersburg floods are signalled by the firing of cannons. The city is highly susceptible to floods. One had occurred in the autumn of 1925, just before the publication of this story.

The Actor

Page 76: *theatrical specialists*. The narrator uses this Sovietism vaguely: he might mean anyone from one of the stage hands to the assistant director.

A Bathhouse
Page 79: *foot-cloths*. Worn by many at this time in place of socks.

Passenger
Page 86: *priced less*. The narrator says '*besplatno*' (for free), when he means '*bes-tsenno*' (priceless). Perhaps this malapropism sums up the human condition in Zoshchenko: the fact that a human being's value cannot be reckoned in monetary terms is likely to confer a lower rather than a higher status.

Thieves
Page 87: *Zhmerinka*. Regional centre in Ukraine and junction station on the South-West railway line.

A Glass
Page 89: *in the traditional way, after forty days*. In Orthodox tradition the dead are remembered with a form of wake after nine days, 40 days and a year.

Crisis
The Soviet Union experienced an acute housing shortage, referred to typically as a 'crisis', throughout the 1920s and particularly in the major cities. A Central Committee resolution of January 1928 recognized that the situation was still extremely bad. For another take on the housing shortage see Mikhail Bulgakov's novella *The Heart of a Dog*, which was published the same year.

Nervous People
Page 95: *on the corner of Glazovaya and Borovaya*. Streets in the central district of St Petersburg, bounded by the Obvodnyy Canal.

1926

Economy Measures
In April 1926 there was a Resolution of the Central Committee of the Communist Party 'On the Struggle for Economy Measures'. This story is clearly Zoshchenko's contribution to the campaign.
Page 100: *opened her women's question up for discussion*. The narrator thinks that the women's question is any question posed by women.
Page 100: *why don't we . . .* The original here is *nekhay*, a ukrainian form of *puskay*. This is one of the occasions where Zoshchenko displays his Ukrainian roots.

Paris – Рахис
Page 104: *Krylyshkin*. From *kryl´ya* meaning wings: he may not be able to do the job of a postal worker, but he has an appropriate name.
Page 104: *Paris – Рахис*. The word 'Rachis' when written in Cyrillic resembles the word 'Paris' in Latin lettering. It seems so Russian to Krylyshkin because of the proliferation of acronyms at the time, many of which began with the first two letters of the Russian word for worker, 'ra . . .' [*rabochiy*.] Typical examples are Rabkrin, the Worker-Peasant Inspectorate, and RAPP, the Proletarian Writers' Association.

The Benefits of Culture

Culture. The Russian term *kul´turnost´* covers culture, civilization, cleanliness and polite manners. In this book it is translated, depending on the context, as culture, civilization and even as 'living properly'.

Lemonade

Page 109: *Ptitsyn.* This name comes from the Russian word for 'bird'. *Tovarishch Ptitsyn* (Comrade Ptistsyn) could also mean 'the birds' comrade', a fitting epithet for a vet.

Page 110: *Even in the old days.* That is, before the Revolution, when vodka was far more freely available.

A Hasty Business

Page 111: *Business.* The word is *delo* – business deal, criminal case, or simply 'matter'.

Page 111: *fact.* It is characteristic of the language of the time to overuse the word fact (*fakt*), employing it as a near-synonym for 'incident'.

Page 111: *Gorbushkin.* The name comes from the word for a hunch-backed salmon (*gorbusha*).

Page 111: *GPU.* Abbreviation for the State Political Directorate, the secret police force, which replaced the Cheka in 1922 and went through further name-changes before becoming known as the KGB in 1953.

1927

Guests

Page 114: *shchotochka.* A game the rules of which are now unknown even to Russians; or it may be purely imaginary. In any case, judging by the name, it would seem to have something to do with brushing, since *shchotka* means a brush.

Red Tape

Page 117: *a certain much-esteemed office.* Soviet bureaucratic cliché standard in the 1920s.

Page 117: *bentwood chair.* In the original, 'a Viennese chair', by which Russian designates the type of bentwood chair pioneered by the Wiener Werkstadt.

Page 118: *I can do without that sort of fact.* This incongruous use of the word 'fact' (*fakt*) was typical of the way in which Russians spoke in the 1920s. Cf. note 2 to page 111.

Page 118: *Social Security.* In the original, *SObes* (*Sotial´noye obespechivaniye*).

Pushkin

In 1927 the Soviet Union commemorated the 90th anniversary of Pushkin's death. Pushkin's last apartment, on the Moyka Canal in St Petersburg, was turned into a museum in 1925.

Page 120: *in a right welfare state.* The character uses the word *utopiya* in the original, which he understands as linked to the Russian word *utopit´*, to drown. This is an example of the misunderstanding of foreign terms which flooded the language immediately after the Revolution.

Page 120: *irritable genius*. The narrator in the original uses the word *nesterpimyy* (unbearable) instead of *nesravnimyiy* (inimitable).

Page 121: '*The bird hopped on the branch.*' That these words bear no resemblance to any lines by Pushkin should not surprise the reader.

Page 121: *Pushkin estate*. The Pushkin family estate of Mikhaylovskoye, south of Pskov; the reconstructed house is now a museum.

Page 121: *Demyan Bedny* (1883–1945). Pseudonym of Yefim Pridvorov, poet famous for his folksy satirical verse in the 1910s and '20s.

Page 121: *Dmitry Tsenzor* (1877–1947). Poet and colleague of Zoshchenko in the 1920s satirical press, particularly *Begemot, Smekhach* and *Pushka*.

The Tsar's Boots

Page 123: *Palace of Labour*. Formerly the Kseninsky Institute, but from November 1918 the centre of the Petrograd Trade Union Council.

Page 123: *Vasilyevsky Island*. A district of St Petersburg traditionally inhabited by the poor.

Does a Man Need Much?

Page 127: The title ironically echoes that of Tolstoy's story 'How Much Land Does a Man Need?' (1886), which was one of his 'Tales for the People'.

The Cross

Page 142: *Shchukin*. From *shchuka*, a pike. Another example of Zoshchenko's pervasive animal imagery.

Rostov

Page 143: *The debates section*. This was a newspaper supplement covering the important debates at a Party Congress.

Page 143: *in his underpants*. Although *trusiki* could also mean shorts, it has here been rendered as 'underpants' so as to stress the narrator's shock on first seeing the man jumping over him.

1928

No Hanging Matter

Page 145: *civilized*. The Russian is *kul´turno*. This relates to the concept of *kul-turnost'*, a notion of correct behaviour that Zoshchenko's characters repeatedly infringe. See also note to 'The Benefits of Culture' (1926).

Page 145: *petit-bourgeois*. The Russian is *meshchansky*. See note to page 39.

Sobering Thoughts

Page 147: *In the whole of May*. Many celebrated the public holiday on the 1st of May by drinking.

Foreigners

Page 149: *Hospital. Graveyard.* In the Russian '*Mariyinsky Hospital. Smolensky grave-yard*'. The proper names have been dispensed with for the rhythm of the paragraph, which creates one of the central comic effects of the story.

An Unpleasant Story

This story was rewritten for the *Sky-Blue Book* as 'An Interesting Incident at a Party,' first with the name of Trotsky replacing that of Rykov and then without any name.

Page 151: *free professions.* Under NEP, a term for those employed by other organizations than the state.

Pawning

Page 154: *Autumn could occur.* The clumsy, bureaucratic or journalistic cliché 'occur' is applied to a natural phenomenon. This grotesque stylistic feature, common to many of Zoshchenko's characters and narrators, serves to contrast the spheres of the bureaucratic and the natural to comic effect.

Page 154: *for five kopecks.* A copy of *Pushka*, in which this story was first published, cost five kopecks.

1929

A Summer Break

Page 155: *petit-bourgeois.* In the original *meshchanstvo*. See note to page 39.

1933

A Trap

Page 162: *She ordered herself some meat-balls. Schnellklops* in the original (German meat-balls).

1934

How Much Does a Man Need?

See note to page 127.

An Incident on the Volga

Page 169: *Thunderstorm.* In Russian *groza*, which also means fear or terror, as in 'Ivan the Terrible' (*Ivan Groznyy*).

Page 169: *the former Penkin.* The word 'former' became over-used in the Soviet era as a shorthand way of keeping up with the sometimes dizzying pace of politically motivated name-changes.

Page 169: *Korolenko.* Vladimir Korolenko (1853–1921), a famous prose writer. Despite his condemnation of the Bolsheviks, his timely death soon afterwards removed all obstacles to interpretation of him as a proto-Bolshevik, acceptable writer.

1935

Water Sports

Page 172: *Gagry*. Abkhazian town on the Black Sea coast. Its subtropical climate made it a popular holiday resort. The town has also been known as *Gagra*, its Georgian name.

1936

The Story of an Illness

Page 175: *more radiant*. This was one of the buzz-words of the 1930s, most famous in the notion of the 'radiant future' towards which the Soviet Union was supposed to be heading.

Page 176: *cleaning point*. The Russian word *obmyvochnyy* also suggests the washing of a corpse.

1937

The Pushkin Centenary Celebrations

In 1937 there were commemorations of the 100th anniversary of Pushkin's death.

First Speech about Pushkin

Page 182: *Tsaplin*. Another example of Zoshchenko's pervasive animal imagery: the name comes from *tsaplya*, a heron.

Second Speech About Pushkin

Page 185: '*A serf-boy takes his dog . . .*' Alexander Pushkin, *Eugene Onegin*, trans. Babette Deutsch, Harmondsworth: Penguin, 1964, V ii, p. 116.

Page 186: "*Tell me, branch of Palestine . . .*" Mikhail Lermontov, 'Branch of Palestine' ('Vetka Palestiny', 1837).

Page 186: '*Whence comes the noise . . .*' An attempt to quote the opening lines of Pushkin's dithyrambic ode 'The Triumph of Dionysus' ('Torzhestvo Vakkha', 1817/18). The first line should actually begin: 'Whence comes the wondrous noise . . .'

1938

In Praise of Transport

Page 188: *GAZ*. A type of car made in the city of Gorky (formerly and subsequently Nizhny-Novgorod).

Page 188: *Nevskaya Zastava*. A region of St Petersburg, then far from the centre.

1945

The Photograph

Page 194: *Pushka*. This means 'cannon'. It is possible that the camera is an imported 'Cannon' camera, and that the Russians have translated the name.

Page 194: *Barnaul*. A town in Siberia, near Lake Baykal.

Further Reading

Editions in Russian

Zoshchenko, Mikhail, *Rasskazy* [Short stories], Moscow: Khudozhestvennaya literatura, 1974

——, *Sobranyie Sochineniy v tryokh tomakh* [Collected works in three volumes], ed. Yury Tomashevsky, Leningrad: Khudozhestvennaya literatura, 1986–87

——, *Uvazhayemyye grazhdane: parodii, rasskazy, fel´etony, satiricheskiye zametki, Pis´ma k pisatelyu, odnoaktnyye komedii* [Much-esteemed citizens: parodies, short stories, feuilletons, satirical articles, 'Letters to a Writer' and one-act plays], ed. Mikhail Dolinsky, Moscow: Knizhnaya palata, 1991

——, *Sobraniye sochineniy v pyati tomakh* [Collected works in five volumes], ed. Yury Tomashevsky, Moscow: Russlit, 1994

——, *Apollon i Tamara: izbrannoye* [Apollo and Tamara: a selection], St Petersburg: Limbus Press, 1999

——, *Sochineniya 1920-e gody: rasskazy i fel´etony, Sentimental´nyye povesti, M. P. Sinyagin, rannyaya proza* [Works of the 1920s: stories and feuilletons, 'Sentimental Tales', 'M. P. Sinyagin', early prose], St Petersburg: Kristall, 2000

English translations of Zoshchenko

Zoshchenko, Mikhail, *Scenes from the Bathhouse and Other Stories of Communist Russia*, trans. with an introduction by Sidney Monas; stories selected by Marc Slonim, Ann Arbor MI: Ann Arbor Paperbacks and University of Michigan Press, 1962

——, *Nervous People and Other Satires*, ed. with an introduction by Hugh McLean, trans. Hugh McLean and Maria Gordon, London: Gollancz, 1963

——, *Before Sunrise: a Novella*, trans. with an afterword by Gary Kern, Ann Arbor MI: Ardis, 1974

——, 'About Myself, My Critics, My Work,' trans. Jacqueline Cukierman, *Russian Literature Triquarterly*, 14 (1976), pp. 403–05

——, *A Man is Not a Flea*, trans. Serge Shishkoff, Ann Arbor MI: Ardis, 1989

Criticism in English

Carleton, Greg, *The Politics of Reception: Critical Constructions of Mikhail Zoshchenko*, Evanston IL: Northwestern University Press, 1998

Hicks, Jeremy, *Mikhail Zoshchenko and the Poetics of 'Skaz'*, Nottingham: Astra Press, 2000

Murphy, A. B., *Mikhail Zoshchenko: A Literary Profile*, Oxford: W. A. Meeuws, 1981

Popkin, Cathy, *The Pragmatics of Insignificance: Chekhov, Zoshchenko, Gogol*, Stanford CA: Stanford University Press, 1993

Scatton, Linda Hart, *Mikhail Zoshchenko: Evolution of a Writer*, Cambridge: Cambridge University Press, 1993

—, 'Writing for the New Reader', in Nicholas Luker (ed.), *After the Watershed: Russian Prose 1917–1927: Selected Essays*, Nottingham: Astra Press, 1996, pp. 93–106

Shklovsky, Viktor, 'On Zoshchenko and Major Literature,' trans. Jacqueline Cukierman, *Russian Literature Triquarterly*, 14 (1976), pp. 407–14

Zholkovsky, Alexander, '"What is the Author Trying to Say With His Artistic Work?": Rereading Zoshchenko's Oeuvre', *Slavonic and East European Jour-nal*, 40:3 (1996), pp. 458–74

Criticism in Russian

Starkov, Anatoly, *Mikhail Zoshchenko: sud´ba khudozhnika* [Mikhail Zoshchenko: the fate of an artist], Moscow: Sovetskiy pisatel´, 1990

Tomashevsky, Yury (ed.), *Litso i maska Mikhaila Zoshchenko* [The face and mask of Mikhail Zoshchenko], Moscow: Olimp, 1994

— (ed.), *Vospominaniya o Mikhaile Zoshchenko* [Recollections of Mikhail Zoshchenko], St Petersburg: Khudozhestvennaya literatura, 1995

Zholkovsky, Aleksandr, *Mikhail Zoshchenko: poetika nedoveriya* [Mikhail Zoshchenko: the poetics of suspicion], Moscow: Shkola, 1999

Soviet culture, society and politics of the 1920s

Boym, Svetlana, *Common Places: Mythologies of Everyday Life in Russia*, Cambridge MA: Harvard University Press, 1994

Brovkin, Vladimir, *Russia After Lenin: Politics, Culture and Society, 1921–1929*, London: Routledge, 1998

Chapple, Richard L., *Soviet Satire of the Twenties*, Gainsville: University of Florida Press, 1980

Sources

Editions used as source texts (for full references see Further Reading) are followed by details of first publication.

R   *Rasskazy* [Short stories], Moscow, 1974
SS   *Sobraniye sochineniy v tryokh tomakh* [Collected works in three volumes], Leningrad, 1986–87
UG   *Uvazhayemyye grazhdane* [Much-esteemed citizens], Moscow, 1991

1923

A Thief (Vor) *SS* I; *Ogonyok* 5
A Speech About Bribery (Rech´ o vzyatke) *UG; Drezina* 7
A Crime Report (Protokol) *SS* I; *Krasnyy voron* 37
An Anonymous Friend (Neizvestnyy drug) *SS* I; *Drezina* 9
A Victim of the Revolution (Zhertva revolyutsii) *SS* I; *Krasnyy voron* 41
Classy Lady (Aristokratka) *SS* I; *Krasnyy voron* 42

1924

Love (Lyubov´) *SS* I; *Krasnyy voron* 1
Host Accountancy (Khozraschot) *SS* I; *Drezina* 16 (1). Original title 'Zhertva vremeni' [A victim of the times]
A Dogged Sense of Smell (Sobachiy nyukh) *SS* I; *Smekhach*, 1. Also published as 'Rasskaz o sobake i o sobachoy nyukhe' [A story about a dog and a dog's sense of smell]. The opening and concluding paragraph from the original magazine-published version are included in the present translation
A Forgotten Slogan (Zabytyy lozung) *SS* I; *Krasnyy voron* 9
A Bad Habit (Plokhoy obychay) *SS* I; *Krasnyy voron* 11
Electrification (Elektrifikatsiya) *UG*; *Krasnyy voron* 17. Also published as 'Bednost´' [Poverty]
Casual Work (Otkhozhiy promysel) *SS* I; *Leningrad* 22. Also published as 'Al´fons' [A gigolo]
Domestic Bliss (Semeynoye schast´ye) *SS* I; *Krasnyy voron* 32
What Generosity (Shchedryye lyudy) *SS* I; *Krasnyy voron* 35–36

1925

Monkey Language (Obezyanyy yazyk) *SS* I. First published in a 1925 collection of Zoshchenko's stories
Firewood (Drova) *UG*; *Smekhach* 1
The Actor (Aktyor) *SS* I; *Buzotyor* 5. Also published as 'Iskusstvo Mel´pomeny' [The art of Melpomena] and 'Vyssheye iskusstvo' [The highest art]

The Match (Spichka) *UG*; *Buzotyor* 5
A Bathhouse (Banya) *SS* I; *Begemot* 10
Live-bait (Na zhivtsa) *SS* I; *Begemot* 11. Original title: 'Chestnaya grazh-danka' [An honest citizen]
Passenger (Passazhir) *SS* I; *Begemot* 21
Thieves (Vory) *UG; Begemot* 23
A Glass (Stakan) *SS* I; *Smekhach* 27
Crisis (Krizis) *SS* I; *Begemot* 44
Nervous People (Nervnyye lyudy) *SS* I; *Begemot* 47

1926

Connections (Protektsiya) *SS* I; *Begemot* 21. Original title: 'Byvayet' [I could tell them]
Economy Measures (Rezhim ekonomii) *SS* I; *Begemot* 22. Original title 'Khudo li?' [Not bad, eh?']
A Workshop for Health (Kuznitsa zdorovya) *SS* I; *Begemot* 28
Paris – Paruc SS I; *Begemot* 29. Original title 'Neschastnyy sluchay' [An unfortunate incident]
The Benefits of Culture (Prelesti kultury) *SS* I; *Begemot* 46
Lemonade (Limonad) *SS* I; *Begemot* 47
A Hasty Business (Speshnoye delo) *UG*; *Begemot* 49

1927

Guests (Gosti) *SS* I; *Begemot* 1
Quality Merchandise (Kachestvo produktsii) *SS* I; *Begemot* 2
Red Tape (Volokita) *UG*; *Buzotyor* 5
Pushkin (Pushkin) *SS* I; *Begemot* 7. Original title 'Grob: iz Povestey Belkina' [The coffin: from 'The Tales of Belkin']
The Tsar's Boots (Tsarskiye sapogi) *SS* I; *Begemot* 10
The Galosh (Galosha) *R*; *Begemot* 15
Does a Man Need Much? (Mnogo li cheloveku nuzhno?) *SS* I; *Begemot* 25
Fantasy Shirt (Rubashka fantazi) *SS* I; *Pushka* 29
Hard Labour (Katorga) *UG*; *Begemot* 34
Green Merchandise (Zelyonaya produktsiya) *SS* I; *Begemot* 35
A Fight (Draka) *SS* I; *Begemot* 36
Of Lamp-shades (Kolpak) *SS* I; *Pushka* 37
Three Men and a Cat (Koshka i lyudi) *SS* I; *Pushka* 41. Original title 'Pechka' [The stove]
The Cross (Zakoryuchka) *SS* I; *Begemot* 48. Original title 'Lyogkaya zhizn´' [Easy life]
Rostov (Rostov) *SS* I; *Begemot* 50

1928

No Hanging Matter (Pustoye delo) *UG*; *Chudak* 1
Sobering Thoughts (Trezvyye mysli) *UG*. Details of original magazine publication unknown. Published in collection under this title in March 1928

Foreigners (Inostrantsy) *SS* I; *Begemot* 21. Original title 'Vsyo v poryadke' [Nothing to worry about]

An Unpleasant Story (Nepriyatnaya istoriya) *UG*. According to Dolinsky, this story first appeared in September 1928, but Yury Tomashevsky claims that it appeared in *Begemot* 27 (1927) but was censored. See note on this story

Pawning (Lombardiya) *UG*; *Pushka* 43

1929

A Summer Break (Letnyaya peredyshka) *SS* I; *Revizor* 7

1932

Loose Packaging (Slabaya tara) *R*; *Krokodil* 10

1933

A Trap (Zapadnya) *SS* II; *Krokodil* 8. Original title 'Lich n aya zhizn'' [Private life]

1934

How Much Does a Man Need? (Skol´ko cheloveku nuzhno?) *SS* III; *The Sky-Blue Book* (1934–36). A rewrite of an earlier story titled 'Karusel'' [The merry-go-round] which appeared in *Drezina* 1 (1923) and was reworked under the titles 'Besplatno' [Free] and the present title

An Incident on the Volga (Proisshestviye na Volge) *SS* III; *The Sky-Blue Book* (1934–36). A rewrite of 'Parokhod' [The steam-boat] which was originally published in *Begemot* 33 (1927)

1935

Water Sports (Vodyanaya feyeriya) *SS* II; *Krokodil* 28–29

1936

The Story of an Illness (Istoriya bolezni) *SS* II; *Krokodil* 28

Go On, Sleep! (Spi skorey) *SS* II; *Krokodil* 32

1937

The Pushkin Centenary Celebrations:

First Speech about Pushkin (V pushkinskiye dni. Pervaya rech´ o Pushkine) *SS* II; *Krokodil* 2

Second Speech About Pushkin (Vtoraya rech´ o Pushkine) *SS* II; *Krokodil* 5

1938

In Praise of Transport (Pokhvala transportu) *SS* II; *Krokodil* 2

1945

The Photograph (Fotokartochka) *SS* II; *Leningrad* 3